Forever WINTER

CHRISTOPHER SCOTT WAGONER

OMNIFIC PUBLISHING
LOS ANGELES

Omnific Publishing
1901 Avenue of the Stars, 2nd floor
Los Angeles, CA 90067
www.omnificpublishing.com

First Omnific eBook edition, May 2015
First Omnific trade paperback edition, May 2015

The characters and events in this book are fictitious.
Any similarity to real persons, living or dead,
is coincidental and not intended by the author.

Library of Congress Cataloguing-in-Publication Data

Wagoner, Christopher Scott.
    Forever Winter / Christopher Scott Wagoner – 1st ed.
    ISBN: 978-1-623421-04-2
    1. Love — Fiction. 2. Professional Wrestling — Fiction.
    3. Japan — Fiction. 4. Cover Bands — Fiction. I. Title

10 9 8 7 6 5 4 3 2 1

Cover Design by Micha Stone and Amy Brokaw
Interior Book Design by Coreen Montagna

Printed in the United States of America

This one's for my sisters, Kerensa and Eileen.

Chapter 1

He gripped Parker tightly around the neck, his knuckles turning white. The look of sadistic glee on his face was more disconcerting than the murderous act itself. Perhaps feeling that Parker had not suffered enough, he grabbed him by the feet and slammed his head a half dozen times on the hard table.

"Go easy on Spider Man," Steve said, hovering nearby. He adjusted the spray bottle and stained rag in his hand and straightened up a bit. "He's a hero, too."

"He's Marvel," said the young child, perhaps six or seven. His brown eyes narrowed as he regarded the Spider Man toy lying in a pool of ketchup. "I only like DC."

"DC…" The big man lifted up his ball cap to scratch his scalp. The hat was decorated with a poorly rendered depiction of Zeus, the Greek god of Thunder. "That's Superman and Batman, right?"

"Yeah!" The boy's swarthy face crinkled up in a smile. "How come you know that? Grownups don't read comic books."

"This one does." Steve smiled widely. A UPS truck parked just outside had turned the restaurant's large windows into surprisingly effective mirrors. The man staring back looked tired, most of all. He was broad shouldered and tall, positively dwarfing the tiny child. His blue eyes were striking, though they remained partially hidden by the visor of his hat. His forearms knotted with muscle as he turned to sweep up an errant French fry from under the boy's table, using a grease-encrusted broom.

"I wish my daddy liked super heroes." The boy pouted, the sourness in his pucker causing Steve to chuckle. "He only likes that stupid *Walking Dead*."

They were in the lobby of Greece Hut, a fast food restaurant. It was a slow period, with no cars in the drive-through and no other customers inside. Behind the big man, a group of young people busied themselves with scrubbing every gleaming surface of the kitchen. A heavyset, balding man with a dirty blond mustache came bustling up to the counter from the kitchen. He bumped his belly up against the surface, his head only two feet above it. A narrow-eyed glare crossed his pock-marked face as he leaned on the counter, supporting himself on his pudgy hands. When he spoke, his voice was dripping with irritation.

"Steve!"

"Right here, Glenn."

"How long does it take to sweep the dining room? I need you back here making salads for the lunch rush."

"In just a minute." Steve indicated the child with a nod of his head. "I'm watching the little guy while his mom is in the bathroom."

Glenn's nostrils flared, and his brows rose high on his forehead.

"What?"

Steve sighed. "I said that I am watching—"

"Thank you so much," said a dark skinned woman, giving Steve an appreciative smile.

"Not a problem, ma'am." Steve grinned at her and gave the boy's head a playful pat. "I used to teach kindergarten, so I don't mind kids."

"*Steve!*"

"Duty calls." Steve smiled at the boy and his mother. He turned around and headed behind the counter, looking down on the furious man before him.

"You're taking advantage of me, Steven. Not doing your job is just like stealing from Greece Hut International. You said when I hired you that you would be a good, hard worker, even though this is your second job."

"Third job, if you count my tech support gig."

"Look, Steven, it breaks down like this: Five months ago, when you came in that door, you said you wanted to be a manager. Well, the fact that you used to teach school means nothing to Greece Hut International. You said you were fine with working your way up from the bottom."

"And I have been. I'm always on time; I work my ass off—"

"I'll be the judge of how good a worker you are."

Steve didn't give life to the angry retort on the tip of his tongue, and heaved a heavy sigh.

"C'mon, Glenn. When I started back in June, you said that I could go to manager training in the fall. Well, here we are in late October, which is pretty much the fall, and I'm still working the grill."

"I put you where I need you, Steve. And I said we'd *see* about sending you to manager training. There's no room in the class left this year, so you'll have to wait."

"This year? How long do I have to wait?"

"Until the end of the first quarter, around March."

"March." Steve ground his teeth. "Didn't you put in a request for a spot?"

"Must have slipped my mind." Glenn smiled smugly.

"Well…March? You're not giving me much to work with here, Glenn."

"Whatever. I need you back on the job. You're not being paid to babysit. You don't do anything unless I tell you to first, understand?"

"Whatever you say, Glenn." He fought to contain the hot bile rising in his belly. Glenn made a dismissive wave with his pudgy hand.

"Go take the trash out."

"I thought you wanted me to make salads?" Steve's mouth was pressed into a thin line.

"I do. I want you to do that after you take out the trash."

Steve moved to comply, his shoulders slightly slumped.

"Don't forget to check the bathrooms! I better not walk in there and find any jelly donuts or chocolate eclairs!"

"Mom!" the boy, said patting her on the arm. "They have donuts in the bathrooms here!"

Steve gathered the rubbish from the large plastic bins in the dining room. He cursed as one of them leaked terribly when he lifted the bag free, dripping pink colored fluid onto the tiled floor. He hurried to drag the heavy bags outside where they would cause no more harm.

Stepping into the bright morning sunlight, he blinked for several seconds, then dragged the bags across the parking lot. The weather was unseasonably warm for October, and he felt comfortable in his short sleeved uniform shirt. He arrived at the wooden corral containing their Dumpsters and found it already open.

"God dammit! For fuck's sake, why can't anyone ever close this thing?"

"It's my fault," came a voice from inside the corral. A young woman, who looked about high school age, peeked around the corner, pushing her glasses up on her nose with one hand while hanging on to her cell phone with the other. "Sorry."

"Don't worry about it, Tamara. I take it you're on break?"

"You could say that." The teen smiled at him, showing off metal braces on her teeth. She was cute, if a little bit thin. Her uniform shirt was tucked into pants so tight they could have been painted on. Steve struggled not to notice her body, which was easy when he had a task to perform. Using his long arms, he flipped the Dumpster lid up into the air and sent it crashing against the back of the receptacle.

"I've never seen anyone do that before," Tamara said with a whistle. "They have to inch it up and walk around the side. You must be strong!"

"Just tall, with Sasquatch arms. See you in the trenches, kiddo."

"See you," Tamara said, going back to her cell phone.

Steve shuffled across the parking lot, his limbs growing even more weary at the prospect of spending three more hours inside Greece Hut. He had his eyes on the slimy trail left by the leaking bag.

"What the hell is this?" said Glenn, staring at the pink line.

"One of the bags leaked. I'll clean it up off the dining room floor and foyer."

"What about the parking lot?"

"The parking lot?" Steve looked up at the sky, taking note of the gathering clouds in the east. "It's going to rain. Is it really necessary to mop the parking lot?"

Glenn looked at him with a narrow-eyed smirk on his plump features.

"Steve, you don't understand these sort of things, because the only real job you ever had was babysitting, but Greece Hut is more than just a restaurant. It's an *idea*. It's an idea that people can come to our establishment and get tasty food, but it's also an idea of cleanliness and sanitation. What would you think if you pulled into, say, McDonald's and saw a line of pink shake mix along the ground?"

"Somebody shanked the Pink Panther?"

Glenn's mustache danced as he blew out an exasperated sigh.

"Your humor is not appreciated when you do such poor work. Clean up the lobby, then get the hose and spray this crap off. Do you think you can handle that?"

I can handle kicking your fat ass too, thought Steve, though he managed to keep his anger off of his face.

"Yes, Glenn. I got it."

Steve grabbed a slab of bloody meat, the gore dripping down his exposed forearms. Wrinkling his nose in disgust, he separated it into its component patties and slapped them onto the wide grill before him. Soon they were steaming, the aroma almost unbearable. Sweat dripped into his eyes, and his sanguine-drenched hands were unavailable. He wound up wiping his face on his shoulder, dislodging the headset he wore. Frustrated, he grabbed onto the black console with his bloody fingers and removed it, placing it on top of a shelf containing buns.

"You need to keep your headset on, Steve," said Glenn from a few feet away. The manager was making sandwiches next to him, an empty bun awaiting Steve. The big man scooped up a seared burger on his iron spatula and gently placed it on the bun.

"It keeps falling off! It's way too small, Glenn."

"I don't give a shit. Those headsets are one size fits all, and Tenisha can fit it over her big fat Afro."

"Her 'fro provides a spongy surface on which to grip. My head stretches the metal out until it's not springy anymore. Besides, why do I need the headset? I'm hardly taking orders."

"So you know how much meat to drop on the grill. Put the headset back on or go home without a job."

"Fine." Steve retrieved the device, putting it on joylessly. It nearly slipped off of his head as soon as he looked down at the grill. It was shaping up to be one of those days.

"Don't 'fine' me!" Glenn shot the big man a glare. Steve forced himself to keep his cool, but it took effort. He took out his aggression on the pale pink meat sizzling on the grill, smashing it flat with his spatula.

"Don't squish the patties," Glenn said. "It's grill *pressed* meat, not *smashed* meat."

"Sorry." Steve glanced at a clock over the bun warmer. "Where's Donnell? I'm supposed to be off in ten minutes."

"Donnell is always a little late," Tamara said as she dashed by, her arms laden with stacks of paper cups. "Don't worry, he'll be here!"

True to form, a lanky black teenager came sauntering in the door about eighteen minutes later. Steve gnashed his teeth as the boy laconically made his way to the time clock, chatting with several other employees instead of punching in. When he finally swiped his card and checked the dry erase board outside the manager's office for his position, Steve was ready to explode.

"I'll take that, big man," Donnell said, offering to receive the headset.

"Great," Steve said, grinning ear to ear. "I am so out of here—"

"You can't leave," Glenn said with a glower. "We're in the middle of a rush. You need to go and help Tamara bag in drive-through."

"I was supposed to be gone twenty minutes ago! My girlfriend is probably in the parking lot blowing up my phone."

"You can't leave until the manager on duty says you can," Glenn said.

"Actually," Donnell said without looking up from the grill, "in the state of New York you only have to work fifteen minutes past your scheduled shift. Then you can't legally be forced to stay."

"You heard the man," Steve said, feeling new fondness for the teen.

"Where did you even hear that? This is the first I've ever heard of it, and I've been a manager for this company for seven years!"

"My mom works at the unemployment office," Donnell said with a shrug.

"Bye, Glenn." He tried to hide his smirk as he punched out—but judging from Glenn's black look, he failed.

Steve went to the rear of the kitchen, to a tiny area that laughingly passed as a break room. He squeezed past a rotund black lady as she broke down cardboard boxes into flat shapes. Steve grabbed the hemline of his Greece HuT-shirt and pulled it over his head, revealing a densely muscled chest and abdomen. Each of his thick arms bore a tattoo: on the left arm, he had a depiction of a tripod from H.G. Wells' *War of the Worlds;* on his right, a beautiful illustration of a maple leaf, nearing the end of its time on the tree. He glanced down at his impressive torso. At least there were some benefits to working fifty-plus hours a week.

"Lordy, lordy," the woman said as she stared at him, "Steve be strippin' up in here!"

"Sorry, Sandy." Steve dragged on a much cleaner T-shirt over his tired muscles.

"Don't be sorry," she said as he passed by her, her eyes running up and down his body. "I didn't know you got tattoos. Why'd you get a leaf on your arm?"

Steve glanced down at his arm and saw the realistic illustration of a maple leaf. Its rich tapestry of oranges, yellows, and reds made it seem like it had fallen from a tree on an autumn day and gotten stuck to Steve's skin.

"Long story."

Steve grinned at her before skipping past Glenn on his way out of the kitchen. He elbowed his way through the long line of impatient patrons and at last stood breathing the outside air. He squinted in the late afternoon sun until he spotted a little blue car parked in a shady patch near the Dumpster corral.

Steve used his hand to shield his eyes from the bright red sun. He approached the car on the passenger side and opened it wearily. Sliding into the clean vinyl seat, he was immediately greeted with an enthusiastic kiss from the young woman behind the wheel.

She was beautiful despite her unconventional appearance. Her hair was black as pitch, pulled into pigtails that dangled next to the varied piercings in her ears. Colorful tattoos were visible on her arms, her black tank top baring her arms. A white skull with a pair of eyeglasses was emblazoned on the tank. A pair of black pants with a snug fit and dozens of shiny zippers adorned her lower half. Her eyes were large and colored a deep, rich brown. Her eyebrows were a bit angular, which made her seem a bit annoyed even when she was not. She had light tan skin, which was complimented by the smoky lavender eye shadow and pale purple lipstick she had applied.

Her tongue was nimble in his mouth, and he responded in kind. She lightly bit his lower lip as their mouths parted, just a bit over the line of being painful. That was what he expected of Autumn. Even the best moments around her seem tinged with a bit of pain. It was hard to look at her without thinking of the way she'd left him, what, six months ago? Had it really been that long?

Autumn's nostrils flared twice and she giggled. "You smell like french fries."

"I know, and it makes me want to barf."

"I think you smell good…" Again their lips met again in a kiss. Steve broke it off first, which elicited a disappointed *awww* from Autumn.

"Try working here a week. Then nothing they make will smell even remotely good."

"You look tired." Autumn put her hands on his cheeks and peered at the dark circles under his eyes.

"I *am* tired."

"Too tired to eat dinner?"

"Not if it's real food, and doesn't come in a white wrapper with a horrible depiction of the Greek god of Thunder printed on it."

"I was thinking surf and turf."

"You hate shrimp."

"You don't." She kissed him deeply, breath mingling with his own. Their lips lingered, and for that moment Steve forgot about the aches in his body and the abuse he'd suffered in the restaurant.

"I love you," he said when they parted at last, pressing his forehead into hers.

"I love you. And I'm sorry you have to work these shit jobs because of me."

"*You* didn't get drunk then punch out a transvestite hooker, and get fired for the resulting scandal."

Steve glanced up from rubbing his tired eyes and locked gazes with her. The guilt, the pain were clear on her exotic features. He *wanted* to forgive her, so much, but he just couldn't. With effort, he managed to keep his conflicting feelings out of his tone.

"You had your reasons," he said simply, sitting back in his seat and luxuriating in the flow of cool air from the dashboard vents.

"Stupid reasons." She pursed her painted lips and ruffled his damp hair. "I shouldn't have put you through that."

"No, you shouldn't have."

Steve winced at his own harshness. He hadn't intended to be so full of venom. He stared out the window in the awkward silence that followed.

Autumn chewed her bottom lip and put the car in gear. Slowly, she pulled out into traffic, mulling things over silently.

"All I can do is say I'm sorry, Steve. I'm not sure what you want from me."

"You don't have to do anything. Don't worry about it."

"Uh, no can do, sugar. Obviously you still haven't gotten over it-and I'm not saying that you *should*, really—but I don't know what else I can do! I came back, doesn't that count for anything?"

Steve looked over at her, the memory of her return still fresh in his mind. For a brief while, when she had strode into his classroom on his last day of work, he'd felt as if all would be right with the universe. Soon enough, the feeling had faded and he was left with the reality of their time apart and what it had done to him. He loved Autumn, truly and deeply, but he wasn't sure if he had faith in her anymore.

"It counts. It does, and I'm still very happy you changed your mind…"

"But?"

"Nothing. Don't worry about it. Let's just have a nice dinner and—"

"No."

Autumn's angular brows lowered, and she tightened her grip on the steering wheel. Amid the screeching of tires and numerous blaring horns, she cut off two lanes of traffic and slid next to a length of curb painted yellow. Steve's face had turned white because several cars had narrowly avoided slamming into the erratically steered sedan. She ignored the angry shouts and threats from the other motorists and instead fixed Steve with a withering glower.

"Are you crazy?"

"Quite possibly. Goddamn it, Steve, I'm tired of creeping around this. No more walking on glass around each other."

Steve's jaw set hard, and he put his hand on her knee.

"I need you Autumn, I really do, the way grass needs rain."

She put her hand on top of his, eyes boring deeply into his own.

"I know. I need you too, Steve. Don't you believe that?"

"I do believe it. But I need more than that. I need you to believe. I need to know that you believe in me, in *us*."

Autumn's jaw fell open, and she stiffened. Her voice had a scoffing note to it when she spoke.

"I believe in us!"

"Do you?" Steve said, but she had stuck her head out the window to yell at a particularly nasty driver she had offended.

"Blow it out your ass, you cum stain!" she bellowed at top volume. *"Yeah, I'm talking to you! What? What you gonna do? My boyfriend is huge! He'll kick your ass!"*

When she pulled her head back inside the car, he had to smile a bit.

"Let's go before we end up on one of those video clip shows where people fight in the middle of traffic."

"I like those shows," she said with a giggle, causing more bedlam in traffic as she rudely pulled out in front of another car. "Especially the ones with Sheriff John what's his name, you know the guy with the orange spray tan and that annoying 'told you so' voice?"

"These fugitives," Steve said in a high pitched, annoying way, "thought they were going to get a free ride. But they couldn't drive far enough to escape the long arm of the law!"

Autumn chortled so hard she nearly slammed into the rear of a huge pickup truck. Steve swallowed hard as the chrome bumper loomed before them, feeling quite vulnerable in the little car. As they waited at the light, she turned to smile sadly at him.

"It sucks! A guy like you, with an education and shit, shouldn't have to sling burgers."

"Going back to teaching's just not possible."

"I guess it backfired, having a famous father."

Steve yawned and stretched.

"Yeah. Deathslayer Jr. really brought honor to the family name that time."

The light changed and Autumn accelerated. They headed toward the Hudson, crossing over the bridge to the Bronx. Steve stared wistfully at a muscle car as it thundered past.

"I'm sorry you had to sell your car." The brakes squealed as she had to stop at another signal light.

"Don't be."

"But it's all because I got sick —"

Steve straightened up and focused his gaze on Autumn.

"Are you feeling okay?"

"I'm fine, that's not what I meant. Dammit, Steve, I keep fucking up your life. Don't sit there and pretend that everything is okay. *Talk* to me, don't keep it all in."

Steve leaned his head on the window, eyes sagging shut.

"There's nothing to talk about. I love you, and that's that. I'll accept whatever comes as long as we're together."

"God, you sound like a pussy."

Steve ignored the jibe. He felt the cool glass sucking away the kitchen's heat, wanting badly to drift off to sleep. A moment later he was glad he hadn't.

"I mean, it's sweet. What you said, the things you're always saying, they're really sweet. They help me get through the day."

Steve pretended to snore, hoping it was a good performance.

"Poor baby." She stroked his hair gently until the light turned green and he felt the car lurch forward. Then his mouth broke into a grin and his eyes snapped open. He thrust his finger under her nose and laughed maniacally.

"Ha! Now who's fucking with who? I have you on record that I'm not a pussy. I'm sweet!"

Autumn slapped him smartly on the cheek.

"Shut up, pussy!"

The tiny spider crept noiselessly toward Crawley. She was seated before a microscope, watching the approaching arachnid with a touch of amusement. Its legs moved rapidly for a moment, then paused, holding as still as death. Eight eyes reflected the lights from the fixtures overhead as it crept toward her. First one leg brushed her white sleeve, then another, and soon the hairy creature was crawling along her forearm.

"Portia," Crawley said, smiling at the arachnid, "how did you get out?"

She rose from her rolling chair and walked across a gleaming white tile floor to a wall filled with glass aquariums. Inside each one of them were one or more spiders. There were long-legged orb weavers, yellow like bananas, hanging motionless in their webs. They were joined by massive, furry tarantulas the size of dinner plates, and most dangerous of all were the little Styrofoam cages holding the black widows. She opened an empty aquarium and gently plucked the spider from her sleeve. With great care, she placed it inside and closed the lid.

She stood back and stretched her slender body. Crawley shook out the long, flowing hair that cascaded in a thick sheet down to the middle of her back. Almond-shaped eyes with a slight epicanthic fold peered intently back at her as she made sure the glass cage was closed properly. Her nose was slightly wide for her face, but did nothing to diminish her obvious beauty. She had a small but firm bust, and a narrow waist that flared out into womanly hips. A white lab coat was draped over a tight red tank top and even tighter jeans with strategic holes ripped in them. Her white and pink sneakers made little noise as she strode across the floor to a wooden staircase. She tromped up out of the windowless basement lab, flicking off the lights before she went.

She passed by a cheery kitchen and into a spacious living room with an L-shaped burgundy sofa and matching easy chairs. A wide screen was flush against the wall, tuned in to a news channel though the volume was off.

"Eleanor?" said a woman's voice from another room. An older woman with dirty blonde hair and red rimmed glasses came striding down a flight of carpeted stairs. She was wearing a flower print blouse and tan slacks. Though she was Caucasian, the resemblance to the younger woman was obvious.

"In here, Mom," Eleanor said, sitting on the couch and scooping a sleek black remote off of the back.

"Did you get a chance to look at the funnel web venom?" Her mother's gaze flashed to the tight pants she was wearing and then back to her face.

"Sure did," Eleanor said with a smile. "Everything looks good, no contamination. We can send it off to make rabbits really sick whenever you're ready."

"Don't say that. You know it pains me to think of them having to suffer."

"Better a rabbit suffer than a human die," Eleanor said.

"I know, honey. I just don't like thinking about it."

"Where's dad?"

"Lighting candles at St. Augustine's," her mother said a bit admonishingly. Eleanor rolled her eyes.

"This is about Autumn's Dad's wedding, isn't it?" Eleanor said. "I told you I'm not even invited to the ceremony, just the reception."

Her mother sighed, taking off her glasses so she could rub her nose. She walked across the polished hardwood floor to sit on the sofa next to her daughter.

"You're an adult," her mother said, fixing her with a stare carefully bereft of judgment. "You are free to do whatever you want."

"But…"

"But…your father and I don't have to like it."

"I'm sorry, Mom, but I just don't see anything wrong with it. I mean, if two people are happy together, isn't that what's important?"

Her mother pushed her glasses up on her nose and fixed her with a stern gaze. "You young people don't get it. You have too many choices, and too many people telling you that those choices are okay."

"Choosing to be with the person you love *is* a good choice." Her brow furrowed, and her eyes stared expectantly at her mother. "Isn't it?"

"Ah, we're talking about you and Phil now, aren't we?"

She patted the young woman on the shoulder sympathetically.

"I love him, mom," Eleanor said, her eyes fixed on the silent news broadcast. "I really do love him, and I think he loves me, but…"

"But what?" her mother asked after several seconds of silence.

"He has this…wandering eye problem," Eleanor said after a deep sigh. "Like last week, we were playing our gig, and this hipster chick in a leather skirt kept buying him drinks. He had this stupid grin on his face every time she sashayed over to the stage. And that's hardly the first time he's paid attention to every woman in the room but me. I feel like he takes me for granted."

"Oh, honey, your father checks out other women all the time."

"What?" Eleanor said, a short bark of laughter escaping her painted lips. "Dad? No way."

"He thinks he's pretty subtle about it," her mother said with a chuckle, "but I can still tell. It doesn't mean that your father stopped loving me, or wants to have an affair."

"It's not just the wandering eye thing," said Eleanor. "It's his whole skittish attitude too. Every time I talk about the future, about having kids or getting married, he gets twitchy and uncomfortable. I'm afraid that, because I'm his first girlfriend, he might be thinking he wants to play the field more. Or maybe I'm afraid because I've never felt this way for someone before. And it's not like Phil makes it easy, avoiding the subject like the plague."

"That's men for you," her mother said with a laugh. "They're stupid, what can I say?"

Both women laughed at the comment, but Eleanor's face quickly fell.

"I know that a lot of guys are scared of commitment, but I never thought Phil was like that. I mean, OMG, his friend Steve proposed to his girlfriend after about three months!"

"Don't say OMG. It's the same as taking the Lord's name in vain!"

"Sorry. I guess I just…those two are so good together, they, they…"

"Complement each other?"

"Yeah, that's a good way to say it. They complement each other really well. I don't know that Phil and I do that. I definitely love him, though."

"Well," her mother said, scratching behind her ear and looking a bit sheepish, "maybe it's time you saw other people…"

"I'm not dating a Catholic man, mom," Eleanor said with a grunt.

"Why not?"

"Because I don't want to be a brood mare for the Church," Eleanor said, her lips drawing into a tight line. "I want two children, a boy and a girl, and that's it! Catholic men seem to think the only thing Catholic women are good for is making more little Catholics."

"Eleanor!" her mother said, growing a bit tense. "I'm really starting to worry about you. I put up with the rock and roll music, and your…wardrobe, such as it is, but now you're starting to sound like a, like a *heathen*."

"Motherrrr…it's the new millennium, no one says heathen anymore."

"Well, what else do you call it?" Her mother rose from the couch. "I have to start dinner."

"I'll help, Mom."

"You've been working in the lab all day, Ellie. Just sit down and rest. Maybe give Phil a call and talk about things."

Eleanor waited until her mother was around the corner before thrusting her tongue out. Still, she dug in her pants pocket and extracted a shiny smartphone. She scrolled through her contacts until a picture of a young man with short curly hair and glasses was at the top. Her finger tapped the image twice and she held the phone to her ear. It rang for about half a minute before going to voice mail.

"Hey, honey! I guess you're still working. I was wondering if I could come over later, maybe watch a movie? Call me back when you get this. I —"

She paused for a moment.

"I love you."

Sighing, she lay down on the couch and set her phone down on her sternum. As she stared at the ceiling, she thought of how things had gotten to the point they had with Phil. After their road trip to find Autumn's father, and the many misadventures they had along the way, she had felt bonded with the young man. For a time, they were clicking in every imaginable way: on stage, with her parents, even in the bedroom.

Crawley tapped her nails on the gorilla glass shielding her smartphone. The sex had been *very* good. That was the one arena of their relationship that had continued to get better. Silently, she wondered if all nerdy, awkward people were secretly sex maniacs. The idea of what her mother would think about some of the lascivious thoughts coursing through her head made Crawley giggle. Her sudden movement sent the phone sliding down to the floor.

Admonishing herself for being careless, she retrieved the phone and checked it carefully. Seeing no damage, she cycled through her contacts and sighed again. Except for Phil and her other bandmates, she had few people in her friends circle. Autumn was there, though she wasn't sure if the caustic young woman truly cared for her company or just felt obligated to speak to her.

Then there was the fact that when Autumn had left Steve, she had been the one to drive herself and Phil upstate. There they had confronted the seemingly callous young woman on what she had done, in the process reminding her of how much she actually cared for Steve. Crawley licked her lips, feeling a bit guilty. No one would ever know just how tempted she had been to use Autumn's absence to make her own play for Steve…

The sound of her mother calling for her help setting the table drew her out of her reverie. She lost herself for a time in the familiar pattern of dinner with her parents.

Chapter 2

Steve was practically dead on his feet as he and Autumn stood in line at the steakhouse. His eyes were mere pinpricks that blandly gazed at the floor as they waited. Deep circles lurked beneath his blue orbs, and he felt much older than he actually was. Autumn slipped an arm around his waist and stood on her tiptoes to kiss him on the cheek.

The contact seemed to stir him, as his eyes widened and a slight smile played across his face.

"What was that for?"

Autumn leaned her head on his shoulder and sighed.

"No reason."

Soon a cheerful waitress seated them near one of the front windows. Cars passed by on the street outside, some with their headlights on in the fading sunlight. Steve's eyes narrowed at the menu, then glanced up at Autumn.

"This place is expensive."

"Don't worry about it, sugar. Dad sent me some money, for the car payment, really, but he sent some extra."

"We need that extra for bills, food…"

"Sit the fuck down."

"Autumn…"

"Sit. The. Fuck. Down." Autumn grabbed him by the forearm and dragged downward. Steve allowed himself to be reined in, though he raised an eyebrow as he did so.

"This is a tad irresponsible…"

"You've worked your ass off all week. You deserve a good meal."

"As Clint Eastwood once said, 'Deserving's got nothing to do with it!'"

"It should. I mean, after all we've been through in the last year, we deserve normal time as a couple."

Steve glanced up at her, a hint of eagerness in his blue eyes.

"So let's get married."

"Steve, I love you. You know I do. But…"

"…not enough to marry me."

"Why does it matter if we're married?"

"Are you guys ready to order?" the waitress asked, stopping by their table to drop off two glasses of ice water.

"Not yet, thanks," Steve said, unable to muster up a smile.

"Why does it matter if we're married?" Autumn put her elbows on the table and leaned forward. "We're together, right? Isn't that what counts?"

"Of course that's what counts. But getting married is the next logical step, right?"

"Hey!" the waitress said, popping back next to their table. "You folks ready to order yet?"

"Go away," Autumn said with a growl.

"What she means is we need a few more minutes, please."

"Take your time," the waitress said before flitting off.

"Why don't you want to get hitched? You said yes before—"

"I thought I was dying."

"I see…so till death is only good if death is pretty damn close, right?"

"That's not what I meant, Steve. God, you can be such a dick! Everything just has to be your way, doesn't it?"

"What the hell does that mean? I bend over backward to take care of you."

"That's just it, you think I need to be taken care of. I did an okay job of it for years before I met you, Steve."

"Well, at least I'm committed to us."

"You should be committed all right."

"Why can't you ever take anything seriously? Everything I say you cut to pieces so you don't have to deal with it."

"Can we just drop this, please, and enjoy our dinner?"

Steve was taken aback by the moisture in the corner of her eyes. Autumn sniffled, hands twisting nervously on the spoon in her hands. Her bottom lip trembled, chin dimpling up as she strove to hold herself in check.

"Okay, let's drop it. Sorry if I just...I'm sorry."

Autumn dabbed at her eyes, then smiled weakly at him. Her hand cupped his own and squeezed it tight.

"I did this to us. You still feel betrayed, and I can't blame you."

"Don't say that. I don't feel betrayed."

"Yes, you do."

Autumn picked up his hand and brought it to her lips. Steve felt his anger fade away, at least for the moment. He could believe in her skin, warm against his own, at least.

"I love you, Steve. More than anything. So much it's terrifying."

"I love you too. And I've always been a little terrified of you."

"Me? You're like six and a half feet tall, weigh a quarter ton, your father is the Deathslayer from Hell, and you're scared of *me?*"

"Gotta watch out for those chicks with tattoos and piercings. You know they're wicked and will tempt you to destruction!"

"You have tattoos of your own now, sugar, so what does that make you?"

"Hungry. Where's that pesky waitress when you actually want her?"

"Probably spitting in our food."

"Only if she has a time machine. We haven't ordered yet."

"Shut up, dumbass!"

Steve's back hit the wall outside their apartment with a resounding thud as Autumn mauled his face and neck. He responded with equal enthusiasm, his hands sliding along her spine to cup her generous buttocks. One of their upstairs neighbors inched past, offering a nasty sneer at their public display. Steve's apologetic smile did nothing to assuage his ire.

Autumn fumbled inside his pocket in order to extract his key ring, allowing her hand to linger for several seconds. She looked him right in the eyes as she went spelunking around, her nimble fingers finding everything but his keys. He found himself hard as a rock, straining against his black work pants. Finally withdrawing the key ring, she was hampered in her efforts to open the door by the attention Steve was paying to her neck and chest. She barely had the door open halfway when Steve swept her up into a fireman's carry and sidled through the entrance.

"Damn," she said, kneading his prominent bicep, "you're getting *strong*, sugar!"

"Hard work makes hard bodies."

He enveloped her lips in a passionate kiss.

"You better be hard," she said in a sultry tone, "because I'm not letting you get any sleep tonight!"

"I'll sleep when I'm dead." Steve used his heel to shut the door behind them.

"Don't say things like that." Autumn wrapped her arms around his neck and gave him a tight squeeze.

Steve did a circuit of the apartment, dropping his keys on the wooden peg near the door, then sidling over to the television to turn it on.

"You really want to watch TV at a time like this?" Her eyes lit up and a slight grin crept onto her face. "Oh, did you rent a dirty movie?"

"No, cover noise."

He smothered her face with kisses, tasting her sweat. His body was straining hard against his pants. Her scent, the feel of her soft body's curves pressed against him already had him sweating.

"We need to move," Autumn said when her mouth was free.

"With what money?" Steve slowed down in his amorous ministrations.

Autumn grabbed him under the chin and kissed him forcefully.

"Never mind…right now, I don't give a shit who hears us."

She squirmed in his arms playfully as he swept her off to the bedroom. Steve dropped her onto the mattress. Autumn got on all fours facing him, eyes half-lidded and a coy smile on her face. She reached out her hand and unbuckled his belt. Steve stroked her silken hair gently, a slightly perplexed smile on his face.

"What?" Autumn said, pausing when she had his fly half undone.

"Nothing. I was just thinking you're beautiful."

"Pffft." Autumn rolled her brown eyes. "There's better looking chicks, sugar."

"Come on, you could have any guy you wanted."

"Shut up and take off your pants."

Steve laughed, then slipped out of his shoes and then his trousers. He was ready, his member lunging out of his boxers at her. Autumn leaned forward and put her mouth to work. She kneaded his buttocks with her hands, playing him the best way she knew how.

"God," he said, putting his hands gently on the back of her head. A soft rain pattered against the window, the subtle hiss of it falling masking the street noise. Her soft, brown eyes enveloped him in a gaze which suggested he was the only thing that mattered in that instant. Autumn's lips and tongue worked together, slippery and sliding along the length of his cock. He tried to hold out, but she knew him very well at that point, knew just how to please him best. She felt him spasm, receiving the results of her efforts even when he tried to warn her it was coming.

"You're so bad," he said as she leaned back on the bed and smiled.

"Aye," she said, affecting a Scottish brogue, "the way you like it!"

"Was that a *Highlander* reference?"

"Is that the one where the guys are hacking at each other with swords in the middle of New York?"

"Yeah."

"Never seen it. I'm not a *nerd*."

She burst out laughing when Steve sputtered. His face was crossed with a playfully sinister look. He crawled onto the bed, lightly shoving her on her back when she rose to try to kiss him. Wordlessly, he lifted her shirt over her head, revealing her generous bosom covered by a black lace bra. His fingers nimbly undid the clasp between the cups, releasing the soft, pliant skin beneath. He dragged off her pants so quickly his nail left a tiny scratch near her waist. Their bodies slid across each other as he lay atop of her. He started at her neck, leaving a swarm of kisses down her sternum. Carefully, he kissed each of her breasts, lingering on the nipples. His teeth gently tugged on her piercings, eliciting a long moan from her.

Slowly, deliberately, he worked his way down her stomach, his mouth brushing the Anarchy tattoo over her navel. He ran his tongue lower, then lower still, until he was mired in her soft mound. Autumn reached back with both hands and grabbed the pillow under her head. Her eyes were closed, her mouth open as she writhed under his wickedly clever tongue. He felt a rough patch of skin on her heel drag across his back, pulling him to her more tightly.

Steve lifted his head just a bit away from her labia, using his fingers to spread her open. Delicately, he blew on her clitoris, smiling as her flesh quivered and a helpless moan escaped her painted lips. Gingerly working his tongue all around her hood, he avoided actually pressing it against her most sensitive spot.

"Stop teasing me," she said desperately, her body rearing against his.

"What do you want me to do?"

"You're so mean!" She tried to force his head down on her.

"Say it! Come on, tell me what you want, you dirty little girl."

Autumn grabbed the pillow under her head tightly and moaned.

"Lick it…and suck it, please."

"Lick what?" He kissed the inside of her thighs and teased her skin with his tongue.

"You know what!" A second later she gasped as his tongue flicked for the briefest of moments across her clit.

"I can't read your mind, so I don't know what."

"Lick my clit," she said harshly, nails digging into the back of his head. "Lick it and suck it right n —"

Her head was thrown backward, body arching as he complied. Steve took her entire hood inside his mouth and held it with his lips. Very, very gently he ran his tongue over her clitoris while applying suction with his mouth. He knew her responses well, too, and he felt a certain amount of pride in his performance. As his efforts reached a crescendo, she put her right hand on his shoulder, midway between holding him down and trying to shove him away. When she reached the summit, she left long red weals across his flesh with her black painted nails. Her scream nearly had the window rattling, and soon their upstairs neighbor was stomping hard on the floor/ceiling.

"Guess we got too loud," Autumn said between gasps for air. She was covered in sweat, her legs quivering slightly.

"I take it as a sign that I did a good job." He wiped his mouth with the back of his forearm, then grabbed her under the small of her back. Simultaneously, he dragged her forward while getting to his knees. They remained that way for a moment, her staring up at him with a glassy eyed grin while he toyed with one of her pierced nipples.

"You're beautiful…" He ran his other hand over her inked flesh. "I could just touch you for hours."

"I'm wide open," she said, reaching down below her waist to try to connect their bodies.

Grinning, Steve raised up on his knees and assisted her. She gasped as he entered her, putting her hands behind her head and arching her back. He stared down at her, eyes tightly shut and a warm smile on her face. At moments like that, he had no problem believing that they were inseparable, presenting a united front against whatever the Universe could throw at them. He gasped a moment later, as Autumn gripped him tightly with her cunt lips. Despite being underneath him, she was quite active, gyrating her hips in concert with his. As always, he was amazed at their ability to get in sync. Sometimes, it was if they had one body with two brains.

Steve leaned forward, bracing one hand on the headboard with his jaw pressed against Autumn's cheek. She nibbled on his ear between moans, her legs wrapped firmly around his buttocks as they melded into one.

The headboard cracked repeatedly against the wall, muffled somewhat by old towels wrapped around the wooden posts. He reared up on his knees again, and Autumn shifted her hips to the side, throwing the back of her left leg over her right knee. Steve bore down deeper, crushing her into the mattress. Her chin was pressed up against her breasts, her body folded nearly in half, but Autumn showed no sign of discomfort. She ground her hips against his, giving him permission to release. He did, eyes tightly shut as his body was wracked with pleasurable spasms. They gently disengaged, then lay wrapped in each other's arms, their bodies glistening.

"That was amazing!" Autumn giggled, running her fingers through his chest hair. "So, it's still pretty early. Do you want to head out to the Dew Drop Inn? They have hot wings on special…"

Steve struggled to listen, quite sincerely, but soon felt himself drift into dreamless oblivion.

Crawley tried to smile as she raised her margarita glass for a toast.

"To Danielle," said the bubbly blonde to her left, lips covered in shiny gloss. "Enjoy your last few months as a free woman!"

The other young women tittered and howled as if something funny had actually been said. Crawley took a small sip of her drink, wondering how she had allowed her mother to talk her into this situation.

Upon finding out that Phil would be in a meeting until late, and that Autumn and Steve were turning in early, she had been determined to return to the basement and finish some paperwork. Her mother had been aghast, loudly imploring her to go out and "have a life" for a change. Despite Eleanor's protests that she was fine, her mother had jumped on her Facebook account to bemoan her daughter "wasting her life in the basement."

One of her friends, who had a daughter the same age as Crawley, had been equally aghast. The woman insisted that Crawley's mother go downstairs immediately and invite the hard working young woman to join her own daughter for a night out.

Crawley had been mortified, feeling humiliated that her mother felt the need to set her up for play dates at her age. Nevertheless, she had agreed to go out, if only to shut her mother up for at least a week or two.

"Oh, honey," her mother said, "you're going to have so much fun! Charlotte is such a nice girl."

"She is? Are we talking about the same Charlotte O'Malley who picked on me in high school?"

"She didn't pick on you, dear."

"Bullshit!"

"Language!" her mother gasped, slapping her on the bicep.

"Sorry, but she really did pick on me. Not just me, but a lot of people who didn't fit in."

"Oh, maybe she was snide and teasing when she was a teenager. For heaven's sake, Eleanor, she's grown up now, and you have too."

"She and her popular friends put me on trial once, mom. For the crimes of being ugly and having no fashion sense. They found me guilty and sentenced me to death while we were in study hall!"

"I'm sure she was just kidding."

"Yeah, it was so funny I forgot to laugh."

Her mother stopped in her tracks and sighed. She rubbed her nose and closed her eyes as she collected her thoughts.

"You need to do this, Eleanor. You can't just hang around a bunch of men all the time. People will talk."

"I don't get along with most girls, mom. So what if a lot of my friends are guys? Besides, I hung out with Autumn last week."

"Oh. Well, I just don't think that Autumn is a good influence on you."

"What?" Crawley said, stopping at the bottom of the wooden staircase that led to the second story of their house. "What's wrong with Autumn?"

"She works in a tattoo parlor, hanging around with degenerates and crooks, and look what she did to that nice Steve boy. He used to be a teacher, and now he's mixed up with...strange street people..."

"He's not mixed up with them, mom. It's just that he got into a fight with one. Some of those street walkers can be pretty aggressive."

"Well, whatever. It would still be nice if you hung around with some different kinds of people than you're used to. You know, Charlotte and her friends are all dating nice Catholic men with good jobs..."

"Do you want me to go out or not?" Crawley said, hand gripping the safety rail so tightly her knuckles were turning white.

Her mother stopped speaking and just smiled. Her hands wrung nervously as she stared up the stairs.

"Hurry up, dear. Char says they'll be here to pick you up in half an hour."

"What?" Crawley said, sticking her head back out of her bedroom door. "Mom, I want to drive myself! Can't I just meet them somewhere?"

"Don't be rude."

"Don't treat me like a child! You didn't even wait for me to say yes, you just told them 'come on over!'"

"Wear something nice, but ladylike!"

Crawley stared down at her tight red T-shirt and denim jeans with rips. Pursing her lips, she decided not to change, only spritzing on a bit of perfume and touching up her cosmetics. She retired to the sofa, waiting with arms crossed over her chest defiantly for the arrival of her ride.

Char tsked at Crawley's mostly full glass, drawing her mind back to the present.

"Drink up. We've had like four each already and you're still sipping at your first one!"

She tried to smile at the blonde woman, but Crawley couldn't help remembering what Char had put her through in high school. Physically, Charlotte had not changed much. She still had the same shoulder-length blonde hair, though she no longer held it back with a blue ribbon as she often had in high school. Her face was perky and pretty, with the full lips and sultry eyes that drove men crazy. Her body was stacked, with larger breasts than Crawley's, though her hips were not as sweetly curved. Char had worn a blue dress with a flared out skirt that terminated an inch above her knees. Shapely legs tapered down to her feet, clad in stiletto heels that Crawley would have only worn in the bedroom.

"I have an early day tomorrow, and there's a half dozen Athena orb weavers due to arrive from Micronesia—"

"What's she talking about?" said one of Char's friends, a brunette with narrow, flashing eyes and a nearly-perpetual sour outlook.

"Spiders, Lexi," Char said, giggling into her drink. "Ellie here is a scientist! She sucks their venom out and uses it for medicine, or something."

"Gross," Lexi said, favoring Crawley with a disdainful grimace. She, like all of Char's companions, was incredibly attractive, from her finely featured face to her shapely body. Lexi was wearing a very tight burgundy dress with opaque tights underneath. The skirt was so short it regularly rode up, which caused Lexi to yank it down whenever she rose from her chair. Crawley giggled as the woman stood up for a visit to the restroom.

"What?" Lexi said, eyes narrowing dangerously at Crawley.

Crawley swallowed hard, looking up at the woman with wide eyes.

"Nothing. You just did the Picard maneuver."

"The what?"

"Picard Maneuver," Danielle said, piping in from Crawley's right. "Travis likes that nerdy Star Trek stuff too. Apparently Patrick Stewart liked to adjust his uniform every time he got up."

"Star Trek?" Lexi said, looking at Crawley as if she were an alien life form. "You have got to be kidding. Get a life, will you Ellie?"

Shaking her head, the comely woman left their table. The bar they were in was fairly crowded, the dance floor barely having enough room for the two dozen sweaty patrons who swayed to the music. Crawley sighed, hating the repetitive electronic psuedo-hip hop being blasted at high volume. When she hung out with the guys in her band, they went to less crowded places where real music was still played.

It also occurred to her that she was, perhaps, a bit more fond of snuggling on the couch and watching Trek reruns with Phil than she thought.

"Don't mind her," Char said, mistaking her disdain as a reaction to Lexi's harsh words. "She's just a little bitchy because she caught her man sexting with some girl at work."

"Oh, no," Danielle said, hand going before her mouth. Crawley could remember the red haired woman from high school, albeit barely. She had been possessed of a heavier frame then, not really fat but more round and curvy than was popular. Now she looked almost emaciated, as if she were trying to coax her more voluptuous body to being a skinny rail like Charlotte and Lexi. Dani had been one of the "band geeks" in high school, but she and Crawley had never had any extended interaction.

"Oh yes," Char said with a tittering sigh. "Men. You just can't trust them."

"I trust my man," Dani said with a smile.

"Oh, of course, baby," Char said, smiling sweetly. "Travis is a great guy!"

"I have to hit the little girl's room, too," Dani said, setting down her drink. Crawley rose up from the booth so the redhead could squeeze past. As soon as she sat back down Char put a hand on her forearm.

"Oh my god, Dani has like, no clue whatsoever, but Travis is a freaking lothario! There's not a woman in this bar he hasn't taken home at least once."

Crawley looked at her askance.

"I haven't. You haven't!"

Char chewed on her index finger and giggled girlishly.

"Well...you haven't."

"Wow." Crawley bit her tongue on a snippy retort.

"Oh, he's definitely good in bed, but he's a face licker, you know? Ewww. Dani thinks she's all that, but the only reason he even proposed to her is she's skinny now! Wait until after the wedding and she gets all gross again, then she'll see!"

Crawley sucked down the rest of her margarita, needing the help to stay silent. There were many reasons for the gulf she felt between herself and most women her age, but one of them was their propensity for being two-faced. Crawley liked to play her cards close to her chest, but if she didn't like someone she wasn't nice to their face only to turn on them the instant they walked away. For a moment, she wished she were more like Autumn. A grin came to her lips. Autumn would have called Char on her hypocrisy, probably right in front of Danielle. The grin faded from her lips a moment later. Autumn would never have allowed herself to be put in that situation in the first place. Either you were worth her time or you weren't, that was Autumn.

"Oh my God...you must think I'm a total bitch right now!"

"No," Crawley said, though the sentiment was right on the money.

"I was kind of snotty to you, back in the day."

Crawley winced, taken aback by the unexpected confession.

"Don't worry about it."

"No, I totally was! I thought I was the be all and end all just because I was cute. I guess maybe I was jealous of you."

"Really?"

"Yeah! I spent like two hours every morning making sure I presented a perfect package, while you just threw on some big, tent-like dress and left the house. I don't have the confidence for that."

"Oh," Crawley said, hands clenching into fists beneath the table.

"But look at you now! OMG you're gorgeous! Even in those ratty old jeans half the guys here still want to get with you!"

Crawley tried to smile at the compliment, backhanded though it was. She wished, very dearly, that she was anywhere else in the world at that moment.

"I swear, Phil, I wanted to *scream*."

Phil nodded his head, blinking rapidly as he stared at the menu on the table before him.

"I mean, I'm so glad you were still up so I didn't have to go with those harpies to whatever yuppie bistro they think is trending."

"Uh huh," Phil said, rubbing his eyes.

"Phil, have you been listening to me?"

"Huh? Yeah." He looked up from the menu and smiled slightly. "You're glad I dragged myself out of bed to grab a midnight bite because it got you away from Charlotte the Harlot—"

"Charlotte the Harlot?" Crawley burst out laughing, causing the smattering of late night patrons to glance over their way. "That's pretty good."

"That's what they called her back in the day," Phil yawned and closed up the menu. "I think I'm ready. You?"

"So you weren't listening when I told you I wanted French toast with powdered sugar, and eggs over easy," she said. Then Crawley adopted a pseudo-eureka face, as if she'd just stumbled upon a great discovery. "Oh, wait, that was when Miss Short Skirt Waitress was bending over to pick up a fork off the floor. *Of course* you didn't hear me."

More patrons grumbled at her outburst, and Phil scanned the room with a nervous smile.

"Ellie, dear, I think you're a little bit drunk," he said softly.

"Don't call me Ellie Dear! That's what my mom calls me. Fucking bitch, always telling me I'm not doing things right! There's the wrong way and her way, and that's it."

Crawley unclenched her fists and folded her hands in her lap. Taking a deep breath, she composed herself.

"Okay," she said, "I might have had just a few too many margaritas. I'll have coffee with my French toast."

"You got it." Phil flagged down the waitress and she came cheerily to their side. Crawley didn't like the way she leaned on the booth behind Phil while they ordered, and liked it even less when the flirty blonde ruffled Phil's curly hair before she left.

"Slut," Crawley muttered.

"What? No, she's just friendly."

"A friendly *slut*."

"What's gotten into you?" Phil wasn't looking so tired anymore. His nostrils flared and his eyes were clear but narrow. "Just because you're mad at your frenemy Charlotte you have to take it out on your boyfriend?"

"My boyfriend shouldn't spend so much time staring at other women."

"Well, maybe my girlfriend shouldn't call me up on a goddamn work night because she wants me to hold her hand while she bitches my head off."

Crawley's eyes opened wide. Her mouth opened, but she couldn't articulate anything other than a gasp. Phil seemed a bit abashed, not able to meet her gaze and rubbing the back of his head.

"I'm sorry. I guess I'm more tired than I thought."

"This keeps happening." Crawley stared at her own reflection in the window and realized she seemed close to tears. "It's not good. We keep fighting lately."

"Over little crap. Couples argue over little crap all the time."

"Autumn and Steve don't."

Phil laughed, a derisive bark.

"Are you kidding me? Steve told me the other day that he thinks it's only a matter of time before Autumn goes poof!" He held his hands together and then quickly swept them apart.

"You mean, dies?" Crawley's heart thumped, her mouth gone dry.

"No! I mean, up and dumps him again."

"That's not going to happen. Those two are just..." she sighed, "...just made for each other."

"Here we go again," Phil said, throwing his hands up in the air.

"What do you mean, here we go again?"

Crawley hadn't meant to put so much menace into her voice, but Phil's reaction suggested otherwise.

"Uh, nothing. Never mind."

"Phil."

"I said never mind."

"*Phil!*"

"Ellie…" Phil drummed his fingers on the table, "you may find it hard to believe but Steve and Autumn do *not* have the perfect fucking relationship, okay?"

"I never said perfect—"

"You didn't have to. It's written all over your face. I think it's got to do with how instrumental we were not only in finding Autumn's dad but in getting them back together."

Crawley forced her alcohol-soaked brain to settle down and listen, though she wanted to hotly deny his words.

"You're emotionally invested in them, now. Hell, I am too. Rex, Sven, even Rich. We're all pulling for them after everything that's happened, but face the facts: The divorce rate in this country is over sixty percent. Odds are that you'll always meet someone at some point who's a better match for you than your spouse."

"So, you're just hanging out with me until you find someone better, is that it?"

"No! Ellie…" Phil's hands were shaking as he covered his face. "Can we just drop this and eat?"

"Fine."

Despite the fact that her food was well-prepared and fresh, she didn't taste a bite.

Chapter 3

Steve banked the ten-speed hard, narrowly avoiding a collision with a woman pushing a stroller. She swore at him as he passed, her voice dwindling behind him as he zipped down 103rd street.

"Great way to talk in front of your kid." He was wearing shorts which revealed his thick hairy legs all the way to the thigh, and a tight spandex top. Autumn had insisted that he wear an orange reflective vest over it, but he was regretting having listened to her. The day was quite warm for late fall, and a sheen of sweat ran in rivulets down his forehead.

He glanced down at the vinyl bag with the Velcro snaps lashed to his bike frame. It still held steady, though he really didn't think that it would come loose unless he was pasted under a bus. Glancing up in alarm, he realized the intersection he was approaching was about to have a red light. He poured on the speed, legs pumping wildly, and managed to sail past the crosswalk just as the light turned red. He jumped a pothole by doing a fairly impressive bunny hop, and skidded to a halt outside of the glass revolving doors of an office building.

Steve cursed when he realized that there was no decent place to chain up his bike. The only object remotely suitable was a street sign, and he had a clear memory of someone trying to jack his ride by slipping the chain and bike all the way over the sign post.

Grumbling, he simply seized the frame and lifted the bike to his shoulder. Carefully, he tried to navigate the revolving door, but the awkward bundle soon became wedged halfway. Backing up, he tried to stand the bike on its rear wheel and balance it against his chest. This worked well enough, but he left tread stains upon his reflective vest.

Making it through the revolving door at last, he dropped the bike to the floor with a loud clatter. A plump security guard put her arms akimbo and gave him the baleful eye.

"You can't ride that in here," she said.

"I had no intention." Steve put the bike back on his shoulders. He rummaged around in his fanny pack and withdrew a slip of paper. "Which way is suite 908?"

"Ninth floor, take a left—HEY! You can't bring that bike up there!"

"Well, there's nowhere to lock it up outside."

"That's not my problem," said the woman, rising to her feet and putting her hands on her hips.

"Um, okay…listen, can you watch it for me? I'll only be a—"

The woman's jowl's flapped noisily, so vehement was her head shaking.

"Mmm-mmm, MMM-MMM! I ain't your damn slave! I ain't watching nothing but this here front door."

"I have to do something with it. Maybe your building should put in a bike rack."

"Maybe you should get a real job."

Steve sighed. There seemed to be no pleasing the woman. Realizing he still had to work at Greece Hut later, and thus did not have time to argue, he set his jaw and turned toward the elevator.

"Where you think you going?"

"I'll only be a second. I promise not a single wheel will touch the carpet, okay?"

"It is *not* okay—" the woman's voice was cut off by the sliding elevator doors as they closed. Sighing, Steve leaned against the wall as a horrid Muzak rendition of "Brown Sugar" wafted through the speakers.

"God, I'm tired." Steve studied his wan reflection in the mirrored walls of the elevator. He looked ridiculous to his own eyes, like a grown man trying to dress like a child. The elevator dinged, and he forced his body to move once more.

Dropping off the documents was easy enough, though the receptionist raised an eyebrow at the bike on his shoulder. He was on his way swiftly, taking the elevator back to the ground floor.

"I'm calling your boss," the guard said as he exited. She was on a corded phone, the curly wire stretched almost straight with tension. "You gonna get fired."

"Make sure you tell them about this!" Steve put the bike down and jumped on the seat. He rode it the last ten feet to the door, which he eschewed in favor of the emergency exit. The alarm blared painfully in his ears, and he regretted the decision almost immediately. Still, he felt a slight thrill go through his body at the deed.

"I'm turning into Autumn," he jested with himself. Legs pumping, he strove to make it back to the dispatcher. Perhaps he could do one more run before he had to go home and change for his other job.

Autumn unwrapped the Pop-Tart, silver cellophane crinkling. She withdrew the frosted treats and laid them on top of the wrapper on the reception desk. Sal, who was busy counting inventory nearby, looked up in amusement as she broke off the dry outer edges and tossed them in the trash can at her feet. Crawley sat on the edge of the reception desk, cocking an eyebrow at Autumn's customization of the breakfast staple.

"Still eating only half the Pop Tarts?" said Crawley.

"Shut up." Autumn spat out crumbs while uttering her garbled words. "I don't like the parts without fruit."

"You should get those toaster strudel things."

"We don't have a toaster here, and anyway, those things cost an arm and a leg. Box of Pop Tarts is under a buck most places…well, the no-name brand, anyway."

Sal's brow knit with little lines. Stout arms propelled his wheelchair over to her side.

"Money still tight?" He patted her on the shoulder.

"Yeah, but don't worry about it. I know you can't afford to give me a raise."

"Well, remember that Dwayne guy I served with back in the 704th?"

"The guy who said he was gonna be a millionaire when his grandpa croaked?"

"Yeah, that's some rather specific memory you got there. I mean, you don't remember his Pekinese named Cha Cha, his gay father-in-law or his penchant for collecting Yu-Gi-Oh cards, but you sure can recall that he was going to be rich."

"I was drunk most of the time we were together, Sal, and you were too!"

"Yeah. Those were good times, what I can remember of them. Still don't know how you kicked the sauce without going to rehab."

"Being drunk is a lot like being sick. Besides, I only have one kidney now and I'd like to take care of it."

"What, is your dad gonna want it back?"

"I hope not. I've gotten kind of attached to it."

All three laughed, Crawley the hardest of all.

"Anyway," Sal said, "Dwayne, as it turns out, wasn't as full of shit as we all thought. He really did inherit a fortune, and now he fancies himself an art dealer. I showed him some of your work, and he —"

"You WHAT?" Autumn said, nostrils flaring.

"What's the problem? I was trying to help!"

"Sorry…it's just that…I don't paint so someone else can look at it and go 'oh, that's so pretty!' I paint because it…I don't know, it just…centers me."

Crawley's brow furrowed at the statement. She wondered what she could do to feel centered herself. Her parents tugged her in one direction, and her feelings for Phil in another.

"Spoken like a true artist. Oh come on, Autumn. Are you going to work in a tattoo parlor for the rest of your life? I mean, I love having you here, and god knows I'd lose clients if you quit, but —"

"If you ever wonder why we aren't together, besides the fact that you're an asshole when you drink, it's this father dearest bullshit. I don't need you to 'motivate' me, Sally."

Sal sighed, then rolled himself back to the low table where he had been counting pigments.

"Okay, but he was wanting to display your paintings, maybe commission some for a show he has coming up…"

The chair screeched across the floor as Autumn practically jumped to her feet. She came over to Sal's side, eyes shining.

"He really said that?"

"Oh, I don't want to bother you — far be it from me to tell you how to live your life…"

Crawly stifled a laugh at their continuing antics.

Autumn issued a frustrated grunt, bending low enough that she could seize Sal by the shirt collar.

"Don't think I won't kick your ass just because you're a gimp!"

"Gimp, is it?" Sal said, but he was laughing.

"I'll roll your crippled ass in the street, let a concrete mixer run you over."

"Okay, fine, I'll text him your number. Try not to blow this by being *you*."

"No promises."

"I never heard that you paint," Crawley said, rising to her feet.

"Really? I guess you've never been to our place, have you? I got a big mess going on in one corner, what with the easel and half-finished canvases and what not."

"Maybe Phil and I can swing by later tonight, play some cards or something?"

"I don't play Magic, or Yu-Gi-Oh. I'm not a nerd!"

"Hey!" Crawley pouted theatrically. "I'm proud to be a nerd!"

"It's probably a better career choice than edgy artist chick." Autumn grumbled down at her Pop-Tart repast. "I mean, you have time to stop in here most every day and bug me, and I've never seen you eat anything that comes out of a silver wrapper. It's always high end artsy fartsy salads with monkey balls on them and squished caterpillars for dressing."

Crawley laughed, her eyes tearing up.

"I don't remember eating one of those. What would monkey balls even taste like?"

"Chicken. I bet you enjoy what you do, though. Like a mad scientist trying to come up with a doomsday spider that can devour the world!"

Crawley giggled.

"I like my work well enough, but sometimes I wish I didn't work with, let alone live with, my parents."

"Oh, so the old folks are in the way of you and Phil getting your freak on?"

"No, we can go to his place for *that*. My mom wants me to meet a nice Catholic man and start squeezing out grandbabies. My dad is always pushing me to take our business more seriously."

"Oh, bullshit," Autumn said, spraying crumbs onto the desk. "You work your ass off all the time, like seven days a week!"

"Yeah, sometimes. I work hard on the lab stuff, but Dad wants me to start handling all the other ends of it too. You know, meeting clients, brokering deals, dealing with our attorney. I'm not good with people, Autumn, I can't charm the pants off of them like you can."

"Aw, you think I'm charming?"

"In your own way, yes. You're not afraid to be yourself, and people pick up on that. Me, I don't even know who I am yet."

"Well…" Autumn ticked off her points on her inked fingers. "You're a good Catholic girl who never takes the lord's name in vain, and yet you're like this raging nympho—"

"Hey! I'm so not a nympho! Phil's the only guy I've slept with in the past year and a—"

"Calm down, squinty, I don't want you to use any of that chop saki stuff on me! I never said you were a slut, I said you were a nympho."

"They aren't the same thing?"

"No, of course not! A slut has no standards. A nympho loves sex, worships it even, but still respects herself."

"I'm not sure that's true…I'm pretty confident that nymphomania is a real psychological condition—"

"Oh, for fuck's sake, there you go being Miss Know-It-All again. No wonder the popular chicks pick on you."

Crawley started to protest, then bit it back.

"You think I'm a know-it-all?"

Autumn picked up on her serious tone, sat up a bit straighter and cleaned crumbs from her shirt.

"I don't…not really. It's just kind of how you are, you know? You're *smart*, Ellie, smarter than most of the people on the planet. You're going to keep running into people like Charlotte that just don't understand you, and what people don't understand, they fear."

"So what should I do?" Crawley wrinkled her wide nose.

"Do? Do? Who says you do anything? Just be yourself and fuck all those haters who can't stand you. That's my philosophy."

"Easy for you to say. You hate most everybody anyway. Of course you don't care what they think."

Autumn closed her mouth for a moment, her face impassive.

"You really think I hate most everybody?"

"Yes," Crawley said, licking her lips nervously. She wondered if she had pushed the volatile young woman too far.

Autumn's face split in a vicious, jubilant grin.

"Thank you, but flattery will get you nowhere!"

Crawley hid her face in her palm while Autumn's shoulders shook with laughter.

Skidding to a stop, Steve left two black trails in his wake, smearing the sidewalk. He leaped off the bike and hastily chained it next to several others. He nodded at a Latino man as he elbowed his way through the busy sidewalk to enter *What a Rush*, the bike messenger/delivery company he worked for.

Dashing down a short flight of stairs below street level, he left streaks of moisture from his sweaty palms on the railing. The blast of air conditioning that hit him as he entered the dispatch office was such a shock on his hot skin that he nearly swooned.

Shaking off his light-headed feeling, he blinked in the dimmer light. A receptionist typed a rapid tattoo on the keyboard before her. Another rider nearly ran right into him in his haste, trying to get out the exit Steve was blocking.

"Move your faggot ass," he said, glaring up at Steve.

"Not a very enlightened attitude, Zach." Steve nevertheless moved aside for the bellicose little man with the goatee.

"I'll show you enlightened."

"Was that a threat?" He leaned out the door to holler after the man as he dashed up the stairs. "If it was, it was derivative!"

"Steve," the receptionist said in a stage whisper, phone receiver cradled between her chin and shoulder. "Boss wants to see you."

"I was just hoping to get a run, Beulah." Steve scratched the back of his damp head.

"I think you better talk to Reed first, sweetie."

Steve shrugged and crossed the office, the top of his head inches from the low ceiling. He reached a door with a frosted glass window, the lettering on which had long since worn away. Rapping on the glass with his knuckles, he was promptly rewarded with an angry voice from within.

"Not on the glass, gawd dammit!"

Steve suppressed a snicker and swung the door inward. The office was tiny, barely as long as he was tall and maybe three quarters as wide. Most of the space was taken up by a rectangular metal desk with peeling paint. A short, scruffy man with a bald pate squatted behind the desk, his belly coming up on top of it. He blew out a long stream of smoke, adding to the acrid air that was already stinging Steve's eyes.

"What's up, Reed?"

"What's up Reed?" the man said back in a mocking tone.

"Uh, did I miss something?"

"Yeah, you missed the part about how our clients are our life's blood. You want to tell me why you're intent on pissing them all off?"

"I don't follow, the last delivery went off without a hitch. I barely talked to anyone—"

"Oh, so you *didn't* mouth off to a security guard, *didn't* drag your bike through their lobby and screw up their door, and *didn't* use the emergency exit when you left?"

"Uh, no, all those things happened, but you have to understand—"

"You're fired."

"What? Oh, come on, that's the first time in weeks that I pissed somebody off—"

"It's also the last time. Get out. Your last check will be in the mail on Friday."

"In the mail? That's not fair! Friday is payday, and I need that money!"

"Legally, all I have to do is stick it in the mail."

"You fat piece of shit." Steve glanced over at the extra-large iced coffee sitting on the desk. So inviting, with beads of condensation dripping down the side…

"Don't you fucking *dare*," Reed said, his face turning red.

Steve reached out and knocked the drink over, spilling it on Reed's white shirt.

"Oops! How clumsy of me."

"Fuck you, this is assault! I'm having you arrested!"

"Yeah, I'm sure the cops will make this a priority." Steve slammed the door on his way out. "Have a good one, Beulah."

"Bye," she said, which drew Reed's ire. She looked behind her innocently and shrugged. "What?"

Steve hit the street and fumbled with his bike chain, biting back tears. He got on the bike and willed his sore muscles to action once more.

What am I gonna tell Autumn?

Chapter 4

P hil shoved the basement door open ahead of them, a musty scent wafting out. Crawley peered past him at the two men standing next to each other, fussing with a bass guitar, and flashed them a sheepish grin.

"Sorry we're late," Phil said.

"Yeah, yeah," said the shorter of the two men. He had thinning hair on his head, but had grown out the back and sides into a shaggy helmet. His features were plain and blunt, blue eyes twinkling with good humor. "You know, this is what caused Fleetwood Mac to break up."

"Ja," said the taller of the two. He was broad shouldered with short pale blonde hair. Blue eyes sparkled with amusement at Phil's expense. "You and Ellie, you make the beast with two backs on your own time."

"Where is Crawley?"

"Right here, Rex," she said, pushing open the door. Phil made haste to assist her with the heavy amp for the guitar she had slung over her shoulder. She looked at the taller man and giggled. "Sorry, Sven, I wouldn't let him leave until I —"

"Eleanor!" Phil said, his face growing red.

"— got something to eat."

"Thank you," mouthed Phil, which caused her to roll her eyes. How could a man be so dirty in private, but such a prude in public?

"You were gonna say 'until I got off,' weren't you?" Rex said, slapping Phil on the shoulder. "Don't take it bad, Philly boy, women are hard to please. Sometimes you need, heh heh, *mechanical* assistance…"

"What?" Crawley said as Phil slapped a palm over his face.

"He is speaking of vibrators, *ja?*" Sven said.

"Oh," Crawley said, giggling.

"Please stop talking," Phil said, his cheeks flushed.

"You really don't have a vibrator?" Rex said. "I thought all women had vibrators. Shelly has a whole collection."

"For god's sake," Phil said.

"…different heads, different sizes…she even has one that's shaped like John Holmes."

"Who's John Holmes?" Crawley said.

"Legendary porno movie star," Sven said. "He had a twenty centimeter penis."

"Centimeter?" Rex said. "This is America, Sven, we use inches!"

"Actually," Crawley said, "as of 1982, the United States has officially adopted the metric system."

"Really?" Phil said.

"Yeah," Crawley said, "we actually use the metric system in our lab."

"I never could get it," Rex said, dragging a heavy table out of the way so he could set up his drums.

"It's easier than the English method," Crawley said. She plugged her cherry red electric guitar into her amp.

"Hey, Sven," Rex said, "want to tell them what a lazy bitch you are?"

"Shut up," Sven said, shaking his fist at Rex, "or I open up the can of ass whip!"

"What's up?" Phil said, taking the cardboard he used as a dust cover off a full length electronic keyboard.

"Swedish Chef here don't want to sing and play bass at the same time no more."

"It's hard!"

"Well," Phil said, pursing his lips, "if we got another bassist, Sven could play rhythm on a few tracks…"

They engaged in a debate about the band's future. Crawley largely was silent, still feeling like the newcomer despite her exalted position as lead guitarist. When the three men seemed to have reached an accord, she politely cleared her throat.

"I was thinking," she said when all three eyes were focused on her, "that we should play some new songs."

"We just added 'Smokin' in the Boy's Room,'" Rex said.

"No," Crawley said, "I mean something we've never played before."

"What?" Phil said. "Like Nickelback or something? We're known as an eighties cover band."

"I think she means original songs," Rex said, nodding his head. "Like, writing them ourselves."

"That is sounding awesome," Sven said, grinning broadly.

"There's one problem," Phil said. "No bar owner is going to want us to play original songs. They like us because we have a set list full of songs that everyone knows."

"I know, sweetie," Crawley said, "but I'm *tired* of playing only old songs, tired of the same old, same old every day. I want to try something *new*."

"I think it's a great idea," Rex said. "We can start adding new songs to the set list slowly, expand our repertoire, as it were."

"*Ja*," Sven said, "I'm all for it!"

"Great," Phil said as they began to tune up.

Crawley noticed his less than pleased grimace, and gave him back a narrow-eyed frown. She thought he would be happy to hear of just how emotionally invested she had become in Settle the Score. Ever since her first live gig, in front of a small crowd at a friend's New Year's party, she had been addicted to the rush of performing. It was sexual in a way, using your body and heart and soul to make people feel the way you wanted them to.

Maybe Phil thought of it as "his" band—although it seemed obvious to Crawley that Rex was the true leader—and resented her intrusion. All in all, it made for a stiff practice with a lot of sniping about missed notes.

Perched next to him on the sofa, Autumn snuggled up close to Steve, rubbing his sore arm with both of her hands. The light, frequent kisses she was leaving on his cheek and neck said she was in the mood, but the guilt of losing his job the day before weighed heavily upon him. Picking up on his glumness, Autumn stopped what she was doing and muted the television.

"What's wrong, sugar?" She scooted a few inches away from him.

"Nothing," he said, swallowing hard.

"It's not nothing. You're shutting me out. Again."

"I'm not shutting you out." Steve narrowed his blue eyes to slits.

"Bullshit, you've barely spoken at all today. I thought you were just tired, but—"

"I *am* tired. It comes with working three fucking jobs, okay? I'd have every weekend off if…"

His voice trailed off, and Autumn's lips straightened into a tight line.

"What's wrong?" Autumn put her hand on his shoulder. "Don't shut me out, let me help!"

"You can't help the hopeless. Autumn, I got fired."

"Good, you hate that job anyway. Tell me you slammed Glenn's face down on the grill for about ten seconds before you walked out."

"Not Greece Hut," said Steve, though the image created by Autumn made him smile slightly, "the messenger job."

She sat while he explained the circumstances surrounding his dismissal. She laughed when he spoke of riding his bike through the lobby, and became downright hysterical as he told her of giving Reed a coffee bath.

"Oh, sugar, it's not that big a deal."

"Not a big deal? Autumn, we need that money!"

"You still have two other jobs, and I still work at the parlor four days a week."

"Yeah, and I have to start my tech support job in about twenty minutes. Guess I'd better get ready—"

"Nope," Autumn said, dragging him back down to the sofa as he tried to rise. "You can't deal with those mouth-breathing, single-digit-IQ-bearing morons! Look at you, you're all tense and stressed."

Steve's mouth twisted into a grin as she pretended to consider their options, finger before her lips and eyes cast skyward.

"Now, whatever could we do to reduce your stress levels?"

"There's transcendental meditation." He grinned as she took his hand and kissed his fingers. "Yoga, big bag of dope…"

"Mmm," Autumn said, sucking on the tip of his index finger, "meditation's hard, we don't have a yoga mat, and there's not enough junk food in the house for munchies…"

She took his hand and put it against her belly. He flexed his fingers, massaging her skin through the thin T-shirt she wore. Slowly, he wormed the hand downward, fingers sliding beneath the hem of her spandex fitness pants. He gently traced a line with his finger over the panel of satin fabric that separated their skin. Autumn gasped at his touch, mashing her hand atop of his.

When he slid his hand beneath her panties, she was warm and slippery. He craned his neck until their mouths were inches away, her breath hot on his skin.

"I'm wide open," she said, her eyes closed.

Steve took the cue. He allowed her to remove his hand from her pants, busying himself with yanking down her skin-tight apparel. Autumn got to her feet, shimmying her hips so he could drag the pants off of her. She doffed her panties in one smooth motion, playfully tossing them at him. They landed on top of his head and stayed there a brief moment before falling behind the sofa.

"You're so sexy," he said as she turned her back to him and lifted the shirt off of her head. Her bottom swiveled in a circle, prompting him to smack her across both cheeks.

"Oh!" She jumped in the air nearly a foot. Turning her neck so she could stare at him over her shoulder, she shook her rump again. "That's not all you've got, is it?"

"All we have time for. No more foreplay!" With a grunt, he grabbed her around the waist and yanked her down to his lap. She went with the motion, landing sideways across his thighs and kissing him deeply on the mouth.

Steve had one arm cradling her along the spine, the other enveloping her in a half-embrace. His fingers roughly squeezed her breast, encouraged by her soft cries of delight. She ground her bottom into his lap, sliding all over his engorged member. Deciding that he just couldn't wait any longer, Steve turned her around to face away from him. The colorful demon tattoo on her back stared back at him under a sheen of sweat. Gently, he bit her on the shoulder and neck as she put her arms over her head and stroked his thick hair.

Autumn let out a long, low groan as he slipped inside her. They both leaned back on the couch, his hands exploring every inch of her torso. Steve toyed with her nipple piercing, gently rubbing the connected skin between his thumb and forefinger. His other hand found her clitoris and moved in slow, forceful circles.

Steve gasped as Autumn's body suddenly shuddered, her eyelids fluttering like a butterfly's wings. Her limbs, slick with sweat, lay limply against him, and a gentle smile was on her face as he kept kissing her on the cheek. Steve's eyes went wide when he glanced at the muted television and saw that he had less than two minutes to prepare for his tech service job.

"Ow." Autumn hastily got off of his lap. Steve rubbed a spot at the back of his calf that was knotted up tightly.

"What's wrong?" Autumn's brown eyes were large with concern as he limped across the floor toward his discarded boxers.

"Cramp." Steve winced as he painfully donned the garment. "Ow ow ow!"

"Do you want me to massage it?" Autumn tried to hide her smile as Steve hobbled over to his desktop.

"No time." He plopped himself down in front of the computer. He quickly donned a headset and logged onto Azztek, the service he worked for. In a matter of seconds, his queue of ten calls was full, and he sighed at the terrible grammar and spelling of their hastily written requests.

Autumn walked across the floor to stare at Steve's leg. His calf was twitching as the oxygen starved muscles protested their lot. Wordlessly, she dropped to her knees and kneaded the stubborn flesh into limp submission.

"Uh," Steve said, suddenly on line with a customer, "Azztek support line, this is Steve, how can I help you?"

"Yeah," came the vapid sounding female voice from the earpiece, "my computer won't like, connect to the Internet and stuff?"

"I see…" Steve gritted his teeth as Autumn worked his calf over. She was not gentle, but with his thick musculature she couldn't afford to be. "What happens when you try to connect? Is there a message that pops up?"

"It just says no connections are, like, available?"

"What kind of—" Steve grunted as his calf finally gave up the fight and relaxed. "Sorry, what kind of Windows do you have?"

"Just a second, I'll go check."

He heard the sound of footsteps and then a rattling noise. A second later he heard her voice once more.

"Glass, I think."

Steve hit the mute button on his headset and was overcome by laughter.

He turned the volume back on after a moment, as Autumn arched her pierced eyebrow in query.

"I mean," Steve said, still chuckling, "what kind of Windows do you have installed on your PC?"

"Oh, I'm not sure…is it Windows XP?"

"That's what I was asking you. If it says Windows XP on your screen right now, that's what you have."

"Oh, I don't have my computer with me. I'm at work."

Steve hid his face in his palm as Autumn leaned against his bare thigh, looking bored.

"Okay, ma'am, then what you need to do is go ahead and call back when you have your computer at hand."

"Why? What difference would that make?"

"We need to try some things on your computer, and we won't know if they're working unless you can look at your screen and see what's happening."

"Oh, like, duh!"

"Truer words were never spake."

"What?"

"I said have a great day," Steve said, terminating the contact. "God, some people…"

"Another moron, I take it?" Autumn leaned her chin across her arms, which were laid on Steve's leg.

"Yeah! I mean, I asked her what kind of Windows she had and she was like 'glass, I think'!"

"Oh, god!" Autumn laughed gently. He dropped a hand to her head and stroked her soft hair. She responded by turning her head to the side and nibbling on his thumb.

"Stop that! I have more clients."

"They can wait. I have to wait like forty minutes and then talk to someone in India."

"Shh, I'm on…good afternoon, thank you for calling Azztek support, how can I help you?"

Autumn looked up at Steve's face as he took the call, then down at his lap. Idly, she reached out and played with his member, hidden beneath his red boxers.

"I see." Steve glared down at Autumn. "Quit it!"

Autumn ignored him, running her hand up and down his rapidly hardening shaft with a bemused smile on her face.

"No, sir," Steve said, both his hands busy on the keyboard. "I'm fixing that billing snafu for you right now, sir."

Steve bit down on his lip to stifle a groan as Autumn slipped his cock free and slid her tongue up and down its length. He quickly finished typing the new address, which he thought may have been wrong but he was too distracted to double check it.

"Have a nice day, sir!" Steve quickly ended the call. At that point he saw no reason to stop Autumn, who was looking up at him with wide, almost adoring eyes. She closed them and bent herself fully to her task, and Steve could only stare helplessly at the unanswered calls on his queue.

Chapter 5

S teve leaned out of the drive-through window, straining his long arms to reach the shiny dime on the pavement. His legs stretched out behind him for ballast, and he was just barely able to scoop up the coin with his fingers.

"Here," he said, handing it to Tenisha. The little black woman dropped it into the open cash drawer before her.

"Thanks. Fucking Glenn writes you up if yo drawer more'n a penny short!"

"Damn, glad I'm not on register."

"You too damn tall, you look like a gargoyle all lurched over the register and shit."

A tone sounded three times, indicating that there was a car in the drive-through. Tenisha reached up and pushed the talk button on her headset while Steve moved back to the flat iron grill. The burgers were charred, so he threw them in the waste bucket and laid out a new row of pink patties. Wiping the sweat off his brow with his forearm so he would not get blood on his face, he glanced up fearfully to make sure Glenn had not witnessed the lapse. He was not allowed to touch his face at all on the grill.

The restaurant was not busy at three o'clock in the afternoon. It was a time when most of the skeleton crew staffing the restaurant busied themselves with cleaning and food prep for the dinner rush.

Steve glanced at the clock, slapping himself in the forehead when he realized he still had two hours left on his shift.

"I'm gonna take a bathroom break," he said, once the meat had been grilled to Greece Hut's idea of greasy brown perfection. He personally liked his burgers a bit more rare than the charred hockey pucks Greece Hut insisted on for safety's sake. Steve took off his blood spattered, greasy apron and hung it on the edge of the bun warmer next to a half dozen others. His nonslip shoes made loud sucking sounds as he passed through a puddle of slimy water pooling over a clogged drain.

Entering the bathroom stall, he closed the door and took out his cell phone. He sent off a text to Autumn that he would not be able to get out early, sighing when he realized that she would have to wait in the parking lot or drive all the way across Manhattan and back.

He hesitated as his fingers lingered over the touch screen. Autumn had been fantastic about their monetary troubles, but he knew she was getting tired of ramen noodles and draft beer. Hell, *he* was getting tired of ramen noodles and draft beer.

The thought made him grin before Glenn's angry voice reached his ears. His manager was demanding that Tenisha tell him where his grill attendant had gone. Swearing, Steve shoved the phone back in his pocket and went back to the kitchen.

"Did you wash your hands?" Glenn said when Steve started to reach for a slab of pre-sliced meat patties.

"Yeah," Steve lied.

"Your hands aren't wet…" Glenn peered at the offending extremities.

"I dried them really good."

"Bullshit! Go wash your hands before you touch that meat."

"But I didn't even use the—"

"NOW!" Glenn jabbed a finger at the hand washing sink.

Steve sighed and moved to comply.

"SpongeBob never had to go through this shit," Steve said under his breath.

A recent conversation he'd had with his father came unbidden to his mind. He'd been able to feel the disappointment exuding through the phone. Steve felt a pang of guilt when he was momentarily glad that the old man was always on the road and not there to stare at him with loving but sad eyes.

"Stop daydreaming and get your ass back on the grill and lay out some meat. Our four o'clock rush is going to start soon."

"You got it, boss," Steve said, the honorific almost catching in his throat.

Maybe the time *had* come for a change.

Crawley leaned on the sink in Phil's well-scrubbed, spacious bathroom, staring at her reflection in the mirror. Her hair was disheveled, still tossed about from her slumber. She had forgotten to take off her makeup the previous evening, leaving smudges on her face. Dark clouds crossed her pretty features when she thought of what reaction Phil might have if one of his white, thousand-thread count pillowcases was stained.

She became more alarmed when she thought she detected a black hair forcing its way onto her upper lip. A heavy sigh of relief escaped her lips a moment later when she realized it was just a coffee ground. The curse of her dark hair avoided, at least for a day, she smiled at her reflection when Phil came up behind her. His hair was still mussed hair from sleep as well, though his glasses were already perched on his thin nose.

"Good morning, sweetie," she said as he came up behind her and embraced her around the waist. She glanced down at his hands, which bore a pair of neckties. "I like the green one better."

"Doesn't matter, you won't be able to see it anyway."

"What?" Crawley said. Phil used the green tie to blindfold her, eliciting both a wide smile and a pleased squeal from her. "Oh, am I in trouble?"

"Only if you don't do what I say, when I say." Phil got into character, slipping into a rough voice. Carefully but firmly, he took her arms and pulled them behind her. Crawley giggled as he used the other tie to bind her crossed wrists together. She tugged on them a bit, noting with satisfaction that his knot tying had gotten much better.

She gasped as Phil's hand knotted up in a fist at the back of her head, pulling her hair painfully. Stumbling, he led her blind into the bedroom.

"Get on your knees, bitch," he said, applying gentle pressure to the top of her head. Smiling, she did as she was told. Phil arranged her so her torso was laid across the mattress, the soft sheets feeling nice on her belly. She giggled as Phil threw his shirt up over her head, baring her softly curved bottom to him. Crawley was biting the sheets a moment later, groaning as Phil slid inside of her. He was not a very large man, but then she was a petite woman.

Phil thrust his hips into hers, slowly at first and then picking up speed. Her cries reflected off the bed into her ears, seeming louder for the lack of her vision. Crawley clenched her bound hands into fists, yanking on her bonds in a sincere but futile struggle. Phil had gotten much, much better at tying knots.

She moaned loudly as he bore down hard against her. The bed slid on its coasters toward the far wall until it stopped by the edge of Phil's cherry wood nightstand. The blindfold slipped off of her eyes and around her neck as he grabbed a hand full of her thick hair and drew her slowly up from the bed. Their mouths found each other's, Phil aggressively invading hers with his tongue. She accidentally nipped him with her white teeth a moment later when her body reached the apex. Phil slid out of her, gasping for air and covered in sweat.

"You're not tired already, are you sweetie?" She used her bound hands to massage his smoothly shaven testicles.

"Not even close." The fatigue was obvious in his voice. "Sweetie? Aren't you supposed to be my victim?"

"That's right." Crawley adopted a defiant facial expression even while she continued to stroke his balls. "I might scream if you don't stop defiling me this second!"

"Go ahead," Phil said, repurposing her blindfold. He pulled it up over her chin and tightened it, slipping the silk garment between her teeth. Crawley chewed for a moment, unsure if the fit was tight enough that it wouldn't fall out during an epic bout of passion. "Can you breathe okay?"

Crawley looked at him with narrowed eyes, grunting a bit. Not only had he spoken out of character, he should have known that if she was having problems she'd have used their safe word.

Phil seemed to realize his mistake, because he roughly turned her around to face him and ran his hands over her small, firm breasts. His fingers gripped her brown nipples, and Crawley felt the nubs harden almost instantly. Soon he dropped his hands lower, probing her wet pussy with aplomb while he used his mouth on her chest.

Crawley tossed her head back, luxuriating in the treatment. She pulled hard against the necktie around her wrists, fingers clutching at Phil's hands as if to stop them. Rudely, he shoved them out of his way and hooked a thumb between her flesh and the silk, holding her trapped hands fast. Her breath came raggedly against the gag in her mouth as Phil's hand probed into her ever deeper. A muffled scream erupted from her throat, and she collapsed backward onto the bed, but still Phil did not relent. His nimble fingers continued to swirl about within her body, eliciting another climax from her that left his hand and bed drenched.

Phil gently untied the neck tie from around her mouth and tossed it aside. He fawned worriedly at the visible marks left on her skin from its tight coils.

"What's wrong?" she said as he untied her hands.

"You've got marks." He touched her face and a hint of red came to his cheeks. Crawley slid off the damp sheets and walked on rubbery legs to the bathroom. She giggled at the minor indentations on her skin, which appeared as if they were already fading.

"Oh, Phillip." She came back into the bedroom and collapsed on the mattress. "That's nothing. I'd be more worried about the hickeys on your neck."

"I don't have any hickeys on my neck—" A moment later he gasped when Crawley reared up on her knees and mauled his neck with her mouth.

"I…ah—" Phil put his hands on her shoulders and stiffened against her. She stopped, pulled away and took in his sweating, panting face. "I'm not ready yet…and I may be done for the night."

"Done?" She started to make a quip, but it died on her tongue. "Oh, Phil, you've been working so hard lately. Of course you should get some sleep."

Crawley snuggled up close to his side, patting his belly as she rested her cheek on his shoulder. Phil stroked her hair, but he seemed oddly distant.

"What's wrong, hon?" she said, raising up on her elbow so she could look him in the eye.

"I don't know," he said. "I'm mostly just tired, I guess."

"Mostly?" She swallowed, and tried to keep her voice perfectly neutral when she spoke again. "You're not…freaked out by the BDSM thing, are you?"

"No!" Phil laughed, but it didn't seem to dispel the tension. "I love the BDSM thing. I used to tie up my female GI Joe action figures, you know, like Cobra captured them?"

She laughed along with him, but wouldn't drop the subject.

"Come on, Phillip," she said with a sigh, "what's bothering you?"

"You'll get mad." Phil yawned and reached out toward the lamp on her bedside table. "Good night."

"Oh, you are so not falling asleep!" Crawley sat up in bed and crossed her arms over her naked breasts. "What's going on? What's going to make me mad?"

"It's nothing, it's just…" Phil scratched the back of his head and glanced at the window, as if he wished he could hurl himself through it. "…I don't know. I guess you're my first, my only girlfriend ever and I wonder if what I'm feeling is really what I think it is."

"What you think it…" Crawley felt as if she'd been slapped. She didn't keep the venom out of her words when she recovered. "And just what do you *think* is going on between us?"

"I think I love you," he said harshly. "I think I love you, but how do I know if I've never been in love before?"

"Oh, I get it," Crawley said coolly. "This is all about Phil needing to sow his wild oats."

"Sew my…what?" Phil blinked.

"Looking to screw the new office hottie?" She stood up and started getting dressed.

"What are you doing? I thought you were spending the night."

"And I thought you weren't an asshole like Rich," she said, throwing her phone into her purse in a huff. "I'll just get out of your way so you can sleep and dream about screwing other women."

"Would you listen to me for a minute?" Phil followed her as she stormed through his apartment. A picture of the two of them together on his mantle did nothing to abate her anger, and only seemed to intensify it. "That's not what I meant at all!"

He continued to follow her, all of the way into the hallway and the elevator. While she waited, not looking at him, he spoke.

"I'm scared, Ellie," he said. "I'm scared, all right? I don't know if I'm ready to be this in love with someone."

In spite of herself, she met his gaze, and found his eyes somber and wet.

"Phil," she said in a whisper. Then she shook her head. "I love you. If you don't love me you'd better figure it out. Fast."

The elevator arrived, and Phil was merciful enough not to follow. She managed to hold back the flood of tears until she was in her car, but the torrent running down her cheeks lasted all the way home.

Steve swung the door to Autumn's car open and tossed his Greece Hut cap in the rubbish strewn back seat.

Autumn thrust her phone back into the cup holder and smiled broadly as Steve cursed.

"Hey, sugar." She pecked him on the cheek as soon as he slid inside. "How's tricks?"

"Glenn is a fucking little peckerwood whose neck I desperately want to wring."

"That good, huh? Say, I was just texting with Crawley, and your bros and their hos are going out tonight, something about their band I think. I know you have to get up early but—"

"Uh, I was meaning to talk to you about that…"

"What?"

"Well, I kinda sorta maybe got…fired. Again."

Autumn giggled, rolling her brown eyes in mock exasperation.

"Duh. You told me that yesterday. So what?"

"That was the bike messenger job. I got a message from Azztek today. Apparently my services are no longer required."

"Why?"

"Well, it seems like I was taking a long time to get to my next call on the queue."

"Oh. Shit. I'm sorry about that, sugar."

She leaned over and kissed him on the lips. He returned it, but his heart was not in it.

"What if we get thrown out on the street?"

"Then we'll share a refrigerator box," Autumn said with a shrug.

"God, how can you be so…cavalier about all this?"

"Hey, I almost died, remember? You losing another one of your jobs ain't shit compared to that."

"I know. I'm sorry, I know you have your own problems…"

"Your problems *are* my own problems."

Steve tried to smile at the sentiment, but it appeared as more of a grimace on his weary face.

"Poor baby. You really, really need to get out tonight."

"I really, really need to get some sleep."

"Sleeping isn't the same as relaxing. Oh c'mon, drink a Red Bull, splash cold water on your face, and man up!"

"I don't know…"

"You know that Wonder Woman costume I said got lost before I could wear it? I lied. It's at the bottom of our chest of drawers. If you go out tonight I just might put it on…"

Steve's blue eyes widened and his heart hammered in his chest. Strange, he saw Autumn naked almost every day but the thought of her playing dress up was bizarrely stimulating.

"To the bar?"

"No way!" She laughed, then her face was crossed with a fierce snarl. "You'd better hope Wonder Woman doesn't come out to play, because she *punishes* bad boys."

"I am so going to the bar," Steve said with a giggle.

Chapter 6

The glass towers of Manhattan shone in the dusk, pouring their cheery illumination out over the city streets. Phil stared up at the skyscrapers from the passenger seat of Crawley's white Eclipse as she grinned at him from the driver's seat.

"Penny for your thoughts, sweetie," Crawley said as he drew his gaze back to her. She had put her hair into a long braid, baring her smooth neck and shoulders. A pink printed tank top worn over a lace camisole covered her torso, showing just enough cleavage to be sexy without giving away too much. The muscles in her shapely legs played as she worked the clutch, visible due to the shortness of her pleated skirt. The bright colors contrasted nicely with her light brown skin, almost as well as the pale pink eye shadow she wore. Her lips glistened with scarlet gloss, and she was wearing her favorite earrings, golden danglers in the shape of black widow spiders.

"What's on your mind?"

"You," he said, and she could feel how much he meant it. "I'm about three seconds away from attacking you."

"Promises, promises."

"You're so hot…"

"Thanks."

"Steve says that Autumn hates being called that. Hot, I mean."

"It's a little…condescending, I guess. If some construction worker hollered it at me, I might be offended. But when you say it, I like it."

"Look," he said, coughing a bit, "about the other night—"

"Let's not talk about it." Crawley shook her head.

"I *do* love you." Phil sounded confident. If he'd stopped talking right then, she'd have been willing to forget their fight entirely. Then he had to go and ruin it. "I mean, I don't know if it's a forever kind of love, but—"

"Forever kind of love?" She gripped the wheel tightly, the leather creaking. "What's that supposed to mean?"

"I didn't…" Phil pulled at his collar. "That didn't come out right. I just…I'm new at this, all right? I'm not Casanova, or whatever…"

"Phil, I don't want you to be Casanova, I want you to be yourself." She forced her voice to be even we she spoke again. "If…if you're not happy with things—"

"I am happy!" Phil laughed nervously. "I'm so happy it scares the crap out of me!"

"Saying it's one thing, but do you mean it?" They drove in silence for several blocks, the streets slipping silently by.

"Whoa, what are you doing?" Crawley shot him a sharp glare, and he pulled his hand away from her thigh.

"Sorry, I was just—"

"Just what? Trying to distract me from being mad at you?"

"I was trying to show you my…" He laughed. "Wait, was it working? Distracting you, I mean?"

He looked so sweet when he was thinking dirty thoughts, that she felt her anger abate. For a time, at least.

They pulled into a pay parking lot, Phil handing his credit card to Crawley so she could swipe it. She drove the Eclipse slowly, starting to park in a spot quite near the entrance. She caught Phil staring down at her legs once more, forehead glistening with sweat.

"Wait," he said, "park further back, maybe under that light that's burned out."

"What? Why? Do you want someone to jack my ride?"

"It's a guarded lot," he said, motioning to the tired, heavy set man sitting in a booth near the street. "Besides, I want to get a little taste before we go into the bar…"

"Oh, you think you *deserve* it?" Crawley put the car in reverse. She parked in the spot Phil had indicated, the nearest car thirty feet away.

"No one deserves you," said Phil, blushing a bit.

Crawley turned a surprised, pleased glance his way.

"You just got yourself about a thousand points, hon."

"Oh? What can I redeem them for?"

"Something soft and slippery," she whispered, leaning over the gearshift to kiss him on the lips. Her tongue was vigorous, tasting the mint on his breath. Phil put his hand on her thigh and rubbed it heavily. She gasped at his touch, trying to embrace him more fully even though the confined quarters made the motion awkward. Both of them broke contact and laughed.

"I guess this isn't going to work," she said, staring to open her door.

"No, wait. This can work!"

"Oh, nothing human was ever meant to sit in the back seat of an Eclipse, hon."

"Come here," he said, taking her by the hand and pulling her toward him. His other hand was busy with the thin leather belt that held up his black dress pants. Crawley slithered over the gearshift and sat on his lap. She raised up on her knees so he could finish his task, then remained that way while he hiked up her skirt. The sight of her lace pink thong and her musky smell had him fully at the ready. He fumbled with her panties for a moment before she reached down and provided assistance.

"They unsnap," she said with a sensuous laugh. Phil's fingers found the tiny buttons and undid them. Her shaved nether lips were already damp, and they slid their bodies together easily. Crawley grunted as he entered her, throwing her head back and setting the sun visor in disarray.

Crawley tried to give the occasional glance to the parking lot, to make sure they weren't going to be caught, but her body was in full control. The Eclipse began to rock and sway as she ground her hips into his. She wrapped her arms around his slender neck and squeezed their chests tightly together. His hand rand down her spine, and his lips were buried within her cleavage.

"Oh my god," she said, before a long wail escaped her throat. She flung her body back in an arch, her left hand hitting the steering wheel and setting off the horn while her shoulder knocked the rear view mirror off the windshield with a *thunk*. She then collapsed forward, putting her head on his shoulder and sighing.

"Your car…" He looked at the mirror lying on the dashboard, biting his lower lip.

"Never mind that…Oh, Phil, that was so wrong!"

"It's a brave new world…we're expanding our set list, adding a new member…maybe it's time I stepped up my game, huh?"

"Oh, don't be silly." She kissed him on the lips. "You don't need game; you're smart and sweet and you take good care of me. That's all a girl wants."

"And a big bank account," Phil said as she carefully climbed back into her own seat.

"I've got my own money." Her tone was plaintive, but her lips were parted in a slight smile.

"Forgetting something?"

"I've got the keys right here." Crawley jangled them in her hand.

"No," said Phil, picking up her discarded undergarments, "your underwear?"

"Oh." Going commando like a slut? Her mother would just *die*. *At least I wouldn't be wearing dirty underwear if I got hit by a car.* She thought.

She glanced around the parking lot to make sure she was unobserved and then hiked up her skirt and slid them back on. She fumbled with the buttons a bit but had them securely fastened by the time Phil had exited the car himself.

They walked past the guard, barely able to keep their hands to themselves. The man gave them a knowing, creepy look that Crawley ignored and Phil glared back at. Crawley's steps were audible in her high heels, echoing off the masonry to their left as they walked down the sidewalk toward the Dew Drop. When they were about to enter the open door of the establishment, Crawley yanked him back off the low steps and fussed with his hair.

"What are you doing?" he said with a grin.

"You have FF hair."

"Eff Eff?"

She leaned forward and whispered in his ear, his cologne heavy in her nostrils.

"Freshly fucked." Crawley gave his buttocks a playful slap.

The Dew Drop was packed with people, some swirling around the modest dance floor, some occupying seats at the bar, but most were sitting at a dozen or so tables and watching various sports on the big screen HDTVs that hung from the ceiling. There was little hope that anyone could actually hear anything emanating from the TVs, however, given the noise level generated by the overly exuberant patrons.

"Are we the first ones here?" Crawley said, leaning close to Phil so he could hear her over the throng.

"I guess so — wait!" His eyes lit up behind his spectacles. "I see Sven's blond head over there."

"Where?" Crawley strained her eyes in the dimly lit environs.

"There...under the monitor with...is that hockey?"

"I see them...and I think that's curling, hon."

They shuffled across the bar, taking some time to squeeze their way through the crowd. Phil took her hand in his, both to keep them from being separated and because of the many lingering looks that Crawley was getting from the male patrons. Eventually they stood next to the half circle booth that Rex and Sven had claimed earlier in the evening. Phil's eyes widened in surprise when he spotted Steve and Autumn sitting next to Rex.

"You made it," he said pleasantly, taking time to fist bump his old friend. Steve smiled, and was obviously having a good time, but the dark circles lurking beneath his eyes told of his emotional and physical weariness. The blue orbs themselves were a bit dull, lacking their usual verve.

Phil turned to Autumn and nodded at her. The quick-witted woman looked to be having a great time. He arched an eyebrow at the several empty margarita glasses sitting before her.

"You're allowed to drink with one kidney?" Phil said.

"Gotta run to the little girl's room more than I used to," Autumn said with a shrug, "but yeah, I can drink."

Her eyes were glassy, and her speech slightly slurred. Crawley noted that Steve had a half full bottle of beer in front of himself that he seemed to have forgotten about. Crawley gave Autumn a hug, as she had done often of late. She sat down in the booth next to Phil, her hand going on top of his knee.

"Autumn looks healthy," Phil whispered into her ear. "Well, physically healthy anyway. She still scares the hell out of me."

Crawley giggled, her face lighting up.

"Girls who dress like her are actually pretty boring in bed," she whispered back. "It's us good little Catholic girls you have to watch out for."

"So," Autumn said, drawing their attention, "I hear you guys are looking for a bassist."

"*Ja*," Sven said, his accented voice powerful enough to carry over the crowd and loud music. "I want to concentrate on singing."

"We're also thinking of adding original songs," Rex said, motioning in vain for the barmaid.

"Really?" Steve said. "No more friendly neighborhood cover band?"

"Gotta evolve, my friend."

"Where's your wife?" Autumn asked Rex.

"At home. Her sister is in town, and I really needed a break from hearing them argue about which one of them their mother loved less."

"That's mean," Crawley said as Rex and Steve laughed.

"That's life," Rex said, raising his glass to Crawley in mock toast.

"You don't understand," Phil said. "You've never met Rex's sister-in-law. Everything is a competition to see who's the most miserable, and she's eminently more qualified."

"Dammit," Rex said as the barmaid again ignored his wave.

"Told you to tip more," Steve said with a grin.

"I was gonna get some hot wings or something…"

"I'll go to the bar and order some," Crawley said, rising from her seat. Phil caught her hand and made her pause.

"Wait," he said, digging in his wallet. He took out a twenty and handed it to her. "Here."

"Thanks," she said, letting her hand linger on his when she took the bill. Their prolonged smiles made their companions grin knowingly.

"No wonder you guys were late…" Steve said while Autumn catcalled.

"God," Phil said, slapping a hand over his face. "It's like being back in high school."

"Nah," Rex said, "Sven hasn't given you a wedgie yet."

"Sven," Autumn said, narrowing her big brown eyes at the Swede, "were you a bully?"

"Yes," said Steve and Rex at the same time Sven shook his head.

"I was just screwing around, *ja?*" Sven said.

"So how did you guys become friends?" Autumn said.

"Well," Rex said, "Steve decides he's going to beat up this big blond villain what's been picking on his little buddy, and waits on the parking lot after class…"

"And proceeds to start laughing it up with him," Autumn said. "I've heard this part of the story."

"You ever just meet someone you hit it off with? It was pretty funny the first time Phil came to my house and Sven was there."

"Didn't you climb up a tree in the back yard?" Rex said, wrinkling his brow.

"Shut up, asshole."

Crawley listened to their banter with half an ear, smiling prettily until she drew the bartender's attention. As she waited by the bar for her order, she noticed someone standing beside her. She glanced up into the face of a towering man, his hair bleached blonde but with black roots beginning to show. A T-shirt about four sizes too small strained to contain his admittedly impressive pectoral muscles. The Dew Drop emblem was emblazoned on his sleeve, which probably meant he was a bouncer or bar back.

"Hi," she said to be friendly, since the man seemed to be struggling for something to say. He was handsome enough, but Crawley had learned to be wary of men who took too much pride in their appearance. She preferred to be the one they doted over.

"Hey," he said, offering his hand for a shake. She took it, her own hand disappearing within the meaty paw. "I'm John. You're in that band that played here last month, right?"

"Yeah," Crawley said, suddenly adopting a more professional demeanor, "Settle the Score. Were you interested in booking us?"

"Uh, actually, I heard from one of the waitresses that you guys were looking for a bassist. I play bass."

"Really?" said Crawley, eyes widening. She ran her eyes up and down his impressive form, deciding that she would have to hear him play. He seemed too much of a prima donna type to be in a supporting role like bass player, but then how many women lead guitarists were there?

"You can talk to Rex if you want," Crawley said, motioning for him to follow her. "He's kind of in charge."

She led him back to their table, accepting her basket of wings from the bartender first. As they approached the group, she noticed that Steve and Autumn seemed to be arguing. They stopped speaking as soon as she was in earshot, their angry gazes speaking volumes.

"Uh, guys," Crawley said, wary of the tension. Conversation had stopped, and Autumn and Steve were studiously ignoring each other like angry cats that had just been in a hissing match.

"Uh," Crawley said, licking her lips, "I have some hot wings…"

"Great," said Rex, glad to have a change of subject. "Now it's a party, right?"

He arched a brow at the bouncer standing behind her.

"Who's this?"

"Oh," Crawley said, blushing, "I'm so sorry, I forgot…Rex, this is John. He's interested in trying out for the bassist position."

"Oh yeah? Great to meet you, man." Rex brightened up considerably. Crawley sighed in relief as Rex took over the negotiations. She still was feeling guilty about forcing her songs onto the boys in the band, and letting Rex assume his role as leader was soothing.

"You know this guy?" Phil poked her firmly in the arm. She turned, annoyed, to see the jealousy displayed on his face.

"Just met him, hon," she said, putting a hand on Phil's forearm. Leaning closer, she whispered in his ear. "What happened with Steve and Autumn?"

"He's a sadistic asshole who won't stop punishing me for leaving him," Autumn said, who had apparently heard Crawley despite her attempts to be clandestine. "That's what happened."

"It was just an off-hand comment. You're taking it too seriously," Steve said.

"Fuck you I'm taking it too seriously! You're saying shit like that all the time like I'm supposed to, what, drop to my knees and beg for forgiveness every time you bring it up?"

"You treat everything like it's not a big deal. Even us." Steve's face was overwhelmed with a dark glower.

"Oh, shut up. I like to make fun of shit. You used to like that about me. You know what? You're not borrowing my car while I'm at work anymore."

"That's fine. It'll stop running since I'm the only one who puts gas and oil in it."

"They put oil in it at the factory, don't they?"

"You have to check it every three months! You don't know how to take care of things!"

"Oh, that car won't last forever! It had like a gazillion miles on it when my Dad bought it. You fuss over everything."

"I fuss because I care! I can't just blow things off like you do."

"Since when have I ever —? You're still punishing me for leaving."

"I'm not punishing you."

"Yes, you are!"

"Maybe I just want you to act like you give a shit."

"Get out of my way."

Autumn shoved Steve on the arm until he got up. She slid out of the booth and glared at him. Then she stared at everyone else at the table, smiling through her anger.

"Night all. Sorry you had to see that. I'm heading home."

"Autumn," Steve said, standing up. "Autumn, wait!"

Crawley winced as he charged off after her, the crowd dispersing before the burly man.

"The problem is you don't trust me," Autumn said as she walked a few feet ahead of Steve, digging in her leather purse for her keys.

"The problem is you don't listen to me!" Steve strained to keep up with her angry pace. "I never said that I didn't trust you."

"You don't have to say it. It's all over your face. God, you're so fucking *intense* about us, Steve!"

"That's not a good thing?"

"Not if it makes us fight." Her eyes shone in the half light with a softness that let him know he was already forgiven. "Can we drop this, please?"

"Fine. I'm just tired is all. I love you."

"I love you, too." Autumn wrapped her arms around his waist. They stayed that way for a long moment, until Steve gently disengaged himself.

"We should get to the car before we get mugged."

"Or get into a fight with a transvestite. Those don't end well for you."

"Those bitches are mean!" Both of them laughed, holding hands like school children as they traveled along the sidewalk. "I do trust you. I hope you know that."

"Yeah, well…I guess the money situation is getting to me more than I thought."

They reached her vehicle, Steve looking a bit uncomfortable.

"Hey, you sure you're okay to drive?"

"It's been an hour and a half since my last drink."

"Yeah, but you put away four margaritas."

"I'm fine," she said, attempting to jab her hand in his direction. When she did, the keys flew from her grasp to slide across the roof of the car.

"Yeah." He took the keys in his own hand. "I think I better drive."

"Maybe. You look tired, sugar. Are you sure you're okay to drive?"

"Yeah, I didn't drink much. Didn't want to spend much."

"Yikes. And I went and ordered the most expensive drink on the menu."

"Not hardly." They circled around the car, switching places. "Did you see that Cosmopolitan that had the actual gemstones ground up in it? Was like fifty bucks! Anyway, don't worry about it. Pop lent me some dough to get us through till the end of the month."

Steve had to lean over and push the seat back before he could even get inside. Autumn watched, amused, as he then had to tilt the steering wheel up and adjust both mirrors.

"Giant," she said with a giggle.

"Hobbit."

"Hobbit, is it? See if I wear that skirt for you later."

"We both know that you were full of shit anyway."

"Was not! I really did find it the other day."

She looked at him, an inscrutable expression on her face as they passed under the street lamps. While they waited at a red light, she took a deep breath and spoke.

"So, did your dad mention that idea of his again?" She was careful to keep her tone neutral, but her eagerness bled through at the edges.

"Yeah." Steve rubbed his nose and let out a long sigh. "I don't know, beautiful, it's a hard business to break into, even if you know somebody. Not only that, it's a hard *life*. Always on the road, never getting to see the people you love…"

He turned to her briefly, putting a hand on her stocking clad knee. She put her hand on top of his and squeezed it.

"I could come with you when you went on the road. Hell, I could be your manager or something…"

"No!" Steve winced at the volume of his voice. More softy, he continued. "No, Autumn, managers have to bump, and with your… condition…"

"Bump?" Autumn's brows knit in query.

"When you take a hit, or get slammed, they call that 'bumping.' I don't want you getting hurt."

"Does bumping hurt? I mean, I know it can't feel good, but don't you guys…don't the wrestlers get training on how to fall?"

"Sure, and there's a difference between something that hurts and something that *injures* you. I'd say that most of the time, wrestlers aren't in any more or less pain than other professional athletes. The thing is, sometimes a move goes wrong, or somebody gets sweaty and loses their grip. That's when you have problems."

"It's not like I want you to get hurt, either." She stared out the window at buildings as they passed, the car's blue profile reflected darkly back at them. "It's just that…you deserve better than working minimum wage shit jobs."

"On that subject…I was thinking of asking about being a manager at Greece Hut. I wouldn't make as much as when I was teaching, but—"

"Absodamnlutely NOT."

"What? What's so objectionable about that?"

Autumn heaved a sigh and was silent for a time. When she spoke again, he could sense her struggling to keep her words soft.

"Steve, I love you, but you tend to, well…you look at shit with rose colored glasses. You always want people to be good, and give them the benefit of the doubt…at least as long as I didn't used to date them."

"Hey…"

"Sorry, cheap shot. What I mean is, those are great traits for a teacher, but for a fast food manager? You'd end up being walked all over, or you'd have to change."

Autumn leaned across the divide and kissed him softly on the cheek.

"And I don't want you to change," she said.

Steve smiled at her, the darkness fleeing from his face for a moment.

"We'll take it as it comes," he said, patting her knee once more. He left his hand there and gently massaged her skin under the silky garment.

"What are you doing?" said Autumn with a giggle as he ran his hand further up her thigh.

"I don't know, it has a mind of its own! It's hungry, and it wants poon tang pie!"

"Stop it," she said, slapping his hand when it disappeared under her leather skirt. "I bet you were the kind of kid who had to open his toys in the car, couldn't wait to get home."

"So does that mean I get to unwrap it when we get home?"

She teased his hair with her painted nails.

"Only if you spend all night playing with it."

Chapter 7

Autumn slipped out of bed, careful not to disturb Steve, though he was actually awake. Naked, she padded into the bathroom to relieve herself. Washing her hands in the sink, she glanced up at her nude form and grinned at the dark spots on her neck. One of her pigtails was still banded, and she tugged it free, sweeping her black mane over her shoulders. Steve watched her with slitted eyes, enjoying the ruse.

"You animal," she said in a whisper, fingering the hickeys. Not that she hadn't left her own marks upon his skin, raking her nails down his back during their fit of passion the previous evening.

He heard her go into the cozy living room and pull the gray, paint-spotted tarp off of her easel. Curious, he walked silently after her, watching as she prepared to work on a painting. The wooden frame supported a flat canvas, upon which was scrawled a half-finished depiction of a volcano. Sticking her tongue out at what she apparently considered a bad rendering of its Hephaesten glory, she bent low to retrieve a fishing tackle box that had once belonged to her father. Opening its lid, she revealed that it had been repurposed into a receptacle for her painting supplies. Selecting a large tube of gesso, she used a wide brush to paint over the volcano.

Autumn stared at the blank canvas before her. He thought back to the time she had told him of her high school art class, one of the few she hadn't ever cut. Her teacher, Gregory Isom, had been a strange sort. Urban legend had it that Isom had once been a shop teacher, but had accidentally inhaled lead fumes and gotten so addled the only thing he still had the capacity to teach was art.

Autumn shook her head, bangs threatening to get in her eyes. She pulled her hair back in a ponytail. Her brown eyes scanned the plastic palette held in her tattooed left hand, the little mounds of paint awaiting her whims. Autumn had once told him that the difference between coloring and painting was that when you were coloring, you were just performing a task. When you were painting, you were creating something that was alive, that took shape and formed before you almost of its own volition. She had asserted that, at times, she felt as if she were not truly an artist at all, but a conduit for something that yearned to make itself known but had no mouth or hands of its own.

The other students had not thought much of her paintings, favoring the more precise status quo landscapes and portraits. Autumn rarely strove for photo realism in her paintings as she often did when inking a tattoo. Rather, she was what she would have called abstract but what Steve had insisted was called Expressionist.

Autumn glanced down at a *National Geographic* that was sitting on the cup ring infested coffee table. It depicted a savannah lioness roaring, its white teeth bared and stained in spots with blood and visceral meat. The tag line said it was endangered.

She mixed a dark red paste on her palette, using scarlet and black pigments. This she applied to the canvas while it was not fully mixed, its texture marbled. She swirled it about on the canvas, creating a background that resembled stormy skies but for the color. It looked as if the sky were about to rain not clear raindrops, but sticky blood.

Autumn glanced back at the lion's mouth and washed off her brush in a sawed off half-gallon milk carton filled with water. The clear water soon took on a dark brown sheen. Lightly beating the head against the easel, adding to a growing number of colored splotches, she got most of the moisture out of the bristles. She then mixed red, blue, and yellow together, along with a touch of white. Autumn had related to Steve that Isom told her that the secret to making flesh look convincing was to mix brown first, and then lighten it up. Otherwise, one's mermaid would have lobster red nipples instead of creamy pink ones.

For some reason, she felt like painting the mouth first. The snarling maw began to take shape on the canvas as she added white teeth, mirroring the image on the magazine but reshaping it to fit her mood. The teeth became more wicked and savage, elongating to impossible lengths. The gaping cavern of its throat was more detailed, ringed with vicious barbs and segments of muscle. Below the maw, she sketched out a Manhattan skyline being sucked into the maw, now appearing gigantic and monstrous.

Autumn stood back, using the back of her hand to brush a rebel strand of hair that had escaped her rubber restraint. She left a swath of black paint along the top of her eyebrow, even leaving a dot on her golden hoop piercing. Her large, round breasts were similarly stained, though her chrome barbells still shone cleanly where they exited either side of her light brown nipples.

Taking a step back, she stared at her creation. The work was clearly not done yet, but it was, by his estimation, a hell of a start.

"That's very good work," Steve said, startling her. She turned to face his stubbled visage. He was nude, shoulder length dirty blonde hair coming to his broad shoulders. She had joked that his recent exertions had given him two hams on either side of his neck, but he found his toned chest and prominent abs were more flattering than his slightly pudgy old self. His thighs were sleek but very defined, a result of having pedaled all over the city in recent months. From the neck down, Steve was looking top notch. However, the eyes looking back at him in the mirror every morning were looking quite exhausted.

"What's wrong?"

"Nothing," she said, going to him and wrapping her arms around his body. Her skin felt cold against his. "You're warm…"

"Your skin is like ice!" His hands wrapped around her shoulders. "Watching you paint, I don't know, it's almost scary."

"Scary?" Autumn pushed away from him and pouting in mock indignation.

"Yeah, you scare the shit out of me. A lot. After all, you did get arrested last year for breaking some MMA fighter's foot at a party…"

"Shut up. I was protecting your wimpy teacher ass. He would have beaten you senseless."

"I wish you wouldn't do that."

"Do what?"

"Underestimate me all the time. I'm tougher than you might think, you know."

"Steve, that's not what I meant at all. Train fights for a *living*, sugar. He's constantly pushing his body to the limit against guys who are doing the same thing."

"I'm in pretty good shape." Steve flexed a bulging bicep.

"Yeah, you are, hon, but you're a nice guy at heart. Train isn't."

"Nice guy, huh," he said, his voice a low growl.

"Well…yeah, you are, but you screw like a bad boy. That's the perfect combination."

"Oh, ho, you flatter me, miss Autumn Winters, the future Mrs. Autumn Borgia."

"Ah…" Autumn looked uncomfortable. "Look, about that…"

"I didn't mean to bring it up. Just forget it."

"Steve, this isn't about that. It's about my name. You see, dad isn't likely to have any heirs, and he was an only child, so the Winters name is kind of going to die if it isn't preserved…"

"You can't get married because you don't want to change your name?"

"No, dumbass, I still want to get married, I just want to keep my name."

Steve felt his anger drain away.

"Oh. I see. Well, lots of women do that, very proto-feminist of you."

"Steve…"

"No, I'm actually cool with this. Borgia is a terrible name anyway. Why do you think Pop called himself Deathslayer from Hell? It was a step up."

They both laughed at that, though Steve stopped first, his face growing perplexed.

"I just thought of another reason you can't be Autumn Borgia."

"Why is that?" said Autumn, wiping away a tear.

"Because if you took my last name, I would just be Steve!"

"God." Autumn slapped a hand across her eyes.

Steve laughed at the jibe, his mirth winding down as he stared at her nude, paint-streaked body.

"You have paint like literally all over you," he said, his thumb rubbing over a blotch on her shoulder. "All over…"

His hand roamed lower, gripping her breasts gently as he inspected the numerous stains of pigment. He was thorough in his examination, leaving no inch of her skin unattended to. The hard, smooth edge of his nails briefly brushed against her nether lips, asking the question that his mouth did not. He felt her body respond, eager at his touch.

"We just changed the sheets," Autumn said as he took her by the hand and led her to the bedroom.

"Then let's get you cleaned up." Steve tugged her into the bathroom instead.

"You're so bad!" She took the lead, grinning ear to ear with half-lidded eyes. Her back, covered in colorful ink, rippled as she lifted her arms high over her head and stretched like a lioness on the savannah. Steve's eyes roamed over her form as she did so, just as she intended.

"Hey," she said as he pulled back the opaque curtain to reveal a modest but well scrubbed shower/bath combination. "I was thinking of getting a new piercing or two."

"Oh?" His brow furrowed a bit. He finagled the faucets until he had a stream of water suitable to his taste. "Not a labron, I hope?"

"That's labret…and no, I have enough on my face, even I realize this. I was thinking lower…"

She looked down at her love cradle, pulling apart the spongy flesh for his inspection.

"Maybe a ring on each side, what do you think?"

Steve stared at her labia, swallowing hard. He certainly didn't *dislike* the idea.

"Are you blushing?" Autumn said, coming up to grab his cheeks. "You are, you're actually blushing! Such a bashful little boy…"

"I'm not blushing! And it's your body, you do what you want with it."

"Really? I don't want this to be a thing. If you don't think you can deal with it, it won't happen, okay?"

"Uh…Is this one of those tests where you're just trying to see if I'll support you or not, or does my opinion really have weight?"

"It has weight," she said, stepping past him and getting into the shower. Her spine arched, and she thrust out her shapely round bottom more than the maneuver required. "I want you to find me sexy."

"I do find you sexy." Steve licked his lips as he stared at her rounded flanks.

"I want you to find me more sexy…more and more every day."

"You're not afraid there's a limit? I mean, I already find you the most beautiful, sexy, magnificent woman on the planet. How much higher can you go than that?"

"Well," Autumn said, stepping beneath the stream of hot water and gasping as it hit her skin, "there's the galaxy, the universe, the multiverse quantum bullshit Sven's always going on about…"

Steve's laughter stopped when she suddenly wrapped her arms around his neck and kissed him. Their tongues mingled together, long ago accustomed to one another. Autumn gently bit Steve's lower lip and sucked on it gently just before they broke contact. Their eyes met, communicating on a level more comprehensive and subtle than speech.

Taking the soggy, fist sized sponge in his hand, Steve rubbed it gently over her body, making slow circles on her breasts. He had learned long ago to be mindful of snagging her piercings, so he avoided them. His large, powerful hand squeezed the sponge until only a tiny portion stuck out between his thumb and forefinger. Using it, he rubbed very gently along the tips of her nipples. Rougher than a tongue, but still softer than a finger, the touch made her swoon.

He turned his attention to her stomach. By the time he had finished swirling the soapy sponge around her tattooed belly, her skin was on fire. He felt the same way as his iron hard member found itself encircled by her wet fingers.

Steve leaned back against the corner of the shower and braced his long legs on the sides, using a sculpted section designed to hold bars of soap for traction. Autumn put one leg up on the edge of the tub, her toes thrusting beneath the curtain, and eased onto him. Her face was crossed first with an almost pained expression, before it vanished in a wide eyed stare. Steve stared into her shining brown eyes, her face almost impossibly beautiful in that moment. Moments of profound connection between them were what fueled their passion, wherever and in whatever context they occurred.

Steve gripped her under the knee, lifting her a bit in the air before allowing her to slide back down. Both of them gasped, and soon Autumn was working her hips rhythmically. His mobility was limited, as he had to support their combined weight, but the sensation of their wet, soapy bodies sliding all over each other was more than enough compensation. Autumn's body lurched as she was wracked with spasms, and only Steve's hand gripping her behind the lower back and holding her tight to his body kept her upright.

"Don't set me down," she said, gasping for breath, "my legs are like rubber…rubber, you beast!"

"Don't blame me." Steve shifted his grip to hold her more comfortably. "You did most of the work."

Autumn gasped, eyes going wide as he slid deeper into her. She leaned her head against his shoulder, damp hair spreading over his skin.

"Mmm…I think you could almost let go of me with your arms and still hold me up."

Their lips met once more, slowly exploring each other in the steamy air.

Chapter 8

The cherry red Camaro's wide rubber tires squealed as it turned hard into the Greece Hut parking lot. It zipped into a space right next to the door, unmindful of the fact that it was designated for use by disabled patrons. The door swung open, and a long leg thrust itself out. A tall, pudgy black man with a neatly shaven head awkwardly pulled himself out of the low sports car. He was wearing a very nice suit, though the tie was undone and hung loosely around his neck. His face was crossed with a look of profound disgust as he bent low to retrieve an item from inside the Camaro.

He straightened up, his hand bearing a Big Zeus burger, the chain's knockoff of the more popular fare offered by McDonald's. The sandwich was held aloft in the air before him, as if it were a fetid diaper filled with the most fragrant of feces.

"Uh-oh," Steve said, watching the approach as he struggled to tie a knot in a garbage bag with greasy hands. He raised his voice to carry through the nearly deserted restaurant. "Told you that you forgot the extra Zeus sauce on the burger, Tenisha."

"Lordy, lordy! Just look at his face. He about to come up in here trippin'!"

Sure enough, the man exploded into a rush of complaints as soon as he entered the building. Since Steve was standing in the dining room, trying to take out the garbage, the man vented his fury on him. At length he stopped, crossed his arms over his chest and glared at Steve.

"Do you have any idea how long it takes to drive here from my office? Any idea?"

"About twenty minutes," Steve said, easily recalling the fact as the man had loudly stated it several times during his tirade.

"Oh, so you *can* listen. Why didn't you listen when I told you, *extra Zeus sauce?* Is your job that hard?"

"I'm sorry, sir. I don't actually make the sandwiches, but I'll get it taken care of right away."

"Oh, no!" The man held the burger before him as if Steve should be far more shocked about its normal amount of zesty Zeus Sauce. "*Hell* no, we're way past that! I wanna talk to the manager, the manager's manager, the district manager, and CEO Max Buford himself!"

"I'll go get my manger, sir."

"Wait a minute, you're not the manager? How old are you?"

"That's really not any—"

"You trying to make me even madder? C'mon, it's not that big a deal, you're not a woman. How old are you?"

"Thirty-three. I'll go get my ma—"

"Thirty-three?" The man was suddenly seized by a fit of laughter. "No fucking shit? Damn, man, I'm only twenty six and I got my own corner office!"

Steve bit his tongue as the man guffawed at his expense. His hands clenched into fists but he actually managed to smile.

"It's the economy, you know?"

"Damn, now I feel sorry for you and shit. Tell you what man, you make me two Big Zeus burgers, *with* the extra sauce I ordered in the first place, and we'll let it go at that, okay?"

"Sure," Steve said. He went back and stood hovering near Tenisha when she made both sandwiches to ensure they were duly deluged with the amber sauce.

"Is he pissed?" Tenisha said.

"He was, until my patheticness amused him greatly."

Steve glumly collected the sandwiches, wishing he could fling them in the man's face. He stopped suddenly when a bright flash went off in his face.

"Smile! I just had to take a picture of the thirty-three-year-old virgin."

"I'm hardly a virgin, sir. Here you are, made just the way you—"

"You got a woman?"

"Yes, I do, and she's the most beautiful, wonderful woman on the planet."

"Bullshit, what's she doing with you, then?"

Steve watched him go, getting into his fancy sports car and speeding off. Numbly, he gathered the trash together and hefted it out to the wooden corral. A few spatters of rain hit the pavement as he walked. A few of the cool drops hit his face, mingling with tears that seemed to spring up from nowhere. He tossed the garbage bags into the Dumpster and shut the corral door behind him, allowing his misery to vent itself. The rain increased a bit in intensity, drenching his shirt to his body.

Steve swung the gates of the corral open. His strides were purposeful as he went across the parking lot, his eyes burning with fire. Stepping into the bathroom, he washed his hands before extracting his cell phone. His shirt dripped water onto the tile floor, where it ran into a divot surrounding a shiny metal grate.

"Pop," Steve said, blinking in surprise when his father answered the phone. "I wasn't expecting you to answer, are you busy?"

"Not at the moment." The sound of many voices could be heard in the background. "I was just about to grab a bite, but looks like everyone else in Reno had the same idea. This place is packed!"

"I won't keep you long. Look, uh, does the General still run that training center in the Bronx?"

"Yes." Steve could hear the old man straining to keep the excitement out of his voice. "What's up? One of your buddies decide he wants to wrestle?"

"No, I was thinking *I* might need his help…you know, a refresher?"

"I'm sure that he'd take you, Steve!" Deathslayer was unable to restrain his happiness any longer. "But I have to ask, is this just about money? Because that's not the reason to get into the business. You know that."

"I know, Pop, and it's not just the money. When I was teaching, I had a, I don't know, I guess I had a purpose. I had a reason for getting up in the morning besides paying my bills, you know? I want that feeling back, and you know I've always loved getting in the ring."

"Yeah, I know. It was the backstabbing, soap opera drama of the backstage shenanigans that you could never stand. It hasn't gotten any better, son. In fact, it's just gotten worse."

"I know, Susie was saying that the other day."

"Where'd you run into her?"

"I didn't. Facebooking."

"Right, got it." Deathslayer's tone clearly indicated that he was barely cognizant of what Facebook even was. "Well, you have Autumn to keep you centered. What does she think of it?"

"She loves the idea, of course. Hell, she wants to come along, be my manager."

"That's a great idea. Like Randy and Liz."

"Didn't they break up?"

"Right, bad example. Me and your Ma are still together, though."

"Ma didn't go on the road with you, much…Ma was a ring rat, wasn't she?"

"Hey, don't talk about your Ma like that!"

They chuckled, but Steve broke it off first. He had a favor to ask.

"Uh, Pop, I hate to ask, but I'm short of cash, and I know those training academies can be expensive…"

"Don't worry about it. General owes me. You see, once upon a time we made this pact that we would each train one student for the other for free."

"Really?"

Deathslayer broke into laughter.

"Nah, but it makes for a good story, right? General owes me, I fronted him cash to start that place. Besides, he loves you like blood. Says you're too decent for the business."

Steve's mind raced back to a time when he was more concerned with Godzilla and sling shots than his famous father's cronies. General had been different, putting up with his adolescent prattling, teaching him that ball bearings were great ammunition and covering for him when he killed a pigeon in the front yard while testing that assertion.

The General was married, but didn't have children of his own. While Deathslayer was a people person who everyone was naturally drawn to, General was more unassuming. Even in the ring he had struggled to rise to the mid card, despite his crisp delivery of all the required slams and holds. Fortunately, his association with Steve's more famous father had kept him employed during much of the boom periods of the eighties and nineties.

"Thanks, Pop. I won't let you down."

"You better not. General won't go easy on you, because he *can't*. Haven't been sitting on the couch eating pizza for the last month, have you?"

"Hell no! I'm actually in the best shape of my life, at least physically. If I could get eight hours of sleep in a row, I might even feel good."

"Tell Autumn you need a night off."

"Pop!" A pounding on the door alerted him to Glenn's presence outside.

"Dammit, Steve, get the fuck out of there now and throw some meat on the grill! You've had twenty goddamn minutes to take out the trash and use the facilities!"

"Coming!" shouted Steve. More softly in his phone, he said, "Got to go, Pop. Love you."

"Love you too, boy."

Steve went out of the stall and washed his hands, grinning as Glenn's frustrated voice continued to emanate from the other side of the door.

When he stepped out of the bathroom, Glenn's face was the first thing he saw. The little man's nostrils flared like a bull facing down a matador. His face was certainly crimson enough to pass for one of their snapping cloaks.

"My office," he said through tightly clenched teeth. "NOW!"

Steve followed, his lips mouthing obscenities at the manager's back. Tenisha stifled a laugh at Glenn's almost comical expression of rage, but Steve found little to be amused about. They stepped into the small office, and no sooner had the steel door slammed shut than Glenn tore into him.

"Do you think I look like a bitch, Steve?" Glenn said, displaying faux calm with his tone while his hands shook.

"I'm sorry?"

"Do. You. Think. I. Look. Like. A. Bitch?"

Well, you've got boobs like one Steve thought.

"No."

"Then why do you think you can fuck me like I'm a bitch?"

Steve burst out laughing. Glenn put his hands on his hips.

"What is so goddamn funny, Mister 'I'm About To Get Fired'?"

"I'm sorry, man, but I can't help it, the whole *Pulp Fiction* thing…"

"What are you talking about?"

"Samuel L. Jackson, 1994, Quentin Tarantino…"

"I've never heard of it."

"But that was the speech from when—"

"Steve, the only way this business will thrive is if every one of the dogs is pulling their weight. I'm the lead dog. When you guys don't pull your weight, I have to work that much harder."

"Look, Glenn—"

"No, you look! I'm done. This is it. You can consider yourself on probation. If I catch you doing any goddamn thing that is not one hundred percent in tune with the standard operational procedures of Greece Hut International I will kick your ass out of here. No job, no reference, no nothing."

Steve stood there taking the abuse, trying to focus on something other than the enraged little man. Taking the high road was what his parents had taught him, but sometimes he longed to be more like Autumn. She wouldn't stand there and take it.

"You're lucky a degenerate pervert like you can even find work," said Glenn, making Steve's eyes narrow. Glenn nodded, a smile breaking out on his face. "Yeah, I said it. I saw the papers…a transvestite, you sick fuck? You better toe the line, or that hot little girlfriend is going to have to shake her ass in the strip club to pay your—"

Steve took a step toward the much smaller man. Glenn's voice caught in his throat, as he was unable to retreat more than a scant inch or two in the small confines of the office. Steve's blue eyes burned with anger long-buried, released in a burst of righteous indignation.

"Look, Glenn, *sir*," Steve said, a bit of spittle flying from his mouth to spatter on Glenn's nose, "you can run me down all you want. I can take it. You can call me a homo or a loser or the child of a fake wrestler, and that's cool. Sticks and stones, right? Just like I used to tell my kids when I was teaching. Sticks and stones…"

Steve leaned forward further, until his nose was a hair's breadth away from Glenn's own. His eyes locked onto the little man's piggish eyes in a gaze all the more fierce for Steve's calm tone.

"But if you ever, ever, *ever* speak about Autumn again, you're going to *wish* I was using sticks and stones to beat you with just to get it over with more quickly. And if you want to call the police and tell them I threatened you, go ahead. I'll just tell them about the way you run out to your car every hour on the hour and stick your nose in a line or two of blow."

"How dare you even insinuate—"

"Shut up. I'm not finished. Half of the staff has footage of you shot on their cell phones, Mr. Manager *sir*. They're just waiting for you to piss them off."

"Impossible! Who took it, Steve? Who? Answer me, damn you!"

"That's something to think about, isn't it? I'd keep my words soft and sweet, in case you have to eat them later. That's something else I told the kids when I was 'babysitting.'"

Steve glanced up at the clock on the wall, a smile spreading over his face.

"It's four o'clock, my shift's over. I quit. Have a great day and go fuck yourself."

Steve whistled as he exited the office, leaving a flustered Glenn in his wake. Remembering that his uniform shirt was his own property but his hat was not, he tossed it on the counter in front of Tenisha.

"Do me a favor, ma'am, and give that to Glenn."

"Your ass just quit, didn't you?" She cackled as he took a bow.

"I've never felt better...or cleaner in my life," Steve said as he hit the exit. The crisp autumn air that filled his lungs seemed sweeter than any he'd breathed in months.

Chapter 9

Crawley lit the candle with the taper, her tawny complexion momentarily lightened by the flickering flame. Folding her hands, she offered a prayer for her Uncle Trini, missing since the big typhoon last year. She also sent a prayer for Autumn and Steve, not only that they would see the light and accept Jesus Christ (as she always did) but that the latter could find a good job.

Her lips parted in a slight smile. She loved them both in an effortless, soothing kind of way. Crawley had been nerdy in high school, and most of her girlfriends were more or less the children of her parent's friends. Even amongst people she knew well, she had trouble standing out. At least until she hit the age of nineteen and her body bloomed at last.

Then, she had received plenty of attention from men, while many women shunned her or seemed petty. At first, she had been thrilled with the reversal, but quickly she learned that just because someone said kind things did not mean their heart was in it. Certainly, the young men at the university had been willing to say almost *anything* to get her into bed…

She prayed, asking God for help finding her way. Crawley still wasn't sure what the future held for her and Phillip. She loved him, and not in a way that was at all effortless or soothing. Rather, she found herself almost overwhelmed by her feelings for him. When Phil said something, he meant it, at least at the moment it was uttered. She was confident that the young man loved her, but she wondered if that love was enough.

Finishing her prayers, she blew out the still smoldering taper and discarded it in the metal urn next to the rows of candles. She nodded pleasantly at an older nun who passed by with a cell phone laid across her open palm. A few of the faithful sat in the pews, silently mouthing their own prayers or just looking up at the image of the cross with a restless, haunted look.

Crawley passed through beams of sunlight as she headed down the aisle toward the exit. She stepped onto the street, cursing when she realized it was drizzling. Having no umbrella, she took a discarded newspaper and used it as a crude shield from the chilly rain.

"This is what I get for not wearing a bra to church," she said, her thin pink T-T-shirt soon soaked through. She stepped over a rapidly growing puddle and fumbled for her keys. As her hand entered her tight jeans pocket, she noticed a dark smear on the back of her wrist. A greasy streak had been left on her jeans as well, and when the aroma hit her nose she realized *why* the newspaper had been discarded.

"Oh, this isn't happening, this isn't happening, this isn't happening…"

Gingerly, she discarded the newspaper and checked her hair. It was hard to tell, but she didn't think her flowing tresses had been soiled. Using her unspoiled hand, she opened the door and hit the trunk release latch. She did the best she could, using a gallon jug of water her father insisted she keep around for emergencies to rinse the filth from her clothing and hand.

The thought of driving all the way back to Queens with soiled garments was not a pleasing one. A sudden flash of insight occurred to her. Autumn's tattoo parlor was close by, and the woman may have something she could wear. If nothing else, she could use the bathroom to better clean herself.

Crawley bought a newspaper from a nearby metal vending unit and tried to keep it relatively dry as she made her way back to her Eclipse. She used the newspaper to cover the seat, then slid inside. Moaning at the sight of her hair, she gasped when she realized a male pedestrian was staring into her window. He smiled and glanced down at her chest.

Blushing, she grabbed the remains of the newspaper and covered her prominent nipples. The man laughed and went on his way.

"Pervert," she hissed at his back.

Crawley put the keys in the ignition and started the engine. It was a short drive to the tattoo parlor, the name long worn off the battered sign out front. She spotted Autumn's dark head of hair bobbing to some unheard music as she sketched on a drawing pad.

Under the awning, she was no longer being peppered with cold rain drops, so Crawley took a moment to wring as much of the water from her hair as she could. The buzzer that went off when she opened the door had Autumn glancing up. A slow, confused smile spread over her face.

"Crawley?" She eyed the woman. "You look like you zigged where you should have zagged…and what is that smell?"

"Don't ask." She lifted her hand to display the dark brown stain on her blue jeans.

"Oh, baby…c'mon, I'll save you. I'm sure one of Sal's girlfriend's things will fit you."

"Sal has a girlfriend?"

"Don't sound so surprised." Autumn led her past the application room and up a flight of stairs. "His legs don't work, but his other parts work just fine."

Crawley blushed as she followed Autumn's leather clad derriere.

"I love your pants," Crawley said, both because she did find them flattering and to change the subject.

"Thanks. What with all the humidity, it was a bitch getting them on. Steve gave me a hand, but to be honest that man is a lot better at getting clothes off of me, heh heh."

Crawley smiled, but felt a pang of jealousy. Autumn and Steve's passion for one another never seemed to cool. Autumn had once told her that differences made good sparks, and she and Steve were different enough in the right ways.

Are Phillip and I too much alike, or too different? Just right? She wondered to herself as they reached the top of the steps. Autumn opened a door to a small efficiency apartment. She rummaged around the deployed fold away bed until she found an empty shopping bag.

"Here, throw your jeans in there. Sal and his old lady are gonna be out for hours."

"Okay." Crawley unbuttoned her soiled denim trousers. She peeled them from her shapely legs, straining not to touch any of the brown remnants of her fecal encounter. Autumn whistled.

"Looking good," she said when Crawley glanced up at her. "I like the little birds on your thong."

"It's a g-string." Crawley turned about to show off her finely shaped derriere. "And those are little butterflies."

"Really?" Autumn said, though she didn't seem that interested. Instead, she was rummaging inside of a narrow closet just off the main room. She withdrew a flannel shirt, sniffing it carefully. Nodding to herself, she tossed it to Crawley.

"Here, turkey's done, and all that."

Crawley glanced down at her erect nipples and blushed.

"Oh." She took off her shirt and wrung it out, revealing her small but firm bust to the other woman. A sudden, sly thought occurred to her and she glanced up at Autumn.

"Say, you have a pierced nipple, right?"

"What?" Autumn said, nearly dropping the sweat pants she held in her hand. "That's a weird…where did you hear that?"

"Phil told me." Crawley blushed as she realized the chain of information.

"Steve told him? I don't care, I guess. Yeah, I have both of them done, actually. Why? Not turning lezzie on me are you?"

Crawley's jaw nearly hit the floor.

"You're not, actually, are you?" Autumn said. "Oh, my god, I am so sorry—"

"No! I'm not coming out to you, if that's what you mean."

"Okay, 'cause it's cool if you are! I mean, I have to admit, I've always kind of wondered about you. I could have sworn that you were checking me out a couple of times…"

"Uhm," Crawley said, blinking.

"I'm kidding!" Autumn threw the sweats to her. "Here, these are clean. God, you're almost as much fun to mess with as Steve."

"I am a little bit…sheltered." Crawley slipped on the sweats. "I was actually asking because I was thinking of getting mine pierced."

"No shit?" Autumn was smiling broadly. "Well, I can give you my employee discount. I can even do the deed, if you like."

"Wouldn't that be weird for you?"

"No, not really. Besides, it's too late to get modest, you already flashed your tits and panties at me."

Both women laughed. Crawley felt the tension draining from her shoulders, stress she hadn't even realized was there. She thought that Autumn felt obligated to be her friend due to her financial intervention months earlier. For the first time, though, she seemed to be actually enjoying Crawley's company.

"So, how are you and Steve doing?" Crawley didn't want to ask, and as Autumn stiffened she figured it had been a mistake. A moment later, Autumn sighed and dropped her gaze to the folded shirt in her hands.

"Good, I guess."

"You guess? What does that mean?"

"It means that we're together, and we're…happy," Autumn's brown eyes seemed haunted. "He can't get over me leaving him, though."

"So? Tell him to man up, you're together now."

"It's not that simple. I think he's afraid that I'm going to do it again."

"Oh." Crawley wrinkled her nose. Figuring out how to keep venom from degrading during shipment? That was easy. Figuring out how to fix a fractured relationship was more daunting by far. "So… are you? I mean, do you think it will come to that?"

"No!" Autumn's hands twisted the shirt in her hands. "I mean, I don't want to, but…sooner or later I rub everyone the wrong way, y'know? How long is Steve, is *anyone* going to put up with my bullshit?"

"Don't sell yourself short," Crawley smiled, glad Autumn was confiding in her at last. "You're a catch, Autumn Winters."

"I'm a catch, huh?" Autumn's shoulders straightened a bit, and her eyes lit up.

"Oh yeah, if I was a dude I'd totally get witch ya," Crawley adopted a hip hop pose.

"Gawd, that's *terrible*," Autumn said.

"I tried to make it funny so you wouldn't think I was coming on to you."

"You mean, you weren't?" Autumn pouted. "I'm getting some mixed signals here, Miss Crawley. First you flash your tits at me and now you're all being a prude."

They both laughed, though Autumn stopped first.

"You should be careful," she said, "this is where those women went wrong with Kobe and Tyson."

"That's *not* funny!"

"Then why are you laughing?"

"What's that noise?" Crawley tilted her head to the side as she finished tying her sneakers.

"That's my cell phone," Autumn said, her brows scrunching low over her eyes. "Oh, right, I'm supposed to go pick up Steve at four. FUCK!"

"What's wrong?" Crawley followed Autumn as she dashed down the stairs to the parlor.

"Sal won't be back for a while, and when he said he was going to a movie I forgot about Steve needing a ride. He's gonna walk from the gym so he can pick up his last check at Greece Hut. Fucking stupid!"

"I could pick him up. I mean, it's the least I can do since you saved me from being covered in poop."

"You don't mind?" Autumn had cautious optimism growing on her face.

"Not at all. I could pick up dinner for my folks."

"From Greece Hut?" Autumn looked at her aghast. "You want them to disown you?"

Soon Crawley was hustling out the door, setting her phone's GPS for the Greece Hut.

Steve had not bothered to check the message on his phone, figuring that Autumn was just running late. He was busy communicating via social media with General Rexxun. The man was as old as Steve's father, but had adapted to the mobile device age far better. His wrestling school, *The Monster Maker*, had a nifty website with numerous links that were easy to navigate. The General had been blowing up Steve's phone with messages ever since Deathslayer had called in his favor. Indeed, the trainer seemed even more excited about Steve's foray into pro wrestling than his father.

Gonna put you in the advanced class read one of the messages from General.

Are you sure? Replied Steve. *It's been awhile. Ten years.*

You'll do fine. Like riding a bike. :)

Steve glanced up from his phone, noticing a white Eclipse had stopped in front of him. He was sitting on a bench outside Greece Hut, unwilling to remain within its confines for longer than necessary to retrieve his final paycheck. He squinted his blue eyes and recognized the driver.

"Crawley?" he said, walking over to the open passenger window. "Going to eat here? I don't advise it."

"I'm here to pick you up. Didn't Autumn get a hold of you? She's stuck at work."

"I, uh, I didn't notice she left a message."

He crammed his phone back into his pocket and opened the door. The Eclipse had a small profile, and he had some difficulty folding his long legs so they would fit. He had to sit with his knees bent nearly double.

Crawley giggled at his struggles.

"Sorry, it's a small car."

"Curse of being big. I can only imagine what guys like Andre must have gone through. I'm only six foot six!"

"Andre?"

"Sorry. Andre the Giant. I'm so used to Autumn knowing all the wrestling related crap I guess I take it for granted."

Steve, very discreetly (he hoped), ran his eyes over Crawley's form. Even though she was dressed down more than he was used to seeing, her baggy clothing could not conceal the sweet, sleek curves of her slender body. He really liked her hair, the way it was so long and luxuriant. Thoughts of running his fingers through it were quickly banished by intense guilt. Of course, he would never cheat on Autumn. He could not delude himself into thinking he was the perfect man, but Steve had never cheated on any woman before, and did not intend to start now. No matter how tempting thoughts of Crawley's body writhing under his own may have been…

He realized that he had been staring, tried to come up with an excuse. Crawley came unexpectedly to his rescue.

"You're staring at my 'give up on life pants,' aren't you?"

"I'm not gonna judge. I'm in ratty gym gear myself."

Crawley pulled the car around the drive-through. Steve groaned and slapped a hand over his face.

"You're going to eat here, aren't you? Haven't you been paying attention?"

"What's wrong with Greece Hut? My dad likes the Big Zeus, and my mom likes the Harvest Salad."

"The Harvest salad is pretty good…used to be called the Demeter Salad, but people didn't know who she was."

"Demeter? Greek goddess of agriculture, right?"

"Yeah, that's right. Do you read mythology?"

"When I was in school."

"Oh, that's right, I forget that you actually went to college, unlike most of my friends."

They paused their conversation while Crawley rattled off an order. After she had pulled forward and paid, Tenisha peered out the window at Steve.

"I thought you quit," Tenisha said.

"One of my finer moments," Steve replied.

"Do Autumn know your ass in the car with another chick?" the little woman said, her eyes narrowing suspiciously.

"Autumn sent her!" Steve said, blushing more than usual because of his own guilty conscience. "I am innocent of all charges!"

"Whatever, have fun!"

After getting her order, Crawley pulled the car out into traffic. Steve stared out his window, but could feel her eyes upon him. When he turned back toward her, her gaze would snap back to the road. He felt as if, cliché as it sounded, he could cut the tension in the air with a knife.

"How's it going with you and Phil?" he said to break the silence, then realized it might be interpreted as fishing to see if she was available. He was almost grateful when Crawley appeared to consider the question on its own merits.

"Well, good, I guess. I mean, he keeps checking out other chicks when he thinks I'm not looking, but…"

"Is that all?" Steve laughed. "Most of us do it, it's just that Phil isn't good at being subtle."

"He's honest and sweet," Crawley said a bit defensively.

"I didn't mean it as an insult," Steve said quickly.

"No, it's all right." Crawley grinned. "I think I was talking to myself more than you. The thing is Phil and I are great together."

"I'm a believer," Steve said, holding up his hands. "You've helped him come out of his shell, be a bit more confident."

"That might be the problem. He knows he has game now, and he might be willing to play the field."

Steve glanced over at her sharply, sensing the pain edging her voice.

"I'm not so sure about that. You know about Phil's peanut butter and jelly thing, right?"

From Crawley's horrified expression, Steve figured she was thinking of abjectly sexual applications. "NO! Not that way, I mean, he really loves PB&J. Took it for lunch to school for all twelve years of compulsory ed."

"Really? I hadn't noticed."

"Oh, yeah, that guy's got an addiction. He was always wanting to go to Denver and order a Fool's Gold PB&J that had bacon bits mixed in."

"Wow, that's a heart attack on a plate!"

"Elvis ate twenty-two in one sitting, if the stories are to be believed."

"No wonder he shit himself to death!"

They both laughed, which ended with an awkward silence where they couldn't look at each other. Crawley had the road to focus on, but he found himself staring at his own rapidly tapping fingers. He tried to forge on.

"Believe it or not, I know where you're coming from. There's been a bit of tension between me and Autumn since she came back."

A quick, sharp glance, the way that Crawley's hands tightened on the wheel, clued Steve in to the fact that Autumn had been confiding in the petite Asian.

"That's not cool," she said nervously. Steve figured he should let her off the hook.

"Have you tried talking to Phil about how you're feeling?"

"No, I can't. Every time I bring these things up we end up fighting. It's just that he's so sensitive, and takes everything I say so…literally. He's a great guy, smart, sweet…I just don't know if he believes in me. In *us*."

"As I said, I feel where you're coming from."

Steve digested her words as they drove on. He felt as if he should stand up for his friend, but at the same time he didn't want to give out bad advice to Crawley. The passage of a rain cloud overhead momentarily darkened the interior of the car. The low light combined with his heavy fatigue made his face look severe.

"I didn't mean to cause you problems." He glanced over at her. Crawley lips were pursed in a frown.

"It's not that. I was just thinking. It occurs to me that you're his first serious girlfriend. I don't know if I should say it or not…"

Crawley glanced over at him, a mischievous smile on her face.

"That he was a virgin before we slept together?"

"Oh…well, that cat is out of the bag, then. The problem is, he has the same voice that all men have inside his head, telling him to spread his seed far and wide."

Crawley laughed, a more high pitched sound than Autumn's husky mirth. It reminded him of how young she seemed, though he was only about five years her senior.

"I've learned to accept his wandering eye. I bet all men do the same."

"You better believe it. We can't help it, most of the time we don't even know we're doing it! Autumn caught me looking at a waitress last week, and I had to pretend I was offended by her short shorts."

"Did it work?"

"Not a bit. Fortunately, Autumn's not the jealous type. Wish I could say the same."

"Oh," Crawley said, just a hint of optimism in her tone, "has she given you reason to be jealous?"

"No, except for working for her ex and all. I mean, I haven't noticed any hickeys or monkey bites—that I haven't put there myself."

Crawley laughed, but she felt a rush run through her body at his words. Steve seemed very manly when compared to Phil, but also somehow sweeter. Maybe it was the years he had spent teaching kindergarten, but he just came off as someone you could, and should, trust.

"Autumn's a lucky girl," Crawley said.

"Nah, I'm a lucky guy."

The Eclipse pulled up outside of Steve's building. The old brownstone had seen better days, half of the windows were covered with blue tarp for repairs. A loud, dissonant ruckus could be heard as the construction crew busied themselves with their work. Steve pried himself out of the small front seat and turned about to face her.

"Thanks for the ride…and for saving Autumn, in case you've forgotten."

"How could I when you bring it up every time you see me?" Crawley said, though she did grin. "I was just doing what Christ wanted me to."

"Well, tell that Jew Carpenter that I said thanks too."

"Will do!"

"Thanks," he mumbled again, hastily exiting the car. It lurched forward almost as soon as the door shut tight.

Steve watched and waved as she pulled away, the Eclipse rushing into the afternoon sun.

"Man," he said, thoughts of her slender form pressed against his hard to dismiss. "Man!"

He ran up the stairs to their apartment, opening the door and shutting it behind him as if he could evade his traitorous mind with simple physical barriers. The painting Autumn had done helped to focus his mind. She had finished the work, and Steve was honestly impressed with her artistic skill. He was a little put off by the disembodied lion mouth eating New York, but he had to admit that it was skillfully rendered.

"I love her," he said, seeming to be surprised by his own voice.

"I love her!" he said with great conviction, and a smile spread on his face. He did love her, with every ounce of his heart. He just wished he could put the nagging doubts traipsing about his subconscious to rest. *Had* she only agreed to marry him because she thought she was dying? Were they living on borrowed time, whether because Autumn would get bored with him or her health suddenly declined? Would this new direction their lives were about to take bring them closer together or smash them apart?

Dismissing such thoughts as much as he could, he went to the fridge and rummaged inside, trying to come up with something for dinner. He had some pork steaks he'd defrosted a day ago and had done nothing with. Selecting garlic salt and Cajun seasoning, he spiced up the meat before wrapping it in foil and sticking it in the oven. Some frozen broccoli and half a wedge of Velveeta became toppings for the baked potatoes that soon joined the pork steaks in the oven. When he opened a can of sliced peaches, he was feeling like it was almost going to be a real dinner.

The door slammed, and he smiled at the sound of Autumn bitching about the construction workers taking up all the parking spaces. Her heavy boots with the platform soles were hardly quiet as she walked up behind him.

"Hey, sugar." She slipped her arms around his waist and put her head on his shoulder. "Sorry about leaving you stranded."

He put his free hand atop one of hers, and their fingers wove together.

"Don't stress about it, beautiful. Crawley didn't seem to mind."

"She shouldn't." Autumn kissed him on the back of the neck, though she had to stand on her tip toes to do so. "Her family actually likes eating Greece Hut."

"I prefer real food."

"I know," Autumn said, disengaging from him and opening the oven. "It smells great!"

"Home cooking is something we're going to miss. When we're on the road, I mean."

"Living out of a suitcase pretty much describes my life before we met."

"We'll have to book all our own hotel rooms. Unlike most professional sports, wrestling federations don't make travel arrangements for you."

"I have apps on my phone for that. It'll be fine."

"We're going to have to put up with a lot of crap, too. I'm a legacy, and all the boys who've been busting their asses to get noticed will be resentful."

"I'm used to mean people."

"Autumn," Steve said with a sigh, leaving his broccoli to sit for a moment, "I'm serious! This is not going to be an easy life!"

"So?" Autumn said, jabbing a fork into the pot of cheesy broccoli. "Easy things aren't worth doing, isn't that what you used to tell your kids?"

"I was trying to teach them to print."

"But it still applies, right?" she said, popping a golden-green morsel in her mouth.

"I guess so." Steve stirred the broccoli half-heartedly. Autumn seemed quite excited for life on the road, but what if it wasn't to her liking? Then she'd be here at home while he was away for months on end, bored and lonely…

"Steve, you're still with me right? Kind of spaced out there for a second."

"Right," he said, slapping a lid on the pot when she went after seconds.

"Hey!"

"Wait for the potatoes to get done," he said, wagging a finger before her face.

Chapter 10

C rawley and Phil stepped carefully around the young man bent in half in Rex's driveway. As they feared, he lurched forward and a revolting multicolored stream spattered onto the concrete at their feet.

"Looks like our tryouts have turned into a party," Crawley said, wrinkling her nose in disgust.

"What *doesn't* turn into a party at Rex's?" Phil said, carrying her cumbersome amplifier. They went through the door to the basement, which still stood open in the sick man's wake. Crawley closed it until it latched, then turned and smiled when she saw John the bouncer with a bottle of beer in his hand. He was talking to Rex and Sven, and seemed to be getting along fairly well with them.

The cramped, musty quarters were filled to capacity. Crawley had met many of the guests before, but had problems remembering their names. As such, she was forced to smile stupidly while Phil spoke to each of them in turn, hoping that she wouldn't be put on the spot.

She was grateful when she saw that Autumn and Steve were sitting on the wooden steps leading to the house proper. They were talking in low tones, their faces somber but not sad. As she watched, Autumn took Steve's hand and weaved their fingers together. Steve brought her hand, enclosed within his own, to his lips and kissed it briefly.

"That's sweet," Crawley said.

"Huh?" Phil said, looking around with a worried, nervous expression.

"Steve and Autumn."

"That's great, Ellie."

"What's wrong? You've got your head on a swivel."

"Just hoping that a certain someone doesn't show up…" A moment later a rapid, heavy knock came on the door, and his shoulders deflated. "Oh, great."

"What's up, queers?" came a familiar voice a split second after the basement door banged open. A blast of cool fall air heralded the arrival of Rich. Though it was an informal gathering, the good-looking young man had dressed in a dark gray Ralph Lauren polo. His slacks were navy blue and unpleated, hugging his beefy thighs but loose enough that his socks stayed hidden when he walked. His hair was frosted and spiked with heavy gel, and even from across the basement Crawley could smell his potent cologne.

Rich came sweeping in and began holding court. Not a step behind him was Gina, a pretty redhead from Phil's work. Phil swallowed, hard, and tried to disappear behind Crawley. Gina had dressed in jeans so tight she wondered if the zipper teeth were gritted. The dark denim displayed every inch of her curvaceous bottom when she walked. A long sleeved red sweater with a v neck adorned her upper half, displaying a good amount of her generous cleavage. Her hair was down, cascading in a wavy blanket that seemed to shimmer even in the poor light of Rex's basement.

"How's your dick hanging, loser?" Rich said, wrapping an arm around Phil's neck and giving him a vigorous noogie. "Short, shriveled, and always flaccid?"

"Ow! Why are you here, Rich?"

"It's a party," Rich said, shrugging as if the answer should be obvious. "That, and I heard you guys needed a bass player. I'm an *awesome* bass player."

"Hey," Gina said, coming up to stand next to Rich. She smiled at Phil, her green eyes lighting up. "Phillip! I didn't know you'd be here. It's nice to know somebody besides my date."

"Stop ogling my lady," Rich said, smacking Phil on the arm. "Don't you have your own tail?"

"You have a girlfriend, Phil?" Gina said, eyes widening.

"Yeah, believe it or not, this homely little chud is dating that piece of hotness."

Rich indicated Crawley with his index finger. She noticed the attention, then her eyes fell upon Gina. Her nose twitched, just a bit, when the red haired woman put a hand on Phil's shoulder.

"She's pretty! How come you never mentioned her?"

"I have her picture in my cubicle at work," he said as Crawley joined them.

"Hello," she said, smiling. Her tone was friendly, but everyone could see the slight tremor in her hand when she took Gina's and shook it. "I'm Eleanor. You must be Regina, right? I've heard a lot about you."

"Really?" said Gina, "Phil's never mentioned you."

"I have her picture in my cubicle!"

"Oh?" Crawley said to Gina, ignoring Phil completely. When she finally did turn her almond shaped eyes toward Phil, she took some pleasure in his wilting posture. "I wonder why?"

"I'm sure I've talked about Ellie," Phil said, unable to look Crawley in the eyes. "Anyway, I have her picture in my cubicle."

"Maybe you've talked about her to your BFF here," Gina said, putting a hand on Rich's shoulder. "I can't remember you ever talking about her."

"Rich is *not* my BFF."

"Hey, Rich," Rex said, coming up to their little gathering and offering his fist for a bromantic bump. Rich's knuckles collided with the drummer's. "Glad you could make it. Who's the woman? She can't know you too well, or she would have already checked herself in at the VD clinic."

"Oh, ha ha," Rich said in a rare moment of embarrassment. He quickly looked at Gina. "He's joking, of course."

"I'm Gina. Nice to meet you." She offered her hand. It disappeared into Rex's meaty paw.

"Rex," he said, giving her hand a friendly squeeze. He glanced around the basement then turned to face Rich.

"Where's your instrument, buddy?"

"You mean he actually has one?" Phil said.

"Such a kidder, this guy," Rich said. "I'll go get it out of the trunk."

He turned his gaze upon Gina.

"Babe, can you get me a brewski while I'm out?"

"Sure." Rich was out the door before she even finished speaking. "You're welcome, I guess."

"Rich is an asshole. He has no redeeming qualities whatsoever," Phil said.

"Don't say that! You've been friends since high school," Crawley said.

"Since when are you on his side?"

"I'm not on anyone's side!"

"I know what I'm talking about, all right? Rich is a selfish, egotistical skirt-chasing asshole. It's all there really is to him. If he got cancer tomorrow I would probably throw a party."

"That's a horrible thing to say! I can't believe you'd talk like that behind someone's back."

Surreptitiously, Rex and Gina excused themselves, uncomfortable with the growing sea of tension between the young lovers.

"I'm sure Rich knows how I feel about him, and I would never talk about you behind your back."

"Apparently, you don't talk about me at all."

"Maybe I never mentioned you to Gina, but that's just because I don't talk to her much."

"Really? She was rubbing her tits all over your back while supposedly patting your shoulder. Or did you not notice that?"

Phil's eyes narrowed to slits.

"Do you think I'm lying?"

"I never said that."

"You're thinking it, though."

"Well, with the way you stare at every girl in a pair of tight shorts in a three mile radius, it kind of makes me think so, yeah."

"This again? I told you, my mind was wandering. I couldn't even *see* that chick—"

"Should your mind be wandering when your girlfriend is talking? I get the feeling sometimes that you take me for granted."

"Taking you for granted? Like when I get up at fucking *midnight* because you're all 'boo hoo, my frenemy is so mean to me!' Or how about the way I spent a whole damn weekend going over your dad's accounts—for no charge whatsoever? Yeah, I'm really taking you for granted, Ellie."

"Doing nice things for me is great, but—"

"Why is there always a 'but'? I think you're criticizing in me the faults you see in yourself."

"Excuse me?" Crawley crossed her arms over her chest and glared.

"I didn't stutter. *You* are the one who acts like I should be fucking grateful you let me stick my dick in your cooter."

Crawley's mouth fell open.

"That…that was a horrible thing to say! And it's not true!"

"Isn't it? Maybe you should hook up with that musclebound bouncer. He's a 'ten' just like you. You can squeeze out some beautiful little babies and make your daddy proud."

"Stop bringing my father into this! I never said that you weren't good enough for me!"

"Didn't you? Maybe not, but you were shaking your ass for him, weren't you?"

"You don't pay any attention to what I'm actually doing, do you? I was trying to help the band. Used to be you cared about people other than yourself!"

Phil's teeth gritted so hard she could hear them grind. His hand tightened around her arm painfully.

"Why don't you break up with me, then? If I'm such an inattentive asshole, then why stay? Every guy at every gig we go to wants to fuck you, and you give off the vibe that you'll let them do it."

Crawley sucked air in through her teeth, barely able to believe what she'd heard. "I give off a slut vibe, is that it? Let go of me."

"I never said you were a slut! Stop putting words in my mouth!"

"You implied it. Phil, you're hurting me."

Phil blinked, looked down at his hand. He was gripping Crawley's bicep so tightly his knuckles were turning white. He immediately released her, turning purple with shame.

"I'm sorry," he said, but he was speaking to her back. Crawley was out the door, car keys jingling in her hand.

Phil followed her into the night air. The day's warmth had been sucked away by the November evening's chill, and she shivered as he came up beside her.

"Here," he said, trying to give her his jacket.

"I don't want your jacket," she snarled, jerking her shoulder away.

"Well, what do you want?" Phil followed her right up to the car. "How can I make this right?"

"It's not always about making it right." Crawley turned back to face him. "I'm not a spreadsheet that's not coming up right, Phil. I'm a woman, and I have needs."

"I thought I was taking care of that." Phil's brows came together and she grunted in frustration.

"No, you moron, I'm talking about my *emotional* needs. I need to feel like you treasure me."

"I *do* treasure you!"

"But you only say it when I've told you to. Sometimes I feel like I navigate our entire relationship."

"Well, I'm sorry I was inexperienced when we met," Phil said hotly. "Maybe you'd be happier with Rich. I'm sure he can say all the right things to make your heart flutter and your legs spread."

"I might as well be with Rich, because that's exactly the kind of disgusting thing he'd say!" She blinked away tears. Phil had never spoken to her as harshly as he had tonight. She wished she could blame the alcohol but he'd had barely had a sip.

"Don't touch me!" Crawley glared at Phil when he dared put a hand on her shoulder. "Go away and leave me be!"

"Well fine! Maybe I'll go and bang Gina. That's what Rich would do and I'm apparently just like him!"

Crawley turned on the radio and spun the volume knob to maximum. Phil kept talking, though she couldn't make out the words. His face looked apologetic, though, even pleading, but she was in no mood for it. Eventually he threw up his hands and stalked back to the party.

She wasn't sure how long she sat there, but at least four different songs came and went on the radio when she was interrupted.

A tapping on the glass made Crawley jerk. Her gaze softened when she saw Autumn standing next to her car, covering herself with her arms.

"You okay?" Autumn said as Crawley rolled down the window.

"I'm fine. Men are fucking jerks."

"You're preaching to the choir…let me in, it's fucking cold out here!"

Crawley eyed her incredulously as she slid into the seat next to her. Autumn noticed the scrutiny and narrowed her umbra gaze.

"What?"

"Nothing…it's just…Steve doesn't seem like a jerk."

"Ha! If it has two testicles and a dick, it's a jerk, Ellie."

"Oh, come on, I was just watching you and Steve. He's really sweet when he's with you."

"Yeah." Autumn's eyes were shining. "He is at that. I think I may have fucked him up, though."

"How?" Crawley said, her mind roiling with bizarre sexual positions and practices.

"Uh, emotionally." Autumn's hand grasped at the air. "I guess that's what I mean. He's afraid that I don't believe in what we have enough."

"Do you?" Crawley said, using a Greece Hut napkin to dab at her face.

"What's that supposed to—" A moment later she deflated, shoulders slumping. "I guess I deserve it to a certain point."

"You did leave him." Crawley was careful to keep her voice nonjudgmental. "After he stuck by you when you got sick."

"I know," Autumn said through clenched teeth. Crawley could tell she was trying very, very hard not to get angry with her. "I know, okay? I did it because I didn't want him to suffer."

"He suffered quite a bit, Autumn."

"So what?" Autumn's gaze was locked on the smooth white hood outside of Crawley's windshield. "Maybe I didn't do it just for him. Maybe I did it for me. Maybe it was killing me to watch him watching me die. Maybe I'm just a selfish bitch, Eleanor. Did that ever occur to you with your reasons and logic?"

Crawley held her tongue, waiting for Autumn to wind down. The bellicose young woman seemed conflicted, as if she were just admitting out loud what she had long held inside.

"I don't think you're selfish," Crawley said, clearing her throat.

"Yes, I am." Autumn chewed on the first knuckle of her forefinger. "I didn't want to feel his pain, and I'm afraid."

"Afraid of what?"

"Afraid of Steve wising up and realizing that he can do better," Autumn said with a rueful smile. Tears welled up in her own eyes, though she tried to grin through them.

"Oh, Autumn," Crawley said, feeling a pang of sympathy, "you don't have to worry about that. You two were *made* for each other."

"Think so?" Autumn was still sniffling, though she sounded cautiously optimistic.

"I know so." Crawley patted her tattooed hand. "Steve would die without you, Autumn."

"Yeah, well, I would probably die without him." She turned her head toward Crawley. "Don't tell him I said that."

"Of course not, that's something you should tell him yourself."

"Yeah, not gonna happen. Look, you want to go back to the party? You can drive Phil nuts by not speaking with him the rest of the night."

"I think I'll talk to him after all. I kind of lost my temper, too."

"If you say so, but the silent treatment is a great weapon!"

"Well, you know us Asian ladies. We get really good at yelling!"

"Tora tora tora," Autumn said, squinting her eyes and assuming a posture as if she were operating a machine gun, "kamikaze pirots go!"

"You're just terrible! I'm not even Japanese…" She tried to wipe the smile off of her face before she entered the party. Once inside, she scanned around for Phil but did not see him.

"Steve," Autumn said, putting her palm on his chest, "where's Phil hiding? He has to face the music sometime!"

"Uh," Steve said, looking uncomfortable. "Well, he left."

"Left?" Crawley said, sputtering. "I drove him here! What do you mean he left?"

"That little sneak," Rich said, coming up with a beer in each of his hands, "has learned my lessons too well."

"What are you talking about?" Crawley said, growing angrier by the second.

"Philly boy ran off with my date," Rich said with a shrug. "Not a broski move, but I admire his balls."

"That prick," Autumn said, her eyes growing narrow.

"Well, maybe he was just, y'know, helping her out with something work related," Steve said, though it was obvious the big man didn't believe his own words.

"Is that what he told you?" Rex sauntered up, a half full cup of beer in his fist. "He told me she needed her insulin or some shit."

"Well, he needs to get his excuses consistent if he's going to pull this type of stunt," Rich said, stroking his chin. "It seems I have more to teach the boy."

"I never said Phil *told* me he was going to do something for work, I just assumed—" Steve said, but Crawley wasn't in a mood to hear another word.

"Phil," Crawley said numbly, shaking her head. She felt humiliated, betrayed, and more than a little angry. Suddenly she didn't want to be around people, didn't want to be anywhere at all. She scooped up Molly, fighting back tears, and tore out the door.

Chapter 11

The day after the party, Steve arrived at his appointment with destiny. He and Autumn had driven in the Monster Maker late that afternoon. He was nervous, but stoically silent. She seemed to pick up on his slightly pensive mood, and drove most of the time without speaking.

When they were nearing their destination, she finally turned to him and smiled.

"You're quiet, sugar."

"Yeah, guess I have a lot on my mind."

"Don't bottle it up, talk to me, hon."

"I'm scared." He laughed a bit after the confession.

"Of what? Are you scared of getting hurt?"

Steve sighed, the sun lighting his face in spurts as they passed tall buildings.

"Yeah, but that's not really what's got me down. I'm more worried about losing myself. The business has a way of doing that."

"Your dad seems pretty down to earth."

"He wasn't always. Ma says when he first hit it big he had an ego the size of Texas. I think having kids kind of made him settle down and treat it more like a job."

"You have me," she said, ruffling his hair with one hand while the other stayed on the wheel. "I'll tie you down if you start to float away."

"Like the other night?"

"You loved every second of it!" Autumn gave his head a playful shake. "Don't try to change the subject. This is good, this is you sharing."

"Well, since I'm in a sharing mood, I should probably tell you…"

His voice trailed off, jaw working silently as he fumbled about for the right words.

"Tell me what?"

"General's assistant coach is a woman named Barbara Hickock."

"Battlin' Barb? That's great! I remember when she used to be on TV all the time."

"Uh, yeah, that's the same Barb. Listen, I think you should know…"

Steve grew silent again.

"If you don't come out with it, I'm going to run this next red light."

She stomped on the accelerator for emphasis.

"Slow down, you nut!"

"Then talk while I still have time to stop."

The Focus increased in speed, jettisoning itself toward the waiting signal light. They were less than four car lengths away.

"Barb and I slept together!" Autumn applied the brake, causing them to lurch forward into their seat belts. Steve half expected the air bags to deploy. The smell of burned rubber reached his nostrils, and he could look in the rear view mirror and see two long corrugated streaks on the pavement.

"You did? Isn't she a lot older than you?"

"Well," Steve said as pedestrians and other motorists stared wide eyed at the car which had nearly plowed right through a busy intersection, "it was over ten years ago. I was nineteen, and she was thirty nine, or so she said."

"Pfft, is that all you were worried about? It's not as if I thought you were a blushing virgin when we first hooked up."

"She's kind of…physically affectionate. You'll see when you meet her."

"So Battlin' Barb is a slut."

"I wouldn't be so blunt about it."

Autumn parked the car, using a pay lot that could allegedly get validated by the General himself. Steve took a large gym bag out of the trunk and joined Autumn on the sidewalk. Their hands clasped together as they walked, Autumn's vanishing into his much larger mitt. They drew a few stares, as Steve was wearing old denim jeans and a plain T-shirt, while Autumn was dressed more exotically. Black vinyl pants sleekly hugged her hips, flaring out below the knees to accommodate her heavy leather boots. She wore a long sleeved shirt that was completely sheer, showing off her navel piercing and tattoos. Fortunately, she had on a half shirt over the sheer one, but the image she projected was still aggressively sexual. Steve had long ago learned to ignore the lingering stares of other men upon her form. He had never been fond of the idea of other guys ogling Autumn, but he also didn't want to be a jealous, controlling dickwad.

"Hey," Autumn said, "are you sure you should be in the advanced class?"

She paused with one boot up on the single concrete step that led to the glass double doors of the school. A light breeze stirred her hair, and the delicate twilight lighting made her appear all the more gorgeous to him at the moment.

"You're beautiful."

"Thanks...not really an answer to my question, but thanks."

"Sorry. I'm in the advanced class...because I used to work."

"Yeah, as a teacher," Autumn said, stepping up on the slab with both feet and turning to face him.

"No, when you say 'work' in the family business, it means you've gotten in the ring and wrestled."

"What, with your dad, like in the back yard?" Autumn cocked her head to the side.

"No, when I first got out of high school, I didn't go right to college. I tried to be a wrestler, or sports entertainer if you prefer, like my father."

"Shut up," Autumn said, putting her hands on his shoulders. "Why didn't you ever tell me?"

"I think I did mention it once or twice. Besides, I was down playing it in case you were a wrestling groupie."

"Hey!" She dug her nails into his arm.

"Sorry. But once it was obvious that for some reason you liked hanging out with me, I guess…I guess it never came up. I didn't do it for long, anyway."

Autumn kissed him on the forehead, then grinned.

"I like being taller than you for a change," she said, mussing his hair with her hands.

"Prepare to shrink," he said with a grin, stepping upon the slab with her.

"Aww."

They entered the building, standing in a long, darkened hallway. At the end of the passage was a set of double doors, light spilling out through the cracks. A heavy sounding impact reverberated through the air, followed by someone speaking in a baritone.

"Sounds like they're getting started." Steve quickened his pace. Autumn snagged his hand, dragged him back to her side.

"Wait a minute, how come you quit in the first place? Did you get slammed with a steel chair and suddenly gain insight on how to instruct four-year-olds in finger painting?"

Steve laughed. "I quit because I sucked at it."

He turned from her and pushed the door open with his shoulder, still holding her hand. The doors flew open wide, and they blinked in the suddenly bright light. The interior consisted of one large room, about twice the size of a typical yoga studio. The high ceilings were unfinished, revealing electrical wiring and plumbing over their heads. A sturdy looking set of florescent lights, some of which buzzed loudly, provided the illumination. The wrestling ring took up most of the space, a bright blue skirt with faded lettering running around the edge. As they watched, a heavyset man in his sixties instructed a small group of young men. His eyes were small and narrow, heavy jowls shaking as he spoke with passion.

"Any idiot can learn how to slam somebody," he said in a voice every bit as gruff as he looked. "What matters is making the audience *care* that you slammed somebody. There's guys who can flip all over the place like Mary Lou Retton on crack, but the crowd just snores when they're out there. Loudly."

The General's eyes widened a bit when he saw their approach. With a sudden grin he nimbly sprang over the middle rope and landed on both feet outside the ring.

"Steve!" he said, throwing his arms out wide. He hugged the big man so fiercely, Steve could barely breathe.

"How's it going, General?" Steve said when he could speak again.

"Not bad, little of this, little of that."

His eyes fell on Autumn, running up and down her form and lingering on her bust.

"Who's this vision of loveliness?"

"Sorry. Autumn, this is General. General, my fiancée Autumn."

"Pleased to meet you," she said, offering her hand for a shake. General bent his head low and kissed it instead, tickling the back of her hand with his stubble.

"Charmed," he said, arching both brows twice in succession. "If you ever get tired of this clown, look me up. We'll paint the town red!"

"You haven't changed a bit," Steve said as Autumn looked on silently.

"Not if I can help it!" He turned back to the class and raised his voice. "Damn it, Kyle, you want to kill that individual? Stomp on his shoulder before you drop an elbow so he knows it's coming!"

"Where's Barb?" Steve said, craning his neck to stare around the gym.

"She's on tour in Canada, teaching those skinny little plastic girls how it's done!"

"Careful, my sister is one of those skinny little girls."

"Yeah, but she ain't plastic!"

General turned his gaze on the men lined up by the ring, staring intently at the new arrivals.

"All right, punks, listen up and listen up good. This here is Steve Borgia, and unlike you he's actually worked a match or two in his day. He's here to brush up on some basics, but don't go easy on him. I *guarantee* he ain't gonna go easy on you!"

The other trainees laughed, though their eyes were carefully scrutinizing Steve and Autumn. Most of them were in great shape, but were shorter than Autumn. Steve towered over them as he shook hands and made their acquaintance. General barked orders for them to pair off and practice their bumps.

The old timer slid out of the ring as the students squared off. There wasn't much room in the ring, with all eight of them in it at once, but they seemed to know how to give themselves enough space to practice in. General stood next to Autumn as they watched, occasionally shouting out criticism, or more rarely, encouragement.

Steve noted her pursed lips, the way she focused on everything General said to her. Despite her bravado, Autumn seemed sincerely worried about his well-being. He hoped the old timer was setting her mind at ease.

It was a fact: He *was* going to get hurt.

During an armlock that his partner was over-selling, Steve noted that Autumn's face had split into a smile. General had that effect on people. With any luck, he'd give Autumn a quick education on what would be expected of her at ringside, should Reilly be interested in her services as Susan suspected he would be.

This is all for you, babe. He thought to himself. No, he had not lied to his father. It was not for the money that he was returning to the ring.

It was for Autumn.

Once practice was over, and Steve was thoroughly sore, he toweled off and checked his phone while General showed Autumn how to properly grab someone's leg outside the ring and trip them up. His eyes narrowed when he found a missed call from an unknown number. Listening to the voice mail, he slapped a hand over his face and chuckled.

"What's wrong?" Autumn said, coming up to his side and slipping her arm around his waist.

"It's Phil." Steve put the phone back in his pocket and stared at her soberly. "He's in jail!"

Chapter 12

"Hey there buddy," Steve said, smiling as Phil approached his car. Phil didn't respond. He was walking stiffly, like an indignant cat, with his fists balled up at his sides. He got into the passenger seat and stared sullenly at his lap.

"Déjà vu, right? I mean it was like, what, nine months ago when you were bailing *me* out of jail?"

Phil turned a baleful glare on him. Steve noted the black eye.

"Where did you get the shiner? Did you not want to pick up the soap or—"

"Can you stop trying to make light of this? It's not funny."

Steve closed his mouth, cleared his throat.

"So, ah…what *did* happen, exactly?"

"I told you, I got busted for DUI—"

"Yeah, but…y'know, some details might clear a few things up."

"What are you talking about?"

"They give you your phone back?"

Phil nodded.

Steve pulled the car out into traffic and rushed to beat a changing light. "Go ahead and bring up your Facebook account."

"Why should I bring up my…oh, no!"

"There were some witnesses to your accident, and you know how flash bulb happy people are these days."

Steve cringed in sympathy. He knew what image was making Phil choke in rage: the sight of himself, slumped over the steering wheel of Gina's truck, while she was lying unconscious with her face in his lap.

"How did…I haven't even…"

"Rich," Steve said at the same time that Phil shouted, *"Rich!"*

"I'll kill him. How did he figure out my password?"

"I don't know, but that image has gone viral. A lot of people are, uhm, making it into a meme."

"This is awful…oh my god, Crawley's going to think I was… I'm screwed!"

"Well, Phil, they say a picture's worth a thousand words."

"I know you're not judging me, Mr. Transvestite Puncher! It didn't go down like that!"

"I'm listening, not judging. So spill."

"I was just taking her back to her place so she could get her insulin. About halfway there she starts…groping me. I made her stop, and she slapped me in the fucking eye! The eye, Steve!"

"Then what happened?"

"What do you think? I couldn't see so I wrecked the car. I only had half of a beer, man. Just half a fucking beer and they say I was over the legal limit. Aww, what the hell?"

"What's wrong?"

"I can't delete the post—can't even log on as myself! Rich changed the password. I'm going to fucking murder that asshole!"

"Well, before you do, try typing in *Bukkake.*"

"Typing in what?"

Steve spelled it for him, and Phil was able to access his account and delete the post. It was too late, really, but Phil seemed to draw some small measure of comfort from it.

Steve shook his head in sympathy. He wasn't sure why, but he believed Phil—mostly. Phil certainly seemed convinced of his own innocence.

After Steve dropped Phil off at home, he drove back to his apartment. He told Autumn Phil's version of the story while he dealt with a few scrapes and bruises suffered during training.

"Stop laughing, Autumn," Steve said, shaking his head in disgust. He was standing shirtless in front of the mirror, examining a reddish patch of skin, a victim of mat burn. Using a cotton ball soaked in alcohol, he dabbed at the wound, wincing a bit at the sensation.

"I can't help it," Autumn said, coming into their bathroom behind him. She wrapped her arms around his waist and her face appeared from behind his shoulder. She wore a wide grin, mirth lighting up her brown eyes. "You have to admit it's funny. I mean, nobody got hurt — except you!"

"Phil's got a black eye." Steve rubbed antiseptic on the burn while Autumn looked on. "What's her name's got a bruised back or something from when her SUV plowed into the side of the police car."

"You should put some gauze on that or something. I can't believe that prick Rich posted Phil's mugshot on his status update. I mean, Phil's supposed to be his buddy."

"Oh, Rich has better character than most people give him credit for. I mean, he's a little larger than life at times, and he can come across like he doesn't give a shit about anyone or anything, but he actually would stick his neck out for Phil, or me, or even Rex."

"Oh, come on," Autumn said, carefully peering at his abrasion. "Why did he take that picture then?"

"In Rich's mind, he's blameless for the whole thing, because Phil is the one who cheated, or didn't cheat, if you believe him."

"I don't. Too many holes in his story. Did they really have to drive back to her place so she could get her insulin? And why was he driving the car if he was drunk too?"

"He was supposedly less drunk than she was…"

"So you believe him?"

"No, not really, but Phil believes it. That should count for something."

"Well, I'm going over to Crawley's. I'm going to take her shopping, for ice cream, you know, the standard post breakup routine." She glared at him sternly. "Cover that up, Steve, or it might get infected."

"I will, I will! Relax, Beautiful." He rummaged through his medicine chest until he found large adhesive bandages. "I don't know that they're officially broken up, just yet, but go. Be supportive. I'm a bit curious though…when did you two get to be such gal pals? I thought she got on your nerves."

"I guess I just got used to her." Autumn nodded with satisfaction as Steve covered his wound with the bandage. "You're not jealous, are you?"

"No, it's just unusual. I mean, I've barely seen your other girlfriends at all since we've been together."

"I told you, Jenna is doing a nickel for credit card fraud, Jackie moved to California, Becky...I don't know what happened to Becky..."

"I don't remember any of those people."

"Then you don't listen to me, I guess."

"Wait, was Becky the one who had her thong showing at the Journey concert?"

"Oh, that's some selective memory you got there. Yes, that was Becky, how astute of you."

"Uh, I wasn't looking. I mean, how could I not look, what with it in my face and all...not that it was in my face...she was a good, decent girl and wouldn't pull that. I'm sure it was merely an oversight that she forgot to better select denim shorts that would suffice as butt coverage on this particular occasion."

Autumn was laughing before he was halfway finished with his tirade. She spanked him hard on his rump, bereft of protection except for thin underwear. The strike was not gentle, and he yelped, turning an annoyed grimace on her.

"You're lucky you're funny. Why can't you be that, well, spontaneous on the microphone? General says you're great in the ring but total shit during an interview."

Steve's face fell a bit, his hand rubbing his sore flank.

"Shit, is it? Well, I guess General would know...I don't know, I just get so nervous when I'm on the air. My voice sounds weird, and the things I'm supposed to say are stupid. I mean, if I was going to fight someone, I wouldn't *tell* them ahead of time what my strategy is. Does Bill Belichick get on the Internet and say 'Hey, Seattle, I'm going to run a full field blitz on you in the first quarter'?"

Autumn tittered, patting him on the shoulder. "See, that's what I'm talking about. You need to relax and have fun when you're out there. People will respond to that."

"Yeah, you're probably right. Saying it and doing it are two different things, though."

"I have to go," Autumn said, kissing him on the cheek. "Crawley needs me. Practice hard, sugar."

He kissed her, surprising her with his sudden passion. His body strained against the thin fabric of his shorts. Her own half-dressed form melted into his for a long moment. Reluctantly, Autumn pushed him gently away. She stared up at him, her eyes full of promise.

"Tonight I'm going to screw your brains out. But now, I'm going to Crawley's. Have a good workout!"

"Now I need another shower," Steve said, staring down at himself. "A cold one!"

Cold rain pattered against the sloped windows adjacent to their table at the coffee shop. It cast strangely moving patterns on both women's faces. Crawley had eschewed make up, wearing a ball cap and sunglasses despite the overcast weather. Her unpainted lips looked dry and cracked as she toyed with her uneaten fruit smoothie.

"It's just, I don't know," Crawley said. "I feel like it's my fault. If I hadn't just run off and left him like that—"

"Don't go there, hon. He knew what he was doing. Men are jerks, one and all."

"Steve's not a jerk."

"Well, maybe not, but he has his moments, too. We all do. At this point, you can't beat yourself up about it. Either you break up with Phil for good, or you forgive him, believe him, or whatever, and stay together. It's like the Karate Kid, you know?"

"The what? Do you mean that movie with Will Smith's kid? I don't remember anything about breaking up in that—"

"No," Autumn said, slapping a hand on her face, "c'mon, Crawley, I'm not *that* much older than you. In the original, Pat Morita tells Daniel-san that he can't walk down the middle of the road…"

Crawley's incredulous expression lay hidden beneath her shades.

"Never mind…the point is, the indecision is what's killing you right now. It might hurt more to just break things off, but it'll be more…I don't know, peaceful?"

"So you think I should break up with Phil?" Crawley stirred a bit of strawberry at the bottom of her plastic cup around in a swirl.

"No, I'm saying that only you can make that decision, but you had better make it soon. Now, finish your smoothie, we're going out for manicures, and then—"

"I'm sorry, Autumn, but I just can't do this today. I have a lot to think about, I guess, and I do my best thinking when I'm working in the lab."

"Oh, all right. Well, take care of yourself, sweetie. Give me a call if you need to."

"Thanks," Crawley said, a brief grin flashing over her face. "You know, most of my friends have always been guys. It's kind of nice to have someone to talk about this kind of stuff with. You know, girl stuff?"

"Yeah, don't get all mushy. You'll sound like a pussy, like Steve."

"Sometimes," Crawley said, leaving a twenty dollar bill on the table, "I think you give him too hard a time. You'd best be careful, or someone else might scoop him up."

Autumn's mouth formed an O, her eyes wide, and Crawley giggled at the sight.

"I'm just kidding. I'll see you later."

Autumn didn't seem to be happy, but she didn't protest when Crawley left.

"Okay, honey. Take care of yourself and call me night or day if you need to!"

"Thanks, but I just need some time to think." Crawley left a bill on the table and hustled out the door into autumn air that was cold rather than cool.

The rest of the trainees had left over an hour ago, but Steve remained at the General's school, practicing hitting the ropes. He'd remembered how to hit them on his back, but for some reason couldn't quite master the sideways technique. Every time he tried, his ribs stung badly.

Steve cursed when he heard the buzzer go off. Someone was about to wander in off the street, possibly another street urchin. As the footsteps approached, he called out in a menacing voice, "Gym's closed for the day, thank you very much!"

"I'm an invited guest, thank you very much!"

A young blonde woman came striding confidently into the gym, her skin deeply tanned. Muscles stood out on her forearms, and she seemed to exude a powerful presence, as if she were used to being the center of attention and embraced it. Her breasts were on the small side, but due to the tightness of her spandex gym suit it was obvious that it detracted little from her physical beauty.

"Susan!" Steve felt his cheeks aching as he smiled ear to ear. "You're back in the States?"

"For a day or two, yeah." Susan vaulted nonchalantly up onto the apron and Steve held the ropes open for her entry. "Then it's back to Japan."

"Pop said you quit working for Chester Reilly's promotion." Steve tried to keep his voice neutral. "What happened? I thought he had a pretty good market share, at least in the New England area."

Susan shook her head, pretty face wrinkling up. "I couldn't maintain weight. I was 'fat' in Reilly's opinion."

"Fat?" Steve stared at Susan's impressive physique, the sinuous grace with which she carried herself. "Is he fucking blind?"

"The rule of their women's division is you keep your weight under one hundred and fifty pounds."

"Susie, you're six feet tall and you've worked out your whole life! That's not realistic, or reasonable for that matter."

Susan grinned ear to ear. "That's why I went to Japan. Over there, they don't care how much you weigh. They just care if you can *bring* it."

"You've always been able to bring it," Steve said without a trace of bravado. "You're a better wrestler than me, that's for sure. I can't even remember how to hit the ropes on my side."

"Seriously?" Susan stretched out her neck, grunting as the vertebrae crackled like popcorn. "Here, I'll help refresh your memory."

Steve watched while she demonstrated how to keep from breaking one's ribs while doing a side hit. After several botched attempts, he finally met with success. Then muscle memory took over and they were soon Irish whipping each other across the ring.

"There you go!" Susan shouted in glee as he flew past her and hit the springy ropes. There was a moment when he felt suspended in them, right before he got launched back toward the center of the ring, when he felt almost weightless. It was an exhilarating sensation, and the fact that he was sharing it with his sister made it an almost magical moment.

Then they engaged in "free practice," basically going through the motions as if they were having a match but with less urgency or impact. Susan showed him a new escape from a figure four, and he helped her with a Judo sleeper she was having trouble with.

"Man," Steve said, wiping sweat from his brow.

"Getting tired already?" Susan asked between pants.

"No, I was just thinking that it'd be cool if…well, it'd be cool if Pop were here." He laughed. "Seeing us getting along for once, engaged in the family business. He'd probably get all choked up."

"Nah, not the Deathslayer." Susan sniffed at one of Steve's towels and used it to wipe her face. "You got a wrestling gig lined up yet?"

"No, and I'm really starting to regret walking out of Greece Hut." Steve sighed. "Autumn's been breaking into her savings, and that just kills me."

"Well, Chester Reilly wasn't exactly bitter when I chose not to extend my contract." Susan draped the towel over the top rope and dug around in her hoodie until she came up with a business card. She thrust it into Steve's hand. "In fact, he practically *begged* me to give you his card when he heard you were getting back into rasslin'."

"Really?" Steve stared at the card, scarcely able to believe his good fortune. "That's awesome! Thanks, Susie!"

"Don't thank me yet," she said, a scowl marring her lovely face. "Chester Reilly is big on the eighteen to thirty-four-year-old male demographic. Expect to have an offensive, ludicrous gimmick. Oh, and he'll try to push you into the hardcore bull crap too. Do what I did and say no, 'cause it's just not worth it."

"I don't mind getting a little hardcore." Steve ran his fingers over the slick embossed letters on the card. "Don't they do that stuff a lot in Japan?"

"Some feds do, but not the ones I work for. Wrestling is hard enough on your body, Steve. Doing the hardcore Death Matches just takes years off your life."

"Yeah, well, Autumn probably won't let me do hardcore anyway," Steve said with a chuckle. "Thanks again, even if I end up being Baby Deathslayer or something."

"Nah, Dad owns the rights to the name, so you won't be able to use it."

"Unless Pop gives me permission…not that I would ask." Steve sniffed. "I kind of want to create my own legacy. Maybe go back to being the Insane Warrior."

"Ah, Steve," Susan shifted from foot to foot, and stared at the discarded towel hanging on the ropes as she spoke. "About the Insane Warrior…maybe change your outfit."

"What's wrong with the outfit? It's just a pair of shorts and face paint!"

"Yeah," Susan's cheeks were growing red, "maybe get some longer, looser pants."

"What is wrong with you?" Steve folded his arms over his chest and glared. "If you think the Insane Warrior is a terrible gimmick just say so."

"The gimmick's fine, bro," she said quickly. "You're just a little… endowed…to wear those little bitty shorts. Just saying, some things might hang out."

Steve slapped a hand over his face, his own cheeks burning.

"It had to be said!" Susan patted him on the shoulder. "I've got to go. Got an early morning, need to get my new passport photo—"

"I understand." Steve embraced her and they engaged in a warm hug. "Thanks for stopping by. You saved me in more ways than one."

"Ah, it's nothing." Susan slid out of the ring and gathered her hoodie. "Just remember what I said. Don't let Reilly talk you into anything stupid."

"Right," Steve said, staring at the card. "I don't need to be talked into doing any more stupid shit anyway!"

Chapter 13

"Human Hammer," said the massive man, his ebony skin rippling with muscle, "you think you're such a lady's man, like you're some kind of bossanova?"

The man flexed, his bald head showing off numerous veins as if he was having an apoplectic fit.

"Well, you're not good looking," he said, jowls peeled back to show off bright white teeth. "You're ugly! You're so ugly that if ugliness was from France, you'd be the Great Wall of China!"

"*Cut!*" shouted the little man standing next to him, wearing a very dapper but modest suit. "Chris-sakes, Jerry, can you not remember your damn line? It's *Casanova*, not bossanova! And don't get me started on…the Great Wall of China? Really? That's not even in the right continent!"

"I'm sorry," the big man said, sniffling a bit. "Can we start over Mr. Oberland? I think I can do better this time."

"Oh, jeezus," Oberland said, slapping a palm over his face. "Don't cry, big guy. I'm sorry, all right? Just…just *try* to read the lines as written, okay?"

The two men were on the sound stage of Reilly Productions, perched on the thirtieth floor of the Buster Building. The studio was nestled between a law office above and a medical diagnostics lab below. They were standing before a large green curtain, a two man crew operating a camera pointed straight at them. The red light upon the top flickered on once more, and the big man tried to muddle through his lines.

Off to the side, keeping their voices very low, Autumn and Steve watched the proceedings. The mood was so solemn, they almost felt like they were in a church.

"This is it," she said, leaning close and whispering in his ear. "The real deal, I mean. You're going to be on television!"

"I just hope that two weeks' worth of training was enough to get me back up to speed."

"Pfft. You'll do fine. This is…this is awesome!"

Her eyes shone with excitement, and her hands fluttered open and closed upon his own.

"Calm down…it's not all it's cracked up to be. It's hard enough to work a match, but when you have to worry about getting in the camera crew's way…well, it can be dangerous."

"I never thought of that. Oh, sugar, I hope you don't get hurt."

"I'm *going* to get hurt," Steve said, chuckling a bit as he tucked a strand of her jet black hair behind her ear, "but hopefully not bad. Like I said, most of the time it's like any other sport: you play injured a lot of the time."

Autumn hugged his arm tightly.

"I don't want you to."

"Shhh, I think they're filming again. Hopefully I can get a deal where I'm not on the road all the time. I have no idea what kind of contract he has in mind."

"I think we're about to find out."

A man came out of a door adjacent to the spot where Jerry and Oberland were wrapping up their interview. He tiptoed past the scene, then marched toward the couple with his hand outstretched.

"Hello," he said in a stage whisper, "I'm Chester Reilly, how do you do?"

He shook Steve's hand, pumping it vigorously and making eye contact. He had a thin face and a long nose; this coupled with his prominent, large ears gave him an almost rodent like quality. A pencil-thin mustache decorated his upper lip, matching the dark color of his slicked back hair.

"Steve—" Steve said, starting to introduce himself.

"Steve Borgia, son of the legendary Deathslayer from Hell!" Reilly said, still pumping his hand. "We're expecting big things from you, my boy, big things!"

Smoothly, he turned his attention toward Autumn. His eyes went wide, and his thin lips parted in a gasp.

"And who is this beautiful lady?" he said, taking her hand and bringing it to his lips.

"This is my fiancée, Autumn," Steve said, cocking an eyebrow at the gesture while Autumn giggled.

"Enchanted," he said, staring at her longingly. Autumn arched her own brow and twitched her nose, a hint of her annoyance which Reilly subtly acknowledged by turning back toward Steve.

"Man, you're a big guy!" Reilly massaged Steve's bulky shoulder. "How often do you hit the gym?"

"Three times a week, and I try to get in running and biking every day if I can."

"He overdoes it, that's what he means," Autumn said, brow knit with concern. Her fingers felt at the bandage beneath his shirt, as if she were assuring herself that it was still affixed.

"Three times a week, and you look like that?" Reilly said, shaking his head. "Man, those Deathslayer genetics are just phenomenal. We used to joke that your dad is like a classic car, because he still has all his original parts!"

"He never did any of the off the top stuff."

"Do you?" Reilly said, his tone casual but a gleam in his eyes.

"Yeah. I can bust a pretty good moonsault, as long as the ropes aren't too springy. I used to do an elbow drop, but that really hurt my hip."

"You're too big for that, sugar," Autumn said, nose twitching.

"Nah, it'll be fine. When you land a moonsault you absorb the impact with your whole body, so it's not that unsafe."

"I watch wrestling, I know what a moonsault is. Aren't you afraid that you won't make the back flip all the way and come down on your head?"

"Sure, but then I might slip on soap in the tub tomorrow and crack my head open."

"It's not even close to being the same, and you know it! There will be no moonsaults, no top rope, no diving over the ropes to somebody on the floor. At all."

"Autumn," Steve said, smiling nervously as he glanced back and forth between Reilly and his paramour, "you're kidding! Tell him you're kidding."

"You are a pretty big guy to be pulling that stuff, Steve," Reilly said, winking at Autumn. "Guys built like you don't *need* to come off the top rope. You can just fling the boys all over the place like an ape and the crowd will eat it up."

"What sort of gimmick do you have in mind for yourself?" Reilly asked as he led Steve into his office. The room was spartan, with bare metal walls and a simple desk that looked as if it had been swiped from a teacher at a local high school. A beaten and weary looking desktop computer sat buzzing on the desk, the keyboard lost amid a stack of papers. He bade them sit down in the stuffed chairs before the desk, which were comfortable but for the numerous lacerations that covered the vinyl upholstery.

"Well, when I was wrestling back in the day I called myself the Insane Warrior. I was hoping we could build on that."

"Ah," Reilly said, wincing as if in pain. "You see, kid, the thing is, the Insane Warrior was kind of cliché. I mean, how many face paint wearing steroid freaks can the public be exposed to before the whole thing becomes old hat?"

"I never did steroids."

"Sure, whatever kid...Anyway, I heard about that trouble you had a few months back, with the whole losing your job cause of a fight with a TV hooker."

"Uh," Steve said, blushing red while Autumn stifled a laugh, "I can explain that, I'm really not a homophobic or prejudiced person—"

"No, don't misunderstand me, kid. I don't want to hide the fact that this incident happened. I want to *embrace* it."

"I don't follow," Steve said, cocking his head to the side.

"This is what I think: You, Steve, you aren't Steven Borgia anymore."

"I'm not?"

"You're...you're..." Reilly's fingers grasped at the air as if he could pluck the words out of the atmosphere. A light dawned in his eyes and his smile grew wider. "You're *Pimpmaster S!*"

"Pimpmaster S?"

"Yeah, it'll be great! You can get some bling, a big fur coat, oh, and you can come out to 'It's Hard out Here for a Pimp.' I got a guy who can do a knockoff so good, you'd swear it's just like the real thing, but we can prove in a court of law that it's not!"

"Uh, I don't know…"

"I think it sounds great," Autumn said, putting a hand on Steve's forearm. "Should go over well with that eighteen to thirty-six-year-old demographic."

"Yeah," Reilly said, nodding his head, "exactly! And you, Autumn, would you be available to be his ho? I could draw up your contract at the same time I do his."

"Autumn is NOT playing a prostitute," Steve said.

"Shhh," Autumn said, squeezing his arm. "I could do that."

"Autumn!" Steve said, glancing sharply her way.

"Great! Now, you need a name, something exotic but easy to print on T-shirts and signs…hmm, kind of got an S&M goth sort of vibe here…how about CANDY PAIN?"

"Candy Pain?" Steve said, his blue eyes narrowing to slits. "Are you out of your fu—"

"I think I like it," Autumn said, digging her nails into Steve's arm.

"All right," Reilly said, shuffling the papers around on his desk. "This is what I'm offering. Currently, we run about three shows a week, one of which is televised. You sign here, you agree to appear in all of those shows in a performance capacity. You also agree to any promotional appearances that we might deem necessary but no more than five total appearances, matches included, in any given week. You have to agree to our no-compete clause, which means you can't wrestle for any other promotion in North America. However, you are free to book yourself in matches outside the country, so long as they do not interfere with the ability of WWL, LLC to conduct its business."

Steve's mind swirled with the deluge of information. It was a good contract, one that would give him several days off a week to mend and spend with Autumn. His eyes scanned down to the compensation, and went wide.

"Uh, this says you'll be paying me seventy-five grand for a one-year contract. Is that a misprint, or…?"

"No, that's accurate. I told you, we expect big things from you, and I hope you stick around with us after your contract is up, even if you get an offer from the North or the South."

"Probably wouldn't work for the North anyway. I want to spend *some* time with the people I love."

"That's great!" Reilly said. He then turned to Autumn. "Autumn, your contract won't be nearly as generous…unless you know how to bump?"

"She definitely doesn't bump," Steve said quickly.

"Okay," she said, smiling, "I cave. No top rope stuff for you and no bumps for me."

"She doesn't bump," Steve said with vehemence.

"Great in either case. I'll have legal draw up a contract for her and e-mail it to you this afternoon. It's gonna be a hell of a ride, kid! Welcome to the WWL!"

As the man again pumped his hand with fervent enthusiasm, Steve could not help but feel as if he were already losing a piece of himself. Only Autumn's presence at his side made him feel enough conviction to bury those feelings beneath the knowledge that they needed the money, desperately.

Seated next to him, Autumn did not seem to notice his inner conflict. Her eyes were wide, starstruck with the possibilities that their new life might afford them.

Chapter 14

Crawley was determined to go through with band practice no matter how awkward things were between herself and Phil. She was positively radiant, her soft brown skin glowing and her almond shaped eyes full of vigor. After a week of off and on crying she was tired of looking frumpy. She had her long hair drawn up, as she often did to avoid pulling a Van Halen — getting one's hair stuck in the strings of one's own instrument, as the legendary guitarist had once done on stage. It was done up in a bun of sorts, low on the back of her head with a good deal of length still dangling past her shoulders. She was wearing a tank top with a cobalt and sepia pattern of roses on thorny vines, and tight black jeans adorned her hips.

Her mind drifted back to the day after the party. That had been very miserable, indeed. Most of her friends on social media were connected to Phil's in one way or another, so literally everyone she knew online had now seen the snapshot. The snapshot of another woman with her head in Phil's lap.

Phil had called her, of course, and offered his excuses and explanations. Maybe, just maybe, if he hadn't been such a jerk, if they hadn't had that nasty fight, she might have forgiven him. As it stood, she felt so betrayed and humiliated that his words rang hollow, even though she suspected — hoped — they were true.

And even if he was telling the truth, and she was the aggressor, why was he in the car with her in the first place? Part of being in a relationship was keeping yourself out of situations that might make you stray. Not that she would dream of cheating on Phil, but she could find some drunk to go home with too…

She forced herself to relax, driving the miserable feelings back and fencing them in as best she could. Then she flung open the door and stepped inside, careful not to bang Molly on the frame.

"Hey, guys," Crawley said, giving hugs to Sven and Rex. She struggled with her amp until Rex took it from her. She unslung Molly from her shoulder and let it carefully down on the couch, just as she had done twenty times before. "I have to go and get some stuff out of the car."

Her high heeled leather boots clacked on the concrete as she headed back down the walk. Rex approached Phil, coming over to his side and patting him on the shoulder. Crawley winced as their voices easily carried to her ears.

"Sorry, buddy, that was pretty cold."

"Ja," Sven said, "she's not even making with the eye contact."

"She hates my guts," Phil said, "and I deserve it. I have to man up and deal with the fact that I screwed myself out of something good. God, Rich is going to be all over her."

"Probably," Rex said.

"Ja."

"Man, that creep…do we *have* to practice with him? Can't we find someone else, anyone else?"

Crawley's nose wrinkled in disgust. John had been a perfectly capable bassist, while Rich could hardly pick out a tune. If only the bouncer hadn't had to work on their practice nights.

"Look," Rex said, going to the door and watching as Crawley struggled with two paper grocery bags, "I told him if he can keep up and learn the songs, we'd give him a chance. He's not horrible, he knows how to play…kind of."

"He *is* horrible," Phil said, going to help Crawley with her burden.

"Ja, but so were we all once."

"Not you, Sven," Rex said. "How a motherfucker who can't order a goddamn Big Mac at the drive-through because his accent is so thick can sing as beautifully as you do is a fucking miracle. You must have an extra head, like that guy in that alien movie."

"Men in Black?" Sven said.

"No," Rex said, shaking his head and scrunching up his brow, "it had Will Smith in it, and Tommy Lee Jones, old leather face himself. There were aliens, and they were government guys or some shit…"

"*Men in Black*," Sven growled.

"No," Rex said, stifling a grin and striving to remain deadpan, "not that one. Will Smith had a song that went with the movie, they are the…something, something."

"*Men in Black*!" Sven shouted, grabbing Rex around the collar and picking him up off his feet.

"Whoa," Rex said, finding it difficult to escape when he was laughing so hard, "settle it down, Swede Kong!"

"Hey," Phil said, taking one of the paper bags from Crawley's arms. He managed a weak smile.

"Hello, Phillip," Crawley said, somewhat stiffly. "Thank you."

"Listen, I know you're sick of hearing it, but I really was just heading back to her place to help with a spread—"

"You're right." She felt guilty satisfaction at the way he wilted. "I *am* sick of hearing your excuses. We're on a break, now let's just drop it and have practice."

Phil examined the contents of the bag, blinking back tears. Crawley almost…*almost* felt herself cave, to tell him he was forgiven. It was true that she ached for his presence.

"You brought booze? And what's the rest of this stuff?"

They moved past Sven and Rex as they continued their shenanigans, but Sven's nose detected an aroma from one of the bags Crawley bore. He dropped Rex without a thought, releasing the man to land on his feet. Rex had his eyes closed and was red faced, mighty guffaws escaping his mouth.

"Is that barbecue?" Sven said, his mouth watering as he beheld the greasy paper bags within the larger plastic one.

"Sure is, big guy," Crawley said.

"Honey mead?" Phil said, reading the cool dark glass bottle in his hands.

"Yeah, we were always talking about it, and you know I can't stand beer…"

"She brought food and booze," Rex said, recovering from his hysterics. "She must be sucking up to us for some reason. Fess up, you want to do a Lady Gaga song or something, right?"

"No," Crawley said, rolling her eyes, "I want to do *my* song."

"You wrote a song?" Phil said incredulously.

"Yeah, we did have this conversation, right? About adding new music?"

"*Ja*, but then we never talked about it again."

"Let's take a look, Squirt," Rex said, rifling through the bags and selecting a pulled pork sandwich for himself. "Is it in your fake book?"

"No," Crawley said, digging in her purse for her tablet. "I've been putting all our new stuff on here. I can bring it up…"

She spend a few moments swiping at the screen after it blinked to life. Her fingers shook nervously, and her heart hammered in her chest. The fear of disapproval weighed heavily on her, but she believed in what she had written.

When at last she had pulled up the file, she handed it to Sven.

"You read sheet music, don't you Sven?"

"Oh, *ja*," Sven said. He squinted his blue eyes as he stared at the screen. His lips moved silently a moment, and then he sang softly.

"Don't need you…Don't need you in my life. That's for sure."

"No," Crawley said, "more like this 'Don't need you! Don't need-youinmylifethat'sforsure!"

"Whoa," Phil said, "that's a little up tempo for us, don't you think?"

"We could make it work," Rex said, rubbing his chin. "Crawley, why don't you try singing it for us?"

"Oh, no," Crawley said, swallowing hard, "I'm not a singer, I can barely do back up —"

"Oh, it's not that hard," Rex said, gesturing at Sven. "If this defrosted Neanderthal can do it, anyone can!"

"Ouch," Sven said, wincing as if the comment had hurt, "you are racist. I will open up the can of ass whip on your Nazi dick!"

All of his friends exploded into laughter.

"Sven, honey," Crawley said, putting a hand on his arm, "I'd explain everything wrong with that sentence to you, but I'm afraid I would die laughing."

Rex set up a microphone and practically dragged the little Asian woman out in front of it.

"I need Molly." Her movements were jittery as she prepared the instrument and stepped in front of her audience of three. She took a deep breath, summoning up the state of mind she had been in when she had written the song, the day after Phil's indiscretion. Her eyes closed, and when they opened, they burned with inner fire.

The pick strummed down hard, hitting all the strings. Crawley's right hand flew over the frets, shaping the feedback into an aggressive rift with definite hard rock overtones. They were taken aback by the display, used to the more dulcet tones of their cover songs.

She changed to a much simpler chord so she could concentrate on the words. Eschewing the tablet that Sven tried to hold up for her, she ripped into the lyrics.

> *Don't need you!*
> *Don't need you in my life that's for sure!*
> *Don't need you!*
> *Don't you come creeping round by my door!*
> *Put me down!*
> *Don't you trample my heart anymore!*
> *Put me down,*
> *Treat me like I'm your own little whore!*

Crawley went into a solo that was both energetic and darkly uplifting. When she reached the hook, the refrain of the song, her voice was more hopeful.

> *I thought the world was ending, when you were just pretending,*
> *To love me until it all burns down.*
> *So through the air I'm soaring, new worlds that I'm exploring,*
> *Until my true love can be found.*

She stopped, her strings squealing as she abruptly ended the performance.

"That's it, all that I have for now. Maybe repeat the first stanza and add some more—"

"Why'd you stop?" Rex said.

"That was great!" Sven said.

Phil's mouth opened but did not work.

"Wasn't that great, Phil?" Rex said, punching him in the arm.

"It was…" Phil said, "it was loud. Do we really want to play something that hard?"

"Oh, come on," Sven said, "it was awesome, *ja?*"

"You really think so?" Crawley said, beaming.

"Yeah," Rex said, "I can see us doing that. It needs some more work, as far as adding a bass line, maybe another line or two of lyrics, but it seems solid."

"What about keyboard?" Phil said.

"Don't seem like a keyboard kinda song," Rex said.

"Anything you want to contribute is fine, Phillip," Crawley said. "I'm sure we'll all consider putting it in."

Crawley felt a mix of guilt and glee at Phil's downtrodden face, but she had to admit it was satisfying in either case.

The bellhop was clearly mesmerized by Autumn's skimpy leather outfit. His eyes were big as dinner plates as he gawked at her curvaceous figure. Autumn didn't have time to notice the attention, because she was busy mauling Steve's mouth. Her hands clawed at his chest beneath the faux gold chains hanging from his neck. The bellhop cleared his throat several times, but they didn't pause. Finally he got off on the floor just below theirs.

"I think we scared him off," Autumn said as the bellhop beat a hasty retreat. Her lipstick was smudged, some of it on Steve's mouth.

"You scared him, maybe." Steve covered her mouth with his own once more. "I take it you liked my first outing as Pimpmaster S?"

"Oh God, Steve, it was…it was intense! I mean the lights, and the pyro and the people screaming…and you were amazing! No ring rust on my man!"

"You did pretty well yourself. Hit all your cues right on time."

"Well, I thought I was gonna break a nail when I grabbed Hebrew He-Man's boot to trip him up."

"Poor baby." Steve kissed her again, feeling the press of their semi-clad bodies.

The elevator chimed, and the doors slid open. They strode out quickly into the hallway, hands clasped. Steve used his free hand to dig out their key card from his pocket, while Autumn adjusted her skimpy top to keep her pierced nipple from showing.

Steve barely had the door open when Autumn practically tackled him. They stumbled inside the spacious suite. The kitchen area was just off the door, and the room opened up from there into a living room larger than Steve's whole apartment. A big screen TV was tuned to a twenty four hour news station, though the volume was muted. A leather sofa with soft cushions and a massaging recliner sat adjacent.

"I need a shower," Steve said when Autumn paused to slip out of her black lace thong.

"No, I want you like this, all sweaty and dirty…"

She wrapped her arms around his naked torso and nibbled on his neck. Steve's hand slipped down her shoulders, over the lacing of her corset, and down to her rump. He grabbed her buttocks tightly and kneaded the pliant flesh.

"Should we go to the bed?" Autumn said as Steve's hot mouth explored her neck and chest.

"No time," Steve said in a low growl, sweeping her up onto his shoulder. Her legs kicked in mock struggle as he carried her into the living area. He sat her down on the sofa and squeezed her shoulder.

"Don't stop now," she said, pushing him down to his back aggressively. "Once you start, there's no going back!"

"You're feisty tonight." Steve lifted his hips so she could peel off his pants.

"I don't know, seeing you throw that other guy around…I was wide open the whole time."

"I'm sure all the horny teenage boys would have liked to have known that. They were eye humping you all night."

Autumn swung her hips over and positioned herself so that her head was below his waist. Her nether lips were now just inches away from Steve's face, and he breathed her scent in and felt his jealously slip away.

"What was I talking about?"

"I don't know…maybe we should both find something else to do with our mouths?" Steve nodded, his mouth pursed. He lifted his chin and dove between her legs. Autumn gasped, careful not to scrape her teeth along his most delicate of skin. Their differing heights made getting a good rhythm going a problem at first, but Steve was able to prop his head and shoulders on the armrest of the sofa. Then they were perfectly aligned, pleasing one another as they best knew how. Eventually, Autumn had no choice but to come off of him and wail as her body was wracked with spasms. She collapsed on top of him, and they lay there for several moments, sweat mingling as they panted for air.

"Sorry I stopped early," Autumn said, her mouth mumbling into his thigh.

"Early?" He patted her rump gently. "You were, uh, successful."

"I noticed…I was just going for twice."

"Well, now I'm in your debt, one orgasm to zero."

"Pfft," Autumn said, shifting around so they could lie chest to chest. She stared him in the eyes, chin propped up on a hand laid across his sternum. "You know I love you, right?"

"I love you too," Steve said, his brow coming low over his blue eyes. "What's this about?"

"I might not be able to go to Japan with you."

"What? But you've always wanted to go! What's the—"

"My dad and Brad will be in town that weekend, and we haven't had much of a chance to see each other, since, well…"

"I understand." Steve strove to keep the disappointment out of his voice.

"Is it really okay, or are you just saying that?"

"No, it's really okay. I'll be pretty jet lagged, and have to do some promo work, and have to find a place to work out, eat…It'll be a working vacation anyway. All you'd do is watch me sleep."

"Hey, I'm told those Candy Pain T-T-shirts were selling better than yours tonight. Don't go getting a big head on me!"

"That's the problem with this business, you kind of lose touch with reality, you know? It's tempting to spend money as fast as you make it and pretend the party is never going to end, but Pop showed me the *right* way to do it. The people in your life are what's important. Almost losing you, first to the Lupus, and then to, well…"

"To me being a bitch."

"I was going to say fear, but now that you mention it…"

"Don't talk like that to Candy Pain!" Autumn said, sitting up on him and putting her hands on her hips.

"Oh, I'm so scared."

"You better be," Autumn said, slapping him across the face. The hit was not hard, certainly he had been smacked harder in the ring by Hebrew He-Man, but it was more aggressive than Autumn usually was. He clapped a hand to his face, arched an eyebrow at the display.

"What was that for?"

"Oh, be a man." Her gaze narrowed, angular brows coming low as she slipped into character. "Do as I say and you won't be hurt, *worm*."

Steve laughed, but he played along.

"Yes, ma'am."

"Get hard." She kissed him vigorously, biting his lower lip nearly hard enough to draw blood. "I want you inside me, *now*."

"I'm getting there!"

"Do I have to do everything myself?" With a sneer, she reached back behind her. Steve gasped as she expertly handled him. The feel of her hands sliding over his flesh was amazing, and her aggression only seemed to add to the sensation. When he was ready, she lifted her hips and came down on him slowly. Her façade of stern implacability began to slip as she gyrated atop him. Steve put his hands up on her breasts, but she pushed them down to his sides. She leaned forward, using the leverage to get him as deeply inside as possible. When her body released its pent up tension, she reared up backward and let out a long, deep moan. She leaned against the back of the sofa, their bodies still interlocked.

"God, that was intense!"

"Silence, worm…"

"Looks like a good time to escape," Steve said, rising to a sitting position. He threw his legs over the side of the sofa, keeping their intimate parts together the whole time, and arranged her facing him on his lap.

"Oh god…" Autumn nibbled on his shoulder and neck as she bounced up and down atop his lap. Steve's hands slid down her glistening back, stopping when they reached her buttocks. He squeezed her soft rump tightly, using his grip to aid her own sinuous movements.

"Don't…stop…worm!" Autumn's voice was cut off with each bounce.

"You're…not…in charge…anymore!"

Steve grabbed her hair near the back of her head and yanked firmly backward. Autumn gasped as her neck was arched back. He took her lips, tongue thrusting in possessively. Her hot breath mingled with his own, until she filled his lungs with an exultant scream. Their mouths parted and she collapsed sweating against him. Their breath came rapidly for a time as they cuddled, skin sliding on skin.

"No," Autumn said as he tried to disengage their bodies, "let's just stay like this for a while."

"Yeah." Steve wrapped his arms around her. "Yeah, that sounds nice."

At moments like this one, Steve could almost banish his doubts. Autumn's skin pressed against his own, their hearts beating inches from each other. But what would happen to him if she left again? If he was never able to feel her this close, her breath coming hot on his ear? It was almost too horrible to think about.

So he held her close, tried to think positively, but he couldn't lose the feeling that he was holding a ticking time bomb in his arms. One that would destroy him utterly when it went off.

Chapter 15

C rawley did a double take when she saw who was calling. She had been ensconced in her basement, trying to coax some Sri Lankan Huntsman spiders into biting a cotton-swabbed vacuum pump. The arachnids were huge and swift, but were also among the most docile she had ever dealt with.

The flashing of her phone alerted her to the call, since she usually kept the volume off in the lab. She sighed, put her forehead in her free hand for a moment, and finally pushed the accept key.

"Hello, Rich," she said, trying not to sound annoyed. "How can I help you?"

"Hey, Crawley," came his cheerful, isn't-the-universe-clever-to-have-me-at-its-center voice. "Man, you sure slayed with that song you wrote."

"Thanks, Rich!" She was pleasantly surprised at the accolade. "I really didn't—"

"Yeah, you *killed* Phil. He took off work the day after."

"Oh, no…" a pang of guilt stabbed her in the chest. She really hadn't intended the song as a harangue on Phil—well, not *only* that—and never wanted him to be in pain. "That's terrible!"

"Terrible? I was calling to say, nice shot! I could learn a thing or two from your wickedness."

"Please don't talk like that," Crawley sighed. "Do you think I should call Phil?"

"Nah, no way. Let him stew a little while. You should go out and have some fun, maybe with a trusted friend."

Crawley sat up a bit straighter. Was this leading where she thought it was?

"What are you getting at, Rich?"

"I'm saying maybe me and you go out, catch a flick, maybe a bite. Just as friends, you know, and see where it leads?"

It was hard to deal with Rich most of the time, but now he seemed almost reasonable. That made her even more suspicious.

"Look, Rich, just because Phil and I are on a break doesn't mean I'm ready to start dating."

"Did I say date? I don't think I used the word date."

"Well…" she was out of things to say, except for the elephant in the room. "How do I know you don't just want to get into my panties?"

"My desire to enter that particular forbidden zone has nothing to do with my intentions," Rich said. "You have my word as a broski."

Crawley chuckled. "Okay, fine, one of these nights we'll go out. As friends."

"I wouldn't have it any other way. Catch ya later, Ellie."

As she ended the call, she was fairly certain that she'd just stepped in a trap.

Beautiful Jerry watched, dark eyes mesmerized, as the sparkling amber champagne trickled down from the top of the glass pyramid. Dozens of drinking vessels had been stacked upon each other, and as the waiter expertly poured the spirits in the top glass it ran down to be caught in each of the waiting crystal carapaces.

"Stop gawking," Oberland said, coming to stand behind the big ebony-skinned man.

"I'm sorry, I've always wondered how they did that, without making it spill. I tried to do the same thing in my garage once, but it didn't work out so well. Of course, I used beer and Solo cups, but– "

"Just get your drink and shut up," Oberland said, munching on an ear of baby corn.

Autumn and Steve snickered nearby, standing arm in arm. The two of them were in a nicely appointed hotel suite, mingling with other guests of Chester Reilly—mostly talent, but a few investors that the smooth talking man sought to entice into further loosening their purse strings. It was a work night in a way for the wrestlers, and they had to be on their best behavior so as not to spook the wealthy clients. A long buffet table laden with decadent snacks lay next to the champagne glass pyramid. An ice sculpture of two men grappling with each other was a centerpiece around which the party guests swirled. Soft jazz music was piped in, Chester being too cheap to hire live musicians. Still, the affair had an air of elegance to it.

"Could I have the one off the top, please?" Jerry said to the server.

"Certainly, sir," he said with a smile, not bothering to add that removing the top glass was a necessity.

"Oh boy," Jerry said, almost dancing as he took the stem in his huge hands. "It's bubbly."

"Of course it's bubbly," Oberland said. "It's champagne."

Pimpmaster S was gone for the evening, replaced by just Steve. He wore an Armani suit with a subdued charcoal color, vest buttoned and shoes shined to a gleam. Autumn was clinging to his arm, wearing a sweeping evening gown, the elegance of which clashed a bit with her sometimes exotic skin art. One hand was idly playing with a new bauble, which looked to be a platinum pendant on a chain. The pendant resembled a little face with its mouth open, as if in fright.

"This is pretty swank," Autumn said as they moved toward the buffet. "By the way, I love my new shiny!"

"So you've said. I thought you'd like it."

"*The Scream* is one of my favorite paintings, ever. You get me, sugar. You really get me."

"I'd better get something tonight. I bought you jewelry—that's like a gimme."

"You get something almost every night," she said, giggling as they each took a glass of champagne, "except for those delightful three days a month I have."

"Shh! This is a swank party, like you said—"

"Oh, stop, it's not like I'm standing on a chair and screaming out—"

Her chest heaved as she took in a great breath. Steve cringed, knowing what was coming next.

"Hey, I just got off my period!" she said loudly, drawing stares from all over the room. Steve took her by the arm and dragged her toward a set of glass double doors that opened up on a veranda with a spectacular view of the city. She laughed, allowing herself to be taken along and slamming her body against his when they made it outside. A stiff breeze stirred her hair, worn long down to her shoulders.

Steve tucked an errant silken strand behind her ear, his slightly peeved expression softening as he gazed into her eyes. Floodlights provided plenty of illumination, glinting off her nose and brow rings as her own mocking gaze became a more loving one.

He leaned forward and kissed her, very gently, his lips lightly brushing her own. Their lips smacked together a few more times, then they embraced in the evening air.

"I'm glad you're here with me," he said.

"Ditto," Autumn said, patting his back as she breathed against his neck.

"Not just at the party, in my life, I mean. You're the best thing that ever happened to me."

"Oh, ho!" Autumn pulled away slightly to look in his eyes. "I think you're feeling a little worried since Phil lost Crawley."

"It's got nothing to do with that…well, almost nothing. When are we going to get married? You can call yourself Autumn Borgia, Autumn Winters, Autumn Borgia Winters whatever, but why not go ahead and do it?"

"Steve, enough about the goddamn marriage, all right?"

She stiffened in his arms, and he felt as if they were perched on the eye of a needle. He could push the matter, maybe get his fears of abandonment out in the open. On the other hand, he could just drop it and they could enjoy their evening together.

He decided to drop it.

Steve embraced her tightly, strong hands sliding over her back. He tucked a hand under her chin and rubbed her skin lovingly. "I love you."

"I love you too."

"You're so sexy tonight," he said, his hands running over the smooth black satin of her dress. His palm cupped her buttocks and gently squeezed.

"There are people around," she said, taking his hand and moving it to the small of her back.

"Not out here." The other guests remained indoors, and only two rows of tall shrubberies flanking either end of the veranda and a wayward pigeon shared the night air with them. He moved backward, taking her out of sight of the glass doors and near one of the verdant barriers.

Steve smothered her face and neck with kisses, Autumn throwing her head back and shuddering.

"What are you doing? I don't think we should…"

Autumn's hands clutched at him despite her protests.

Steve wrapped his arms around her waist and spun her around to the other side of the shrubbery. There was about a five foot wide, ten foot long empty space, swept clean earlier in the day by the housekeeping staff. He slipped his fingers down her chest and hooked them in the top of her dress. Swiftly, he brought the garment down around her waist. The cool night breeze stiffened her pierced nipples, which he immediately massaged with his fingers. He added a bit of moisture by gently working his mouth over each one before raising back up to kiss her deeply.

"You're so bad…" Autumn kneaded the back of his head with her hands.

Hooking his stout arm under her left knee, he raised her leg in the air. He pulled her lace thong pulled to the side, the flimsy garment stretching easily to allow him entry. Autumn groaned as they melded their bodies together, wrapping her arms tightly around his neck and shoulders. She bit his ear, nibbling the flesh just hard enough to hurt.

The encounter was urgent and brief, due to their potential for exposure, but what they lacked in duration they made up for with passion. Autumn tore a seam on Steve's blazer, and Steve's hand shoved her hair into a tangle of the bush's twigs when he slapped it over her mouth to prevent her passionate cry from reaching inside.

Suddenly Steve gasped, setting Autumn down as gently as he could, as sharp pain lanced through his hamstring.

"What's wrong?" Autumn assisted him as he hobbled a few feet to sit on a stone bench.

"Dunno!" He cried through gritted teeth. "I stumbled a little bit after a lariat last night. Must have pulled something."

She knelt next to him and massaged his tortured leg. At first it was like pouring gasoline on a fire; her fingers only seemed to cause him more pain. Gradually, she kneaded the muscle into limp submission and he was able to relax with relatively little pain.

"Thanks." Steve carefully stood up, then did a few short hops. "I think I'm good now."

Autumn's bottom lip was trembling, dark eyes boring into his own.

"What?" he asked.

"You need to quit wrestling," she said with finality.

"What? Are you kidding?" Steve laughed. "I'm under contract. I can't quit if I wanted to, which I don't!"

"I don't want you hurt all the time," she said with a sniffle.

"Are you crying?" Steve gathered her in his arms and stroked her hair. She didn't sob, but the tears flowed freely onto his shoulder. "Don't cry, beautiful. I'm going to be fine, see?"

He did a little jig, emphasizing how much better his leg felt. The truth was it started throbbing again but he wasn't about to let that show.

"I don't like it." Autumn sniffled, and he offered her his handkerchief. "Thanks. I don't want you getting hurt."

"I know." He kissed her, but she turned her face so that he brushed her cheek rather than her lips. Gently, he turned her to face him. "I love you."

"I love you too." Their lips met, and then their bodies were pressed together. Autumn broke the contact, smoothing down his lapels with her hands.

"What gives?" he grumbled.

"This is a working party, remember?" Autumn led him toward the suite. "We'll pick up where we left off...later."

They were both giggling as they re-entered the party, him picking leaves out of her hair, when they realized that there was a ruckus going on. Most of the guests had turned their attention to the buffet table, where a peculiar scene was playing out. Seated most inappropriately in the center of a rye bread bowl was a little person. He had a tanned complexion and dark hair, his limbs more proportional than many others with his condition. He held a champagne bottle in his hand, tilting it back in order to spill the entirety of its contents down his throat at once. His other hand was being used to hold back the server, clearly at wit's end with the little man's antics.

"Who the hell is that?" Autumn said.

"El Gato Magnifico. He's a legendary mini wrestler from Mexico. Reilly hired him about six months ago because he was going to start a midget division, but as it turns out there's not much of a market for it here in the states."

"I've never seen him at a show."

"He hasn't worked any. Reilly has him under contract but he has no one to work with."

Autumn arched a pierced eyebrow at him and gestured at the crowd.

"There's a whole room full of people for him to work with."

"Autumn, come on, he's a midget! How would it look for a guy Jerry's size to have to sell for a midget?"

"It's pro wrestling, people will suspend their disbelief. They think your dad is from Hell. Why wouldn't they believe that a midget could put up a credible fight?"

Steve started to respond, but realized there was no logical way to argue with her point. A bit of sympathy welled up in his chest as he looked at the little man, who was now vomiting most of the liquid he had just consumed onto the posh carpet.

"Eww. This Gato guy…is he any good?"

"Oh, yeah, he's really athletic for uh, for one of them…is he a midget or a dwarf?"

"I'm not sure what the difference is. So he could work a match with a big man, even if it was spotty?"

"Spotty…I love it when you talk industry jargon."

"Then you should love this. I think you should tell Reilly you want to marry the little guy for a while."

"Feud with him? I don't know, aren't I ridiculous enough with the whole pimp thing?"

"It's entertainment, it'll play great, and it would give the man something to do — a purpose, as you would say."

"Hoist with my own petard!"

"You just dipped your 'petard' in my —"

"Shhh." Steve's hand clapped gently over her mouth. "It's from Shakespeare. It means 'stabbed with my own sword.'"

"Stabbed with your own...how would you even...that Shakespeare dude was a fucking perv!"

Steve rolled his eyes.

"All right, what the hell? It'll go a long way to making the boys in the back respect me, too. Putting over a midget has got to count for paying at least some of your dues."

Autumn cast a furtive glance about the room, then surreptitiously picked at her rear.

"You chafed my butt when you yanked my undies aside."

"I did? I'm sorry."

"Yeah, the little string kind of digs in...next time they're in your way, just rip them off or something."

"How about now?" he said, dragging her back toward the veranda. Autumn allowed herself to be carried along, a wide smile playing at her lips.

"You are so bad!"

Chapter 16

S teve stood still, trying to pay attention to Gato but failing to understand the string of rapid Spanish erupting from his mouth. He had taken a year or two of it in high school, but the little man spoke so quickly he could only make out every fifth word.

Gato finished speaking, putting his hands on his hips and looking at Steve expectantly. The big man turned to look at Autumn standing a few feet away, awaiting her translation.

"He wants to work in a 450 off the top, since that's his finisher. He also said…"

Autumn paused, prompting Steve to raise his brow at her.

"He also says, that if you blow it on the mike tonight he's going to…be upset."

Steve stroked his chin as he gazed at the mini wrestler. The little man's fierce, defiant sneer told Steve that he had used more colorful language than Autumn indicated. Forcing himself to be calm, Steve smiled. Gato was, after all, a respected international talent, and had been in the business for over ten years. In the loose, unwritten rules of the pro wrestling locker room, that made him higher on the totem pole than Steve. The big man nodded.

"I'll do my best, Don Gato."

The three of them were sitting in the locker room of a small venue in Hoboken, New Jersey. It was a television taping night, and all of the WWL talent and staff were in attendance. The sounds of feet in the hallway outside the door mingled with the muffled announcer's voice as he introduced the talent. Steve was dressed in his ring gear: a pair of tight, sparkling silver pants tucked into ostentatious furry boots. His hair had been gelled up, bright blond streaks dyed into it that he thought looked ridiculous but apparently looked good on TV. Gato was likewise dressed for the ring, in a full body black spandex suit, though his feline-themed mask was sitting on the bench next to him.

Autumn shifted from one foot to the other, trying to hide her smile. Her thigh high, shiny latex boots definitely made her appear more exotic and sexy, but the high heels were so tapered she struggled to remain erect. The boots covered more of her body than anything else she wore. A pair of shorts less modest than underwear briefs clothed her lower torso, the same shiny latex as her boots. A pair of handcuffs served as a belt, and her rhinestone studded top showed a great expanse of cleavage. The straps were designed to look like little chains, which was probably not the most comfortable sensation against her skin, but it was not as if she would wear the garment for long.

"Can you translate that?"

"I think he got the gist," Autumn said.

"Where'd you learn to speak Spanish, anyway?"

"When I worked at the fish market that one summer. I know I've told you before."

"You told me about the fish market, but you never mentioned the Spanish thing."

"Bullshit. If you remember it so well, who was my boss?"

"A paisan with a club foot named Vinnie."

"Half the Italians in the city are named Vinnie; that doesn't count."

"You called off whenever this one guy with a harelip was scheduled to work because it grossed you out to look at it."

"Okay, maybe you were paying atten—"

Gato let loose a long stream of Spanish, using his hands to illustrate his point. Autumn paused, staring at the little man attentively and nodding.

"He says he hates to interrupt, but he wants to work in a spot where I jump on the apron and try to distract him, and he smacks me on the butt."

"What?" Steve said, his brows coming low over his blue eyes. "Tell him no way!"

"It's not that big a deal. I mean, it's not like it's going to hurt. He's four feet tall!"

"No way. It's bad enough you have to walk out there half naked and have all the men ogle you."

"All right," Autumn said with a sigh. She turned to Gato and spoke to him briefly. Gato nodded and gave Steve a slight bow of his head. He spoke to Autumn, who turned her brown eyes on Steve for the translation. "He says if you don't want to do it, it won't happen. He'll just gyrate his hips at me or something…I don't know what he said, my Spanish is a little rusty."

"Good. Could you please tell him it's a pleasure to be working with him, and I'll be sure to put him over?"

"Don't worry, gringo," Gato said in terrible English. "I take good care of both you!"

His sinister, sly grin was lost on Autumn, but not on Steve.

A short while later, Gato headed off to prepare for his interview segment. The idea was that Gato would speak in Spanish while Oberland held the mike, and then Steve would come in and harass him for being an immigrant. Steve was not a fan of the slightly racist tone of his character, but he was playing the heel, the bad guy, while Gato was a babyface, or good guy.

He sat with Autumn, going over his lines. They were not complicated, but he felt himself tensing up at the thought of speaking on camera. Steve was skilled at executing the various holds and throws in the ring, but he was not smooth on the microphone. Autumn, on the other hand, had taken to it like a duck to water. He was more than a bit jealous of her ability to relax and get into character.

"This is hopeless. I'm not a pimp, I don't know how they act or how they talk! I can't just read some lines and be this character. God, I wish I was still teaching…"

"Aww." Autumn's eyes were soft, her lips slightly open. "Do you miss it that much?"

"Yeah, sometimes. I don't know, this is…this is hard!"

"Sugar," Autumn said, putting her hand on his forearm and lightly stroking the skin, "the problem is you need to relax. You're going to talk for like three minutes, not deliver Othello's soliloquy!"

"Hamlet. Hamlet has the most famous soliloquy."

"Shut the fuck up, *Crawley.* I don't need you to correct me. Just listen to me for a minute. If you want people to respond to you, you're going to have to embrace your inner pimp."

"My inner pimp?"

"Sure, you can send out your pimp vibe a lot of different ways, like the way you walk."

She rose to her feet, affecting a strange limping gait. Her head was tilted back, and a smug smile was plastered on her painted face.

"You have to pretend like you're the shit, and you've got it all figured out. You try it."

Steve rose to his feet and tried to mimic her, but his comical efforts made Autumn laugh.

"Stop, stop," she said, leaning on him for support. "Oh my god, that was *terrible.*"

"I'm trying."

"You're trying too hard." Autumn pursed her ruby painted lips. A moment later, she looked up at him, her smoky eyes half lidded.

"What are you doing?" he said as she strode over to him and grabbed his crotch. "We've only got like five minutes, woman!"

"You need to feel like a pimp if you're going to act like a pimp." She slipped her hand under the elastic waist of his tights. He gasped as she seized his shaft in a tight grip, massaging the spongy flesh into hardness. His hands reached for her, but she slapped them away.

"Stop it, you're a pimp, you don't care about making *me* feel good. Just stand there and let your girl do her job."

Steve crossed his arms over his chest, not knowing what else to do with them. It was hard not to respond to her touch, not to take her in his arms and stroke her fine black hair. He tried to do as she said, to channel his feelings of self-importance and pomposity. His body did not get the message that they only had limited time, and soon she was dragging his tights down lower. He lunged out at her, and she glanced up at him with a look that was somewhere between desire and stoic task-mindedness.

"You're the man, baby," she purred, her hand busily sliding over him. "You're the man…"

Steve closed his eyes, willing himself not to release early. He opened them again when Autumn abruptly stopped.

"What are you doing?"

"Like you said, we don't have much time," she said, sticking her tongue out playfully.

"You can't stop!"

"Consider it a down payment…Now get out there, Pimpmaster S, and remember, you're the man!"

Steve walked out of the locker room, hoping no one would notice how he strained against the confines of his silver tights. Autumn walked with her arm hooked in his, heels clacking on the concrete floor. They reached the area flooded with light from numerous lamps on tripods. Gato had already begun on his interview. Steve waited for his cue, and then sauntered on camera, donning his shades first.

"Burrrrrrito," he said, rolling his R's like a native Spanish speaker. "Taco grrrrrande chalupa!"

"Pimpmaster S," Oberland said, pretending to be incensed at the interruption, "what are you babbling on about?"

"I thought we were just naming things off the Taco Bell menu," Steve said, which prompted Autumn to laugh in character.

"That's very disrespectful," Oberland said. "This is El Gato Magnifico's time, so why don't you take your floozy and get out of—"

"You're just jealous that you can't afford this, honey!" Autumn said, putting her hands on her hips.

"Quiet down, ho," Steve said, not even looking at her. He squatted down and put his hands on his knees. "There ain't no pee wee division here in the WWL, El Shrimpo, so why don't you go hang out in front of the Home Depot with all the other illegals?"

El Gato nodded for a moment, then reached back and slapped Steve. He had been expecting it, of course, but the impact was surprisingly hard. His face snapped to the side, and a noticeable red welt was rising almost immediately.

"You little freak!" Steve said, having no trouble getting into character.

"Calm down," Oberland said, "this is the WWL, not a knitting circle. Why don't you two settle it in the ring?"

"Oh, we'll settle it all right! I'm going to turn El Gato into my own personal piñata. Let's go, Candy."

Steve sauntered off the set, clapping a hand over his cheek as soon as he was no longer being filmed. Oberland came up behind him and slapped him on his broad shoulders.

"That was great, Steve! The way you reacted when he slapped you, I thought you were pissed for real!"

"Imagine that," Steve said, holding a hand to his face and glaring at the little wrestler. His fierce gaze was returned spark for spark, and Gato even jabbed two fingers at his own eyes and then thrust them in Steve's direction.

"Calm down," Autumn said, amused by Steve's anger. "You broke your toe last week and didn't carry on like this."

"My toe didn't hurt till after the match. Getting slapped really stung! El Gato ain't gonna play around in there."

"Don't play around either, then. You can work stiff, but don't kill the little guy."

"I'm going to be stiff all night, thanks to you. God, you're so beautiful…"

"Don't smudge my lipstick," she said as he moved his face toward hers.

Steve had to admit, El Gato was a consummate professional. He didn't miss any of his spots, was always where he needed to be in the ring, and his kicks stung but did no actual damage to Steve. The crowd seemed to enjoy the match, booing Steve viciously and cheering for the natural underdog, Gato. In a way it was one of the easiest matches he'd had to work yet, as the little man was half the size of his usual "foes."

Not that the little wrestler wasn't rippling with muscle. He weighed as much as a man of average height, and Steve could feel the power hidden in his tiny form when they grappled.

The time came for the match to end, and they set up the spot. El Gato, being the hero, hit his spectacular finisher, flipping in the air twice before crashing down on Steve. The Mexican went for the pin, but Autumn took her cue and climbed onto the apron. She swiveled her hips seductively at the little man, who quit trying to "win" the match and walked toward her. Steve rolled onto his side, pretending to be in pain but actually moving so he could watch for his own cue.

Autumn turned about and shook her latex clad bottom at Gato, which whipped the men in the crowd into a frenzy. Steve's jaw dropped as El Gato reached out and slapped Autumn across both shapely cheeks. It was not a gentle slap, and her buttocks danced for a full second after the impact. Autumn's mouth flew open, and she spun around, hand on her bottom.

El Gato was not done. Going further off script, he climbed under the middle rope and stood next to her on the apron. Without preamble he wrapped his arms and legs around her shiny black boot and ground his crotch against it, like an amorous dog.

Steve was on his feet and charging at the little man, his face a mask of rage. El Gato let go and put his hands on the middle rope, setting himself up for a spot where the midget would ram his head into Steve's belly. The big man allowed it to happen, though he was furious at the mini wrestler.

El Gato sprang up to the top rope, showing considerable agility, and dove onto Steve's now prone form. Steve suddenly rose to his feet and caught Gato, then put him on his shoulders and performed his finisher: a Death Valley Driver, just like his father's. He was careful not to put the little man on his head or neck, but he put as much impact into the move as if he were in the ring with a full-sized man. Gato did not seem to mind, and allowed Steve to lie across his diminutive form and get the "victory."

A chorus of boos greeted him, which felt the same as cheers to a babyface. He grinned, soaking it up. Even though Gato had gone off script, the match had apparently been entertaining enough. Autumn got into the ring and leaned against him, thrusting her hips out and standing seductively.

"Great job, sugar. I mean, my ass is sore, but it was worth it."

"I'll kill him."

She patted his toned belly and laughed.

Chapter 17

C rawley dashed down the hall, carrying a dozen live spiders in a glass aquarium. Oddly, the aquarium didn't look like one of the small ones they used in their lab, but rather like one of the gigantic fish domiciles maintained by the rich and obsessed. Somehow, she managed to keep it from falling out of her slender arms.

"Looks like that's heavy," Rich said, leaning against a wall as she passed. "You need a hand?"

Her reply was cut off when he clapped his hands vigorously. She turned and walked away from him, the hallway seeming to grow longer as she traversed it. The names on the doors she passed were jumbled, as if the letters were close to making sense but the words were actually gibberish.

"Ellie!" hissed her mother, leaning out of a door that for all the world looked like the red painted front entrance to their house. "Ellie!"

Crawley ignored her, continued to look for the lab where she was supposed to drop the critters off. Her mother usually only wanted to harangue her, or tell her about something she already knew, or something that was too late to be changed.

"Ellie," her mother's voice said, "you forgot to put on any clothes!"

Crawley looked down at herself, gasping at the sight of her soft brown nipples pressed against the cold glass of the aquarium. She dropped the glass menagerie, sending broken fragments and frantic arachnids all over the floor. Running, she hid her face in shame as almost every one of the doors opened and someone she knew gaped at her nude form.

She desperately flung a door open at the end of the hall and slipped inside, slamming it shut behind her. Her gaze raised upward, and she gasped in shock. Somehow, she was no longer in the office building, but in Steve and Autumn's apartment. The two were not expecting company, as they were as nude as she was, their mouths and bodies locked in a passionate embrace.

"I'm sorry. I'll go now…"

They stopped, stared at her, and laughed strangely.

"You're trespassing," Autumn said, "and stop staring at my boy-friend's junk. Some BFF you turned out to be!"

"I don't know," Steve said, scratching his chin, "should we just let her go? She kind of deserves some kind of consequence, doesn't she?"

Crawley tried to bolt out the door, but her limbs seemed to move slowly, as if she were trapped in sand. Plus, the door seemed to lack any sort of knob or handle on this side.

She turned around, gasping, holding her arms crossed over her chest. Autumn was inches away from her, leering at her form. The other woman grabbed her by the wrists and pulled her arms away.

"Don't hide yourself, Ellie. You know you're such a hottie."

Autumn leaned forward, pressing her lips against Crawley's. Soon her feeble resistance melted away, and she was enthusiastically return-ing the kiss. Their hands slid all over each other's smooth skin, and Crawley felt her heartbeat pounding in her chest.

"Hey," Steve said, "I can't just sit back and watch."

Both women looked at him. Crawley gasped, as he was standing at full attention. His anatomy was far more impressive than Phil's…

"Look what you've done to him," Autumn said. "You have to take care of that!"

Autumn took her by the arms and pulled her away from the wall. Crawley could not even begin to resist when the dark haired woman took her arms and held them behind her. The slender Asian was forced gently to her knees, Steve right in her face.

"Get to work, you little slut," Autumn said. Crawley closed her eyes and did as she was told. Her jaw ached to open wide enough, and Autumn let go of one of her arms to put an encouraging hand on the back of her thick head of hair. It was not a forceful push, but something of a reminder of her lowly status.

Crawley gasped as the results of her efforts stained her, getting on her chin and sternum. Soon they were forcing her to her feet, dragging her to the couch. They sat down with her lying across both of their laps. Crawley had her face in Steve's lap, continuing to serve, while Autumn was using her hands to explore the conveniently located nether region before her…

Crawley's eyes blinked open, and she rolled over on her back and sighed. She was covered in sweat, her night shirt clinging to her damp body. She giggled a bit at the dream, realizing that it had been over two weeks since she had been intimate with anyone. *Two weeks.*

She sighed, sat up and thought of Phil. She missed him, his laugh, his hands, and his body. Her cravings could not be denied, and she slipped a hand beneath her panties to sate her own lust.

A short while later, she heard the telltale beep of a missed message on her phone. She picked up the device from where it sat on the charger atop her nightstand, and squinted at the screen.

"Phil," she said, noting the time of the message. It had been sent just after eight, and a glance at her display told her it was well after midnight. Her fingers moving almost of their own accord, she brought up his image and pressed the call button.

"It's late," she said to herself as it rang on and on. It went to voice message and she started to hang up, but then Phil's sleepy voice came through.

"Hello?" His voice was thick from recent slumber but held an unmistakable hint of optimism. "Ellie?"

"Hello, Phillip. I'm sorry I called so late."

"No, it's all right, I just got home a little while ago."

"Really? They're working you so hard…"

"That's business, I guess…Look, I've been doing some thinking, and I'd…I'd do anything for another chance."

Crawley put the phone down for a moment, closed her eyes tightly as tears slipped down her cheeks.

"Oh, Phil, I don't know. You hurt me really bad. I don't know if I can go through that again."

"I won't hurt you again, I swear!"

Well, at least he's stopped protesting his innocence, thought Crawley, though she didn't know if that meant he truly was guilty or not.

"You're not stupid, you're a man, and men have trouble controlling themselves."

"I know, men suck, we all suck, I suck…but can you please give me another chance?"

"Phillip," she said, gathering her legs under her Indian style, "I want to, I really do, but it's not just about what happened with you and that bimbo."

"Then what is it about?"

"I don't think you really appreciate me."

"I love you, and not being with you hurts! I'm miserable day and night."

"Phil…I love you too. But that's not always enough."

"Please, I'm begging you, here."

Crawley closed her eyes tightly and tried to steel herself against the plaintive edge to his voice.

"I need time. I need some time, okay?"

"Okay. Uh, you're not really going to the movies with Rich this Friday are you?"

"Yes, it would be rude not to, and Rich is a nice guy."

"Are we talking about the same Rich? You're going out as friends, right?"

"Good night, Phillip," Crawley said, turning off the call.

She lay back down on the mattress and sighed.

Steve leaned over the laptop, scrolling through his ledger. Things were not looking good financially. Despite his recent increase in income, they were woefully behind on all of the bills. He held a pink slip of paper in his hand from the power company, demanding seven hundred dollars by the end of the week or they would be cutting the electricity off.

He was struggling to pay off Crawley for her loan early in the year, trying to catch up on rent and also pay the exorbitant monthly premiums for his insurance, which had gotten even worse due to his high risk profession. Steve stretched in the wooden chair he sat in, his body protesting a dozen small injuries. The thought of getting hurt in the ring was always on his mind. He was an independent contractor, as far as the WWL was concerned, and if he didn't work he wouldn't be paid, simple as that.

Working through the holidays had nearly killed him. The WWL had shows on Thanksgiving, Christmas, and New Year's. Even more amazing, people showed up to the arena on those days in droves. If there had been some sort of bonus associated with working the holidays, it may have made him feel better. Reilly made a big deal of what an opportunity it was for them, and they should be grateful to work on a holiday because it would make them all richer. Steve was still waiting for that to happen.

What they really needed was a big windfall, a large sum that would clear their debt and give them a fresh start. He had been pinning his hopes on the trip to Japan and a possible stake in the ticket sales, but from what Reilly had said the deal had fallen through. Now the weekend of February third was empty, and the WWL staff had those days off.

Picking up his phone, he dialed up Susan and let it ring, expecting to hear a voice mail.

"Hello?"

"Hey, Susie, I wasn't expecting you to answer. Isn't it like midnight in Japan?"

"Two in the morning, actually. I couldn't sleep. What's up?"

"Well, I'm kind of having money problems, and Dad is anathema to the Japanese wrestling circuit, so…"

"You want me to put you in touch with someone? Steve, I can do that, but do you know what you're getting yourself into? They do it a lot harder over here."

"Sounds like a bumper sticker. *Japanese Wrestlers do it harder!*"

"Steve, I'm serious, they don't fuck around here. You can get your teeth kicked down your throat, and no one says anything. That would be a lawsuit in the WWE or TNA."

"I'm not looking to *stay* over there, just fly there for a weekend show and fly home."

Susan blew out a sigh.

"They may not be too keen. Japanese are big on the sins of the father philosophy…"

"That wasn't his fault, though." Steve scratched the back of his head. "The asshole promoter he was working for in the States wouldn't let him work for another fed, even one that was overseas."

"Fine. I'll make some calls, send some e-mails, and get back to you."

"Can you kind of make it a priority?" Steve tried to keep the impatience out of his voice. "Sorry, but we're running out of money here."

"I'll start right now. These little worker drones over here are either up already or haven't been to bed yet."

"Thanks, Susan. You weren't always that supportive of me and Autumn, but this is really going to help."

"Just remember what I was talking about. They're really stiff over here."

Steve smiled ruefully. "I can work 'strong' style, Susie. Hell, I *like* working snug."

"I know, bro, just don't get involved in one of those hardcore garbage matches where they spread out thumbtacks and slam each other on them, okay? Stay pretty for Autumn."

"You got it." Steve rubbed his eyes and sighed. "Thanks again. Love you."

"Love you too, Steve."

Steve set the phone down and leaned back in his chair. Spots danced before his eyes, and he decided to join Autumn in the bedroom for a nap despite the daytime hour.

Chapter 18

Steve stepped out of the shower, toweling off his nude form. He reached past his rippling abs and picked inside his belly button to check for lint, then stepped in front of the mirror. Sighing at the sight of his ridiculous streaked hair, he brushed it out and back.

Eschewing clothing himself for the time being, he went into their living room and sat down in front of the computer there. He leaned back and put his hands behind his head while he waited for the browser to connect to the net, stretching out a hundred tiny aches in his back. Being a professional athlete meant living with a certain amount of pain, and he thought about taking something stronger than the ibuprofen he had swallowed upon waking. He dismissed the notion, opening up his e-mail account and checking the in box.

Sweat stood out on his body as he saw that there was a letter from the AJSP federation. His fingers shook as he opened up the e-mail and read its content.

> Dear Mr. Borgia,
>
> We here at the All Japan Super Pro corporation would like to thank you for your interest in performing even though the WWL has declined to enter a working relationship with us. Our director of international talent relations has seen your recent work, and thinks that you could be an asset when drawing sales at the ticket center. As an attachment you will find our

standard freelancer, single appearance contract. Signing this contract does not obligate you to work for our company for more than a single appearance, and your compensation will be based upon three factors.

1. The take in from the gate and Internet sales.

2. Your overall performance in the match.

3. The type of match you are involved in.

Please send a signed electronic form of this document to the above address, if you find it satisfactory. Again, we thank you for your interest, and have a pleasant day.

Samuel Ashikaga

AJSP Vice President of Operations

Steve's heart raced in his chest. They wanted him! One of the oldest, most prestigious wrestling feds in Japan, and they wanted him to work for them.

New sweat broke out on his body. They were going to be expecting a lot from him. His cardio conditioning had better not be wanting. Taking down his bike from the wall, he almost walked outside with it before he realized that he had yet to put on any clothing.

"Damn," he said, laughing at himself.

Tran stabbed his fork into the mound of hash browns on his plate, swirled the greasy mass around to mop up every last bit of red ketchup that he could, and lifted the fork toward his mouth.

"Daddy," Crawley said, sitting across the table from him, "that's disgusting."

He looked up at her, eyes narrowing as he chewed heartily.

"I love ketchup on my hash browns."

"It looks like bloody brains."

"Ellie!" her mother said, smacking her on the hand, "we're in public!"

"Sorry, Mom." Crawley turned her attention back to her food.

They were seated at a booth of a Denny's a stone's throw from their home in Queens. It was not terribly crowded at that hour, the sun only recently having poked its cheery face over the horizon. The three of them were dressed nicely, prepared to meet with potential clients for their arachnid lab. Crawley was wearing a tan skirt suit that came low on her calves. Slight slits showed a bit of her shapely, hose clad legs. Her blazer was buttoned under her bust, and Tran had repeatedly commented on the slight amount of cleavage sending the wrong message to their prospective clients.

"I think your friend is here, honey," her mother said, craning her neck to see out the glass double doors.

Crawley's head perked up, and she grinned when she saw Autumn coming up the concrete ramp. A memory of her vivid dream the other night came to mind, and her heart skipped a beat even as her cheeks burned.

"Not her again," her father said, rolling his eyes. "At least she's dressed decent today. *She's* not showing off her bosom."

"Daddy," Crawley said with a sigh. "I think Autumn is very pretty no matter what she wears."

"Be nice, Tran," her mother said. "Only God can judge."

Tran grumbled a bit but went back to his hash browns.

"Don't know why you invited her anyway."

"Autumn's my friend, daddy. Please don't embarrass me, please!"

"I'm not gonna say nothing," Tran said, looking a bit abashed.

Autumn stepped into the restaurant, spotted the trio and strode toward them.

"Hello, Crawley," she said, then nodded to her parents. "Mr. and Mrs. Crawley."

"How come she calls you by your last name? Isn't that a little weird?"

"Daddy…"

"Uh," Autumn said, "that's what everyone else calls her, so I —"

"Don't worry about it, honey," Crawley's mother said. "Ellie has always hated her first name."

"No way," Autumn said, sliding into the booth next to Crawley. "At least you're not named after a season."

"I think Autumn is a lovely name," Mrs. Crawley said.

"Autumn totally plays," Crawley said, nodding her head. Autumn's hip pressed against her own, causing her to recall her vivid dream a few nights ago.

Autumn leaned forward, pressing her lips against Crawley's. Soon her feeble resistance melted away, and she was enthusiastically returning the kiss. Their hands slid all over each other's smooth skin, and Crawley felt her heartbeat pounding in her chest—

"Are you all right?" Her father's brow was knit, concern evident in his voice. "You look a little peaked."

"I'm fine, daddy," Crawley said, trying to will her body to stop reacting. It was difficult, as even Autumn's perfume seemed to be quite stimulating. All thoughts of Phil and their problems drifted away for the moment as the dark haired woman filled her senses.

"You do look a little off, honey," Autumn said, putting a hand on her forehead. "You don't have a fever, do you?"

"I'm fine," Crawley said, wishing for a miracle to get her out of the embarrassing situation.

"Tran," Mrs. Crawley said, looking askance at her husband as his phone rang, "I told you to turn that off."

"It could be important," he said stiffly, sliding out of the booth and heading outside before answering the device.

"Dad's all business," Crawley said, grateful for a different subject.

"Yeah," Autumn said, "your text said you guys were going to score some big job today."

"I don't know if I'd call it a big job," Mrs. Crawley said. "We were just going to do some cross breeding diagnostics for a medical research firm."

"Cross breeding?" Autumn said. "If you get a radioactive spider, I'll totally let that shit bite me!"

Mrs. Crawley coughed a bit, nearly choking on her food. Crawley nearly choked as well, but due to the laughter rolling out of her belly.

"Warn somebody," she said, squinting at the pain of orange juice shooting out from her nose.

"Bad news," Tran said, hustling up to the table. "The client wants to meet ten minutes ago and we can't finish breakfast."

"Tran," Mrs. Crawley said, "Ellie has barely had time to eat a bite, and she's not feeling well."

"I'm fine, Mom," Crawley said, growling.

"Well," Tran said, his eyes growing crafty, "Ellie doesn't have to go with us. She can stay here and eat with her friend."

"How's she going to get home?" Mrs. Crawley said.

"I can drive her," Autumn said.

"You have a car?"

"Uh, yeah," Autumn said, her eyes narrowing. "Does that surprise you?"

"Autumn," Crawley said, gritting her teeth.

"Frankly, yes," Tran said.

"*Tran!*" Her mother grabbed the little man by the elbow and pulled him toward the door. "I can't believe you! What is the meaning of…"

Their voices were cut off by the door slamming shut. Autumn shook her head, slithered out of the booth and sat opposite Crawley.

"Man, your dad is something else," Autumn said.

"He means well, but he has his prejudices."

"We should totally get your dad to hang out with mine, you know, not tell them about my dad being gay at first, see how long it takes for it to come out."

Crawley giggled.

"That's mean!" She took another drink of orange juice. "So, I hear you're getting your own art show?"

"Not my own, no, but I get to be part of an exhibit. It's not much, but it's a start."

"It gets your foot in the door. That has to count for something."

Autumn nodded, then turned and smiled at the waitress. She ordered cinnamon toast with over easy eggs and sausage, eschewing sugar or cream for her coffee.

"You drink it black?" Crawley said, amazed at the sight of Autumn sipping the hot, dark liquid.

"Milk is for pussies," Autumn said in a low growl.

"I don't know how you can stand drinking black coffee."

Autumn shrugged, then her eyes grew tense. Crawley knew she was going to say something about her and Phil.

"How's things going with you and Phil?"

Crawley cast her eyes downward, picking at her food with her fork.

"He called me the other night, and we talked a little bit. He wants another chance."

"What'd you tell him?"

"The truth. I don't know, I have to think about it."

"I wouldn't take him back, not after what he did."

"He says it wasn't what it looked like."

Autumn put her hand over Crawley's and patted it gently.

"Honey, that's literally what they *all* say."

"So, if Steve wrecked his car because another woman was giving him a hand job, you'd be done with him."

"Well, that—" Autumn said, her face scrunched up in thought. "Steve would never—I mean, that would…depend…"

"Ha," Crawley said, grinning, "it's not that easy, is it?"

"It would depend on whether or not I'm in the car too, watching."

Crawley spat out a stream of coffee. Autumn giggled, gleefully watching her mop it up with a napkin.

"Well, I'm going to have to trust Steve, since he's going out of the country without me in two weeks."

"Where?"

"Japan. The WWL was supposed to be going there and doing a show, but it fell through, and now Steve's trying to work out his own deal. Supposed to be good money."

"Why aren't you going? I watch you guys on TV, aren't you part of his act or whatever?"

"My Dad and Brad are coming into town that weekend. I'm going to be busy with them."

"That's so sweet. I mean, your dad and Brad, that they've found someone to be happy with."

"That's a very enlightened attitude for a good Catholic girl," Autumn said.

"Well, I try to go by what Jesus said, and he said love your neighbor. He never said only love them if they're not gay."

"Man, if more Christians were like you I might think about going to church."

"It's never too late to accept your Savior."

"Sorry, but I'm gonna need to see some proof. Just how I am."

"Faith is about belief without proof."

"That's also what being insane is about."

"I guess you can see it that way." Crawley had been expecting the response, but she still felt that she had to try.

"This is nice," Autumn said, "just hanging out in a café. Without my Candy Pain getup on, no one's going to recognize me...I hope. Should be peaceful."

"Your outfits on the shows..." Crawley said, sucking in a deep breath.

"I know, they're pretty slutty, but a lot of the guys wear less than I do."

"No, I mean, you look really sexy. I wish I could pull that off."

"Crawley, you're hot as hell. You could wear used butcher's paper and look good."

Crawley looked down at her chest.

"My boobs are small."

"They're not small. More than a handful is a waste, you know! Hell, I'd play with them."

Crawley nearly spat out her drink again. She looked up at Autumn, sputtering.

"Oh my god, your face!" Autumn said, fumbling for her phone. "It's priceless, you should see it..."

Autumn's voice trailed off as Crawley looked a bit forlorn.

"Oh, so, you were joking..."

"Uh," Autumn said.

"Ha!" Crawley said, looking up with a grin. "How do *you* like it?"

They both snickered, but Autumn stopped first. Crawley took note of the haunted look in her eyes.

"You and Steve work everything out all right?"

Autumn heaved a heavy sigh, and it was her turn to poke at her food.

"He doesn't trust me," she said, offering Crawley a weak smile.

"Doesn't trust you? I know he's jealous, but—"

"It's more than just that. I mean, it's kind of flattering that Steve's so jealous, but he takes it too damn far. When I say he doesn't trust me, I mean he doesn't believe that I'm going to stick around this time."

"No way." Crawley couldn't bear the thought of Autumn and Steve breaking up, especially not after she had been so instrumental in their reunion.

"Yes way. I can see it in his eyes, like he's thinking 'yeah, you *say* you're not running out again, but…'"

"What are you going to do?"

"Do? What the fuck can I do? It's my fault. I broke him, and now he can't trust me."

"You didn't break him." Crawley took Autumn's hands in her own, squeezed them tight. They looked strange together, the inked and the pristine. "You and Steve can work this out. I know you can."

"You really think so?" Autumn was trying to play it cool, but there was a tiny bit of hope at Crawley's validation.

"I know so."

Autumn scratched at the flower decal on her mug, flaking away bits of it with her nail. Her eyes were pointed at the tabletop, but they seemed focused far away.

"What's wrong?" Crawley asked.

"It's nothing." Autumn laughed without mirth, raised her tired eyes to meet Crawley's. "Okay, it's not nothing. I'm scared that even if Steve and I *do* get past all his resentment that he'll get hurt in the ring."

"Steve's a tough guy, and trained—"

"Yeah, yeah, I know, but tough, trained guys get hurt all the time!" Autumn's hands shook as she held her mug to her lips. "I've been seeing this shit on the web, former wrestlers who took a bad spill and now they're in a wheel chair! What if that happens to Steve? Or worse, what if he *dies?* If he does, it'll be my fault because I left him and he lost his job and…"

"Hey, hey!" Crawley clasped her hand atop Autumn's decorated one as the woman fought back tears. "It's all right. Try to think of all the wrestlers who *don't* have things like that happen to them."

She closed her eyes, sent a quick prayer asking that Steve be protected. Her eyes snapped open when Autumn squeezed her fingers.

"Thanks," she said, dabbing at her eyes with a napkin. "I mean, I'm an atheist, but…it means a lot that you'd do that."

Crawley smiled and sipped her drink, glad for Autumn's company.

Chapter 19

It was strange, watching a ball bounce when you were hanging upside down. The way it moved, not just in the wrong direction, but how it sort of floated at the apex of its dive before coming back up to strike the blacktop sky.

He was hanging from his feet at the gym, staring out a window at a group of kids playing basketball. All around him other patrons used the various machines. Steve ignored the disgustingly veiny muscle bound body builders, who sneered at his physique, and the pretty, young thing whose eyes lingered on his tight stomach.

Growing dizzy, he curled up his body and started doing ab crunches. It started off easy, and then grew harder, and by the time he was nearing two hundred his belly burned with agony. His personal best was two hundred and twenty-two. Determined to make it to two hundred and twenty-three, he kept up the pace until he hit the magic number. Then he hung, arms dangling limply.

Slowly, agonizingly, he lowered himself from the bar and stood up straight. He pulled his shirt back down and toweled off the equipment he had been using.

After grabbing a shower, he sent a text off to Autumn. When she didn't respond, he shrugged and decided that he would ride his bike for a while, since it was a warm day for January.

As he pedaled through Manhattan, his mind drifted back, as it always did, to Autumn. Why was she so against getting married? The only possible explanation he could come up with was that she didn't want things to be messy if she decided to leave again. Maybe he was being a pushy ass, but shouldn't Autumn have had at least a *little* enthusiasm for the idea?

Then there was her decision not to go to Japan with him. Autumn really didn't like blowing off her father, but it seemed to him like she made the decision awfully easily. What was she going to be doing while he was gone? Hang out with Sal at the shop?

Well, if she's at home then she can't overreact to me getting a little pinprick. She probably just doesn't want me to get hurt so if she bails, she won't have to feel guilty.

Forcing such dismal thoughts out of his head, Steve bunny hopped a curb and slalomed his ten-speed through a variety of obstacles. A man pushing a baby carriage flashed past, then a letter carrier emptying a freshly painted mail box, and finally he swerved around an Asian tourist who stared around himself as if he were lost.

The gears hummed as he hit a clear straightaway and poured on the speed. His knee ached a bit, a legacy from an improperly timed suplex a few days ago, but he pushed on. It was a lot more enjoyable for him to be pedaling the bike when he didn't have a delivery to make. The dry air was cool on his glistening skin, soothing as he sucked it down his parched throat.

He passed the Bronx precinct and turned left, heading for the apartment he shared with Autumn. After being on the road so much recently, he was looking forward to a quiet evening at home. Living out of hotel rooms had lost its appeal for him quickly, and he often wondered how his father still did it after so many years.

Skidding to a stop outside their building, he reached down to the nylon pack attached to the frame of his bike and undid the Velcro clasps. His hand closed around a cool bottle of water inside and drew it into the light. There was a chunk of ice at the bottom, a result of Autumn's penchant for tossing bottled water in the freezer, but there was plenty of liquid left to quench his thirst.

He had about two thirds of the bottle drained when his cell played "No Rest for the Wicked," his ring tone for an unknown caller. Digging the phone out of the pouch, he removed the protective zip lock bag and hit the green key.

"You've reached Steve Borgia. Let me just say, if I owe you money, the check's in the mail."

"Mr. Borgia?" came a voice on the other end. It was thickly accented, deep as the ocean, and sent a chill down Steve's spine. Whoever the speaker was, he had *presence,* so much so that it came through even over the phone.

"Speaking," Steve said, realizing the call was probably someone from the All Japan Super Pro federation.

"I am Jiro Higashi, president of AJSP."

Steve's jaw dropped. Jiro Higashi was a living legend, possibly the most famous and popular wrestler from the land of the rising sun. He had been in the business for thirty years, and while his career had changed to more of a corporate role, he was still known to lace up the boots on occasion. He was also the man who had declared that Deathslayer would never work in Japan ever again.

"Pleased to make your acquaintance," Steve said, striving for formality. He remembered Susie telling him how much the Japanese valued manners and courtesy. "It's an honor, sir."

Jiro grunted on the other line, something he knew from speaking with his sister as a polite way of giving affirmation.

"I saw your name on the contract, and just to be certain, are you the son of William Borgia, also known as the Deathslayer from Hell?"

Steve had to stifle a laugh, because Jiro had pronounced the L's in his father's ring name as r sounds.

"Yes." Was he about to be fired before he even began?

"Excellent! I am pleased that you are interested in working for our humble company."

"Humble? The federation I work for right now sells out bingo halls and fair grounds. You performed before the largest indoor crowd in history!"

"You embarrass me with your appreciation," Jiro said, and Steve could almost imagine the man bowing on the other end. "I would be very grateful if you could fly to Sapporo a week early."

"A week? I can't do a full week early. I have obligations to the WWL—"

"Of course, how rude of me to have forgotten. When is the earliest time that would be convenient for you?"

Steve felt a bit giddy, being on the phone with someone he had always admired. His zeal to please the man made him speak hastily.

"Well, I could hop on a red eye flight as soon as the show was—"

"Excellent! I will schedule your flight immediately. Will two tickets be sufficient?"

Steve started to tell him that one was fine, then realized that it might hurt his Japanese pride.

"That would be fine, but I can pay for my own tickets."

"Absolutely not. Mr. Borgia, you are a guest, not only of mine and the AJSP, but of the Japanese people as well. Your travel and lodging costs will be handled by me, directly. You should not even catch a single glimpse of the bill."

"That's most generous, sir," Steve said. "I look forward to our meeting in person."

"As do I, Steve-san. As do I. My secretary will mail you the travel details electronically. Have a pleasant day, sir."

"You as well," Steve said, his hands shaking as he put away the cell. That he rated a call from the prestigious Jiro Higashi was more than enough to swell his pride. For the first time since he had begun wrestling, he actually felt that maybe, just maybe, he belonged.

Hefting the bike onto his shoulder, he carefully made his way up the narrow staircase to his second story apartment. He left damp smudges on the wall where his bare shoulder brushed against it. Reaching the top, he walked down the hallway to their door. Right when he was reaching for his keys, the door opened and Crawley nearly ran right into him.

"Crawley, hey," he said, surprise obvious in his voice. "How's it going?"

She stared blankly at him for a moment, and flushed a bit red.

"It's going fine. Autumn's fine, everything's fine here…how are you?"

"I'm sweaty and need another shower, but otherwise all right. Is something the matter?"

"*No!* No, there's nothing the matter, everything's just status quo, perfectly normal."

Steve noticed the way her eyes kept running up and down his bare chest. The idea both pleased him and caused a well of guilt to spring up in his belly.

"I have to go," Crawley said, moving much further to the side than was necessary to get past him and the bike. "Well, see you tonight!"

"You will?" Steve said, but he was speaking to empty air. Crawley had zipped down the hall and was out of sight, her heels echoing in the stairwell.

The big man shrugged his shoulders and opened the door. Autumn tackled him as he entered, wrapping her arms around his waist and kissing his sweaty chest.

"Hello, beautiful," he said as she snuggled up close to him.

"Hey."

There was a note of trepidation in her voice, at odds with her normally confident and boisterous manner. Steve gently pulled her face away from his chest and lifted her gaze to meet his by cupping her chin.

"What's wrong?" Steve said.

"Nothing," she said, putting her hand on his cheek and smiling up at him.

"You're acting strange, and so was Crawley, now that I think about it…"

"I'm not acting strange," Autumn said, breaking the embrace.

"You were talking about me, weren't you?"

"It's a girl's prerogative to talk about her man with her girlfriends," she said with a shrug.

"If you say so," Steve said, hanging his bike on hooks set against the wall. "I just got off the phone with Jiro Higashi. *The* Jiro Higashi!"

Autumn cocked an eyebrow.

"Who the fuck is that?"

"Who the fuck is—" Steve said, flabbergasted. "How do you not know Jiro Higashi? You know more about wrestling than I do!"

"First off, that's debatable. And two, I only watched American wrestling."

"Oh…well, he's kind of like Hulk Hogan over there, that is if Hogan could actually do more than three moves and was respected by his peers."

"Don't put down Hogan! I grew up watching Hogan."

"Then you know how much he sucks. Pop used to say that Verne Gagne's grandmother with polio could do a better leg drop!"

"That's kind of your problem, sugar. You think it's all about the moves, and how many different arm locks you can put on, but most of the crowd just doesn't care about that kind of stuff. They wanna cheer, to boo."

"You're right, I'm not saying that you aren't, but there's always that hardcore wrestling fan in the audience. Maybe they only make up a small percentage, but they are the ones who keep coming back year after year."

Autumn nodded, taking in the sight of Steve.

"What's wrong?" Steve said when she was silent for a time.

"You still have these on," Autumn said, grabbing the waistband of his tight shorts and sliding them down to his knees. "That's what's wrong."

"What are you doing?" He laughed as she lifted his feet to remove the garment completely.

"If you need to know where to stick *this*," she said, getting a handful of him, "then you haven't been paying attention!"

Chapter 20

It was a tiny venue, with barely enough room for Settle the Score to set up, and there were not more than thirty people present, but one would never know that from Sven's performance. The big Swede was gripping the mike with both hands, his chest rising and falling as he belted out "Rock Me Like a Hurricane."

Sitting at the bar, the only space still available, Steve and Autumn were enthralled. Steve was wearing one of his nicer pairs of slacks, mostly because they went well with his burgundy collared shirt. He had never been much for collared shirts, but it was a necessary evil to hide the dark spots on his neck. Thinking back to one of their recent wild bouts of passion, he put a hand on Autumn's bare knee.

Autumn put a hand atop his, though she kept watching the performance. She was wearing a short skirt, calf high boots and a white leopard print camisole. Her hair was done in a fountain style, her bangs almost down to her eyebrows. Her brown eyes sparkled as she soaked in the sights on the stage.

"He has the voice of an angel," Autumn said, applauding at the end of the song.

"Yeah, they all sound pretty good tonight. Even Rich has only fucked up a half dozen times."

"Has he? I can't really tell."

"They weren't bad fuck ups," Steve said, brushing a hand through her hair. "I've just heard them play these songs for so long, I kind of know them by heart."

"I'm sorry I dragged you out on your night off." Autumn took his hand from her hair and kissed his fingers. "I wanted to show some support for Crawley."

"I thought you wanted to bitch about me to her again."

"I so didn't! I just talked about our problems, that's all."

"Oh, and she told you how much better you can do, that you're a free woman with lots to offer—"

"No, *asshole*," Autumn said. "Actually, she defended you. Told me she knew we could work it out. But I guess she's not as smart as she acts."

"I'm sorry."

"No, you're not."

"Autumn—"

"Shut up and let's be supportive."

Steve sighed, wondering how they could connect so well in the bedroom and so poorly at times like this one.

Hours later, when most of the patrons, including Steve and Autumn, had long since gone home, the band was taking down their equipment. There was an energy to their movements despite the late hour, their minds dancing with glee at their smooth performance.

Everyone, that is, except for Phil. Crawley kept catching him staring at her from across the stage, his eyes tinged with longing. She was feeling quite conflicted herself and was struggling not to show it. Turning her back, she pretended to be oblivious as Rich approached Phil, sucking on a finger he'd cut yet again on the strings of his bass.

"Stop drooling over my girl," Rich said, slapping a hand across the back of Phil's head.

"Knock it off, Rich," Phil said, glaring at him while he rubbed his head. "And since when is Crawley your girl?"

"Since tonight is our fourth date, nerd."

"What? How in the hell is it your…already?"

"Yep. I'm taking little Ellie to eat, and then we're going to this theater in Brooklyn that shows old time horror movies late at night. Then…"

Rich leaned his head in close to Phil's ear and whispered.

"You're disgusting," Phil said, shoving him away. "You don't care about her at all! You just want to get in her panties!"

"Duh," Rich said, rolling his eyes.

"I won't let you," Phil said, rising to his feet. Crawley stifled a laugh at their exchange. Rich was clearly baiting him, but Phil was eagerly putting the hook in his own mouth.

"How are you going to stop me?" Rich said, smiling ear to ear. "We both know I'd kick your ass, and if you try to tell Crawley yourself you'll just end up looking like a typical jealous ex-boyfriend."

"You lay a lip on her and I'll fucking—"

"Is there a problem?" Crawley said, standing next to Rich and taking his arm in hers.

"Nope," Rich said, patting her hand, "ready to go, babe?"

"Yeah," Crawley said, enjoying the pain that Phil was in and trying not to feel guilty about it. "I'm ready to go."

She could feel Phil's eyes boring into her back all the way to the door.

Steve lay on his back, hands clasped behind his head, naked as the day he was born. Autumn was in the bathroom, the door shut tight.

"What's taking you so long? You said you were going to just brush your teeth."

"It shuts up or it gets the hose!" came her throaty rebuttal.

"Well, if *you* want to get the 'hose' tonight I suggest you hurry it up. I'm close to falling—"

The bathroom door banged open, and Autumn stepped into sight, arms akimbo. Steve's jaw dropped at the sight of her outfit. Tight blue shorts decorated with silver stars struggled to conceal her generous rump, leaving her shapely legs bare until the tops of her knee high red boots. A red corset with a metallic eagle design did little to cover her bosom. Autumn's raven black hair was held out of her eyes by a golden headband with a red star.

"Well?" she said, doing a twirl and spinning her golden lasso.

"Wow." Steve swallowed, running his eyes over her form again. "I thought you threw it away?"

"I probably did, this is a new one." Autumn's grin turned to a nasty sneer. "Are you ready for your punishment, you miscreant?"

"Miscreant, am I?" Steve laughed as Autumn stepped up onto the bed, the mattress bowing crazily with her footsteps. His laugh became an *oof* when she stepped on his stomach. Hard. "What are you—"

Autumn dropped across his torso, knees on either side of his ribcage. Her hand knotted in his hair and yanked his head hard to the side.

"Silence, evildoer!" Autumn grabbed one of his wrists in both of her hands. It looked ludicrous, the obvious size difference almost comical as she took him "captive." The golden lasso—which turned out to be an uncomfortable waxy twine—soon held both of his hands pinned to the headboard.

"That's a little tight, beautiful," he said as she jerked the knots into an even more snug position.

Autumn nodded as if satisfied with her handiwork, then grabbed his face harshly. Her nails dug into his cheeks as she shook his head side to side.

"Criminal scum!" Her voice shocked him with its intensity. For a second, he was genuinely afraid. Then she clamped her mouth over his own and sucked his breath away with a passionate kiss. His hands tugged at the rope, as he longed to touch her body. Autumn had tied the knots well, however, and he only pinched himself.

When Autumn raised up on her knees and began sliding her shorts down, Steve figured he knew what was coming next. He grunted in surprise as she shimmied up his body until her shaved twat was inches from his nose. Her scent, so near and so hot, had him growing erect.

"Lick it!" Autumn's hand grabbed his hair again, reinforcing the order. Steve thrust out his tongue, craned his neck, but due to his restraints he couldn't quite reach.

"I'm trying!" Barely, the tip of his tongue managed to flick against her swollen outer labia. Autumn broke character, shuddering from the sensation. Steve chuckled. "I think I've found Wonder Woman's kryptonite."

Autumn sneered, then thrust her hips forward. Steve's nose was buried between her slick pussy lips, almost smothering him. After a moment she pulled back to a more comfortable distance and he was able to ply his skill set with gusto. He wasn't sure when he'd stopped tracing the alphabet during oral and truly started to enjoy himself. It was empowering, even though he was pretending to be a prisoner, to think he could exert so much control over her body with just his mouth.

The superhero who held him captive threw her head back and wailed, hands gripping the headboard so tightly the knuckles were white. Steve was panting for air but smiling when she lay on her back across his body.

"Do I get time off for good behavior?" he said.

"Not a chance!" Autumn scrambled to her knees and then quickly straddled him. They both moaned when she slid down on his shaft until the head of his member was mired in her soft flesh. As she gyrated up and down, her breasts flopped free of the minimal garment. He longed to caress them, stroke the nipples softly with his thumbs until she was ready to scream. With his hands tied, he just had to stare longingly at her magnificent chest.

"Aaagh!" Steve cried out as a nagging pain in his shoulder increased threefold.

"Yeah, that's right, I'm fucking you!" shouted Autumn.

"No!" he said through gritted teeth. "Shit getoffgetoffgetoff!"

Autumn quickly disengaged from him and went to work on the knots.

"The other one first!" Steve said with a strained voice. "Hurry!"

Once he was free to move his arm, the pain subsided a bit, but it was still more intense than he would have liked. Autumn stared at him with her soft brown eyes full of concern.

"What's wrong? What hurts, babe?"

"My shoulder…" Steve gasped as Autumn's fingers slid over his skin, trying to massage the pain away. "Autumn, Autumn…that's not working."

"Maybe you should get that MRI after all?" Autumn slid around until she was facing him on the bed. "It could be more than just a muscle strain."

"I don't think so…" Another jolt of pain make him wince. "Okay, maybe I should get it checked out. Reilly's trainers were fifty-fifty on whether or not I should."

"Those assholes only care if you can make them money," Autumn said. "Look, Steve…maybe you should try to go back to teaching? If you're going to be hurt all the time…"

"I won't get hurt as much once my body adapts to the rigors of the ring," Steve said quickly. "Trust me."

"But—"

"Autumn, I'm *fine!*" He flexed the bicep of his injured arm, straining not to show how much pain it was causing him. "Good as new!"

"Quit playing the tough guy. We both know you're a pussy!" Autumn smiled at her jest, but there was a heaviness in her manner that made him squirm on the inside.

So he did what he could to change the subject: Kissing her intensely. Gradually her protests stopped, but his shoulder ache didn't.

Crawley's nose wrinkled in disgust at the magazines spread out on Rich's coffee table. They were all pornographic in nature, and not simply tossed upon the mahogany surface haphazardly, as if Rich had forgotten to put them away before company arrived, No, they were in a carefully arranged pattern, the glossy covers fanned out like a hand of cards.

"How's the coffee, babe?" Rich said, joining her in the living room.

"Too hot to drink yet."

"You want to watch some tube?" Rich flipped on the flat screen hanging on the wall of his modest but surprisingly neat apartment.

"I guess—" Crawley started to say, but the words caught in her throat once she saw what was on the screen. A big breasted, bleached blonde bimbo was busily putting her mouth to work on a completely hairless man.

"You don't mind adult movies, do you?" he said, putting a hand on her denim clad knee.

"It's…kind of weird, actually. I mean, this is like our second date."

"This is our fourth, babe," Rich said, sliding his hand slowly up her thigh, "and you know what they say about the fourth date…"

"Ewww," Crawley said, watching as the woman was hosed with genetic material.

"Nothing wrong with a facial." Rich stroked a hand through her hair. "Your face would be beautiful covered in jizz."

Crawley slapped his hand away.

"Excuse me?"

"Oh, have an open mind, baby. I heard from Phil how kinky you like to get."

"Phil said that?"

"Uh," Rich said, oddly at a loss for words, "I had to get him really drunk, and put him in a headlock first…"

"Phil said you were a disgusting pig," Crawley said, flinging the hand away from her thigh, "and now I can see he was telling the truth!"

"Phil's a little wuss. Real men are like *me*. Don't be a tease. Get over here and put out!"

Crawley was aghast at his almost comical attitude. It was a stark contrast to the way he had been treating her. He had barely pecked her on the cheek good night on their previous outings. Silently, she wondered if she were being punished. In her heart of hearts, she knew that she was mostly going out with Rich to upset Phil.

Why was she trying to upset him? All at once, it dawned upon her, how much different Phil was than most men. Phil always tried a little harder than anyone she had ever been with, and while he was not always the greatest lover, he was enthusiastic and willing to take instruction. She toyed with the golden earring dangling from her lobe, remembering how Phil had bought them for her. They were shaped like spiders, which had struck her as odd since the man was known to be an arachnaphobe.

"I'm waiting," Rich said, jabbing a finger at his crotch. "Do I have to get started myself?"

Crawley rose to her feet as soon as he unbuckled his trousers.

"Rich," she said, putting her hands on her hips, "I know what you're doing."

"Yeah, I'm trying to get into your panties and your attitude ain't helping!"

"Oh, bullshit," Crawley said, rolling her eyes, "you're trying to be a, a 'broski,' right? You think that if you disgust me with your porn and misogyny that I'll go running back to Phil. It's just not that simple."

Rich stopped fumbling with his belt, then secured it once more. Favoring her with a type of smile that she had rarely seen on his face, he shrugged helplessly.

"Phil's an all right guy. You ought to give him another chance. It was kind of my fault that he ended up driving her home that night."

"How is it your fault?" Crawley said, rolling her eyes as the blonde porn star got louder. "And can you turn that crap off?"

Rich complied, using the remote next to him on the sofa.

Crawley sat back down on the couch and put a hand on Rich's shoulder. He glanced over at the gesture, a puzzled look on his face.

"Rich, Phillip made his own bed. I admit, I went out with you to get back at him, but you've been surprising me. Underneath all of that frat boy badness there's a real person, and he's a good guy."

She kissed him on the cheek, and he reacted as if he'd been stung. One hand clapped over his smoothly shaven face as his eyes stared at her, mystified.

"I'm going home. Thanks for dinner."

"Are you getting back with Phil?"

Crawley patted his shoulder and headed for the door. Soon she would have to make a decision about Phil. It wasn't fair to keep playing him, and was cruel besides. Her anger had largely faded anyway, and it was taking more and more effort to stay mad at him…

She grinned, then giggled, and finally laughed so hard she had to brace herself against the wall to keep from falling over. The prospect of getting back together with Phil was somehow much more exciting than any imagined tryst she could have with Autumn and Steve.

Maybe, just maybe, what she had with Phil was at least equal to, if not greater than, what Autumn and Steve had. Phil was right, she *had* been looking at her friends' relationship with rose-colored glasses.

Crawley didn't call him, though. It was quite late, and she found herself feeling giddy but exhausted. No, it would be better not to call him tonight.

But soon.

Chapter 21

Crawley smiled, trying to act as if she thought that Charlotte's comment had been funny instead of just mean and crass. To her left, Lexi tittered.

They were sitting around an impeccably well-maintained metal table with a glass top. They were spared the wrath of the stark winter sun by a large blue umbrella deployed overhead. The chairs were padded, which meant that the staff must have had to drag them back indoors anytime it rained. Considering the difficulty Crawley had trying to move the massive wrought iron furniture closer to the table, it must have been quite the feat.

Crawley sipped at her iced tea, lips pursing at the taste. At first, the waiter had assumed that she wanted a Long Island iced tea, probably because her "girlfriends" had ordered hard drinks themselves. It was pretty obvious that the tea had been sitting in a metal urn for some time, and she was not pleased with the flavor.

"What are you doing?" Char said, aghast. Crawley paused with her hands about to rip open a package of sugar.

"Flavoring my tea. I don't think it's freshly brewed."

"With sugar?" Char said, exchanging horrified glances with Lexi.

"Yeah," Crawley replied, unable to restrain her impatience.

"OMG," Char said, slapping a hand over her mouth, "are you insane? Here, use the pink stuff—"

"The pink stuff has some nasty chemicals in it," said Crawley, pushing her hand away. "I usually drink unsweetened tea, but this stuff—"

"Eleanor, honey," Lexi said condescendingly, "how are you going to squeeze into those tight designer jeans when you're all bloated up from empty calories?"

"Actually, that's a misnomer," Crawley said as she dumped the packet into her awaiting drink. "You see, there's no such thing as empty calories. A calorie is the energy it takes to heat up one milliliter of water one degree. There is such a thing as too many calories, but ostensibly there's nothing bad about sugar. It's better for you than the cocktail of lethal ingredients in artificial sweetener."

Lexi and Char stared at for a moment and then started laughing.

"Right," Lexi said, giggling, "sugar is good for you!"

"You never know," Char said. "She was a big time nerd in high school, she might know what's she's talking about."

"You were a nerd, Ellie?" Lexi said, seemingly very surprised by the revelation.

"I studied hard. And I was in Chess club, and worked in the computer lab as an assistant. So, yeah, I guess by that definition I was a nerd."

"Wait," Char said, digging in her purse, "I just uploaded my yearbook to my cell. I bet I can find a photo from our senior year. You are just going to *die,* Lexi!"

Crawley bit her tongue and stared at the cars shimmering in the sun as they waited in traffic. Why, oh why had she accepted Charlotte's invitation? Just to keep her mother off of her back?

"Here it is," Char said, gleefully holding up an image of Crawley from their yearbook. Her thick glasses, unplucked eyebrows and lack of cosmetics were a source of great delight to the two women seated across from her.

"Oh my god, honey," Lexi said, handing Char back the phone. "You look sooooo much better now."

"Uh, thanks," Crawley said, unsure of how to take the statement. Her own phone beeped at her, and though it might have been rude, she quickly dug it out of her purse and checked the screen. It was Autumn, crowing about how she and Steve had just dropped off a half dozen of her paintings to be featured in a humble art show.

"Is that the guy you went out with last night?" Lexi said, her eyes wide and eager for juicy details.

"No, just a friend."

She quickly sent off a text to Autumn, lamenting her terrible company while Lexi and Char argued. Apparently, they had come across a photo of a boy from their class who they had both dated, and were determined to prove that they had been his one, true love.

Autumn quickly sent her a typically acerbic reply.

"Want me and Steve to come and save you from those bitches?" it read.

Crawley laughed, drawing stares from both women.

"I knew it," Char said. "It *is* the guy she was out with last night!"

"Is he cute?" Lexi asked, her eyes shining. "Is he a white guy or Chinese like you?"

"Lexi," Char said, aghast, "she's not Chinese, she's Japanese!"

Crawley started to correct them, then shrugged. She decided that she truly did not care what they thought of her.

"Yes, please!" was the response she sent to Autumn. She followed it up with directions to the sidewalk café.

"So let me get this straight," Steve said, his long legs scrunched up in the front seat of Autumn's car. "Crawley needs us to rescue her from some bullies?"

"Sort of. Apparently this girl Charlotte was a total bitch to her in high school but now her mom's trying to make them be buddies."

"Whose mom?"

"Crawley's."

"So we're supposed to, what, beat them up?"

"That's what I would like to do, but girl bullies are different than guy bullies. They usually don't get physical."

"Tell that to my sister. I think she was in more fights before seven a.m. than Mayweather gets into all day."

"Yeah, well, Susie's kind of a bitch and brings it on herself."

"Autumn!"

"Sorry."

"No you're not. Hey, I think I see Crawley—" Steve used his hand to shield his eyes from the sun "—yeah, that's her all right. Damn."

"Damn what?"

"Nothing."

"Oh, I get it," she said after a quick glance at the café. "Damn, those girlfriends of hers are *fine,* that's what you meant."

"No," Steve said. Autumn parked the car a half block away from the café and then fixed him with an admonishing stare.

"Yes," he said a second later, hanging his head as if in shame.

"Busted." Autumn playfully slapped him on the cheek before sliding out of the car. She was wearing what Steve called her one "normal" outfit, the black skirt suit she had worn the first time she went to meet with Sal's wannabe art dealer friend. The long sleeves hid her tattoos, but the dozen piercings above her neck combined with her bright red lipstick and thick eye shadow still conveyed a less than business-like demeanor. Steve followed her, wincing a bit as he had re-broken his toe in a match two nights prior. Once he started walking he felt fine, but any time he sat down for an extended period the digit protested vehemently.

Crawley saw them coming, and made a frantic gesture with her hands, as if she wanted them to stay away. She spoke briefly to the women sitting at the table and then started hustling off. The blonde woman would not let her leave without being hugged, about which Crawley did not look pleased at all. Autumn giggled at her hasty retreat as she weaved in and out of pedestrian traffic to stand before them.

"Fucking cunts," she hissed, drawing a shocked stare from Steve and raucous laughter from Autumn.

"Yeah, they look bitchy," Autumn said after she recovered.

"You need us to give you a ride home, Eleanor?" Steve said.

"Yeah, that'd be gre—" Crawley began. "No, actually that won't work. My mom thinks I'm spending the day with my new 'friends.' She'd barrage me with questions and then jump on Facebook to gossip with her buddies."

"Well," Autumn said, and Steve did not like the calculating look she got in her eyes, "why don't you come and hang out at our apartment for a while? We'll order some pizza or something, play some cards maybe."

"Okay," Crawley said, breathing a sigh of relief. "I can pay for the pizza."

"No way," Steve said, "I still haven't paid you back for your loan yet."

"Oh, you don't have to pay me back," Crawley said as Steve held open the back door for her.

"It's important to his manly pride," Autumn said, somewhat mockingly.

"Oh, hush, you," Steve said.

They chatted idly on the ride back to the Bronx. Steve found himself staring in the rear view mirror at Crawley's face. She was undeniably pretty, though he preferred more curvy figures like Autumn's.

Soon they were ensconced in Steve's apartment, sitting at the battered kitchen table. Crawley perused the environs while Autumn changed out of her suit.

"I thought you guys would have bought a bunch of new furniture. This place still looks about the same."

"What's the point of buying furniture when you're on the road all the time?" Steve said, shrugging.

"Yeah," Autumn said, coming out of the bedroom. She had changed into an old shirt of Steve's that came nearly to her knees. Her bare legs flashed in the half light as she sauntered into the kitchen. "The only piece of furniture that seems to get used around here is the bed."

Steve's cheeks flushed red while Crawley chuckled. Autumn walked behind his chair and squeezed his face with her painted nails.

"Look at him blush, Ellie. He's so bashful until the slow kissing starts, and then someone gets on top and shit gets real."

"I am not bashful," Steve said, grimacing as she distorted his face, "you just have boundary issues."

"You have boundary issues," Autumn said, trying to affect a deep voice like his.

"Oh, be nice to him, Autumn," Crawley said.

"I'm nice to him," she said, letting go of Steve's face and pouting. She pulled his hair slightly, eliciting a small yelp from him. "Tell her I'm nice to you, god dammit!"

"This doesn't count," Steve said with a grin. "I'm under duress!"

Autumn sat down across from Crawley. They poured over Steve's tablet, using an app to build their pizza pie. Of course, it took a bit of haggling. Steve liked green peppers while Autumn couldn't stand them. Crawley joined with Steve in his abhorrence of the idea of anchovies. Eventually they settled on something they mostly agreed on and settled in to wait.

Steve shuffled a deck of cards and dealt out hands for rummy. During one hand Autumn laid out a card that played on a run in front of Crawley, and Steve slapped his palm over it.

"Rummy!" Crawley had to catch her glass before it bounced off the table.

"Settle it down, Hammer Hands!" Autumn snarled at him while he dragged the card to his own stack. "Can't believe I missed that."

"Well, pay more attention next time," Steve said.

Then they were treated to Autumn slapping her palm down on the table and shouting *rummy* every time anything was played. It resulted in a lot of laughing at first, but after the fourth go around the table Steve found it to be getting old.

"Okay, it's not funny anymore," he said. He took a card with a few drops of soda on it and wiped it on his pants leg.

"In your opinion," Autumn said. Crawley laid a card in the discard pile. Steve and Autumn locked gazes for a split second.

"Don't even think—"

"Rummy! For the love of God, rummy!"

Crawley looked up in alarm as their upstairs neighbor pounded on the floor.

"Uh, calm down, you guys…" she said through clenched teeth.

"Oh, that asshole does that all the time," Steve said.

"Yeah, but usually only when we're having sex," Autumn said.

"There he goes again, Autumn," Crawley said with a laugh. "Red as a beet."

"I'm feeling outnumbered here," Steve said.

"Well, maybe we could give Phil a…" Autumn hissed, then looked sheepishly at Crawley. "Sorry."

"Don't be. I've been thinking about giving it another chance with him."

Steve and Autumn exchanged glances, unsure if they should be supportive or not. Maybe because Phil was Steve's friend, he spoke first.

"Well, that's your decision," he said, trying to be neutral. "I think it's a good idea, though. You and Phil were pretty damn good together, and I for one believe him when he said nothing happened."

"*He* believes nothing happened," Autumn said. Steve glowered at her, but she ignored him. "I'm not telling you how to live your life, Crawley, but please be careful."

"I didn't say I was going to propose to him," Crawley said, looking back and forth between them. "I would like to try again, though. Phil's not the kind of guy I usually go out with."

"What kind of guy *do* you usually go for?"

"Well, Autumn, I don't mean anything by this, but someone more like Steve."

Steve's eyes went wide, and his heart skipped a beat. He turned to Autumn, eyes pleading *she said it! I didn't!*

Autumn raised an eyebrow, but didn't seem offended.

"You mean an over-muscled giant? Or a jealous, huffing misanthrope who picks fights with TV hookers?"

"Hey," Steve said, half-laughing through his glare.

"No, just—" Ellie giggled "—more manly, I guess."

"Did you hear that?" Steve gloated at Autumn. "I'm *manly.*"

"Shut up, pussy." Autumn turned back to Crawley. "Phil's not manly?"

"Oh, he's masculine enough. He's just not a, well, a 'he-man' like Steve."

"Don't sell him short," Steve said. "Phil's tough in his own way. When he has to work a weekend, he just shrugs his shoulders and rolls up his sleeves."

"Yeah, and he saved us from a thousand dollar fine," Autumn said. "He's clever and fearless when he needs to be. Pretty handsome, too."

Steve felt a pang of jealousy, but since she was talking about his friend he felt more mirthful.

"Then why don't you date him?"

"I've gotten used to *your* cock. Don't want to change at this point."

Crawley and Autumn laughed as Steve's cheeks burned once more.

Chapter 22

S teve yawned and stretched, a thousand tiny fires burning in his body. He was grateful to be free of the airplane seat at last. Jiro had paid for first class tickets for himself and Autumn, but the seating was never meant to accommodate a man of his size. Factor in his list of minor injuries and the ride had been quite agonizing. He reached up to gather his carry-on bag from the cabinet overhead, glancing down at Autumn's still slumbering form.

"Hey," he said, gently shaking her shoulder. "We're here."

"Finally." Autumn's voice was thick with sleep. There was a red mark on her cheek from leaning against the window, and a line of unladylike drool on her chin. She wiped it away mid-yawn. "I'm starting to regret blowing off my Dad to come along."

Steve helped her to her feet. He couldn't help but feel guilty about taking her away from her father, especially since it was because of an unspoken agreement that they were in trouble as a couple. Being in a new place was just a temporary fix, and he suspected Autumn knew it as well.

While they waited impatiently for the long line ahead of them to filter outside, Steve's mind went back to two days prior. They were sitting in the locker room of Reilly's studio right after a brutal "hardcore" match where he and his opponent hit each other with a variety of implements. The crowd had certainly been enthralled, but Autumn took it upon herself to give him a hard time.

"Let me see," she said, yanking the bloody towel away from his forehead.

"You're just going to make it bleed more." Steve squinted his eyes tight while she prodded at his dripping laceration. "Ow, what are you doing?"

"Trying to get a piece of glass out of your fucking skull," she growled. "Why did you let him do that to you?"

"Well, beautiful…" Steve flinched as she pried the cut open wider. "Ow! I thought he was going to choke me with the florescent light tube. I didn't know he was going to — OW — break it open and jab me in the forehead with the shards!"

"Duh, he's called *the Butcher*." Autumn let go of his head, and he felt profound relief. "Got it!" She held a tiny crimson-stained bit of glass before his eyes. "Didn't it occur to you there was a *reason* no one else in the locker room wanted to have a match with him?"

"He's world famous." Steve shrugged. "I bet if we checked YouTube there's already a video of that match."

"Well, this is the last time you let someone massacre you with a goddamn broken light bulb." Autumn grabbed his chin, not harshly but firmly, and focused her umber eyes on his own. "If you *ever* let someone cut you up like that again, we're through. Clear?"

He had wanted to argue with her, but right then the trainer finally came in the locker room, medical bag in tow. Fingering the bandage on his forehead, he felt a bit of lingering resentment as he followed the line of slow moving passengers off the plane.

They made their exit and soon stood in the busy Narita terminal. As they were strangers to international travel, they rubbernecked for a few moments to get their bearings. All around them, modern Japanese in business suits mingled with relics of their past, like painted geisha girls.

"Everything is bright neon," Autumn said, holding a hand over her eyes. She was wearing the black business dress she had worn to the art studio, striving for a less exotic appearance at Steve's request. He himself was wearing a shirt and tie, though he had to use a clip-on, as most ties would not go around his massive neck without being ludicrously short.

"Yeah, it stings my eyes! Let's go try to figure out where baggage claim is."

They walked through the busy terminal, hands clasped. Outside the large, arched windows they could see the city, its streets locked in what seemed a perpetual traffic jam. It was a hazy, sultry morning, and a thick layer of mist shrouded the tops of the sky scrapers. With a little effort they found their luggage. Steve had only one additional suitcase, but he was burdened with no less than four bags that belonged to Autumn, while both her hands were full with tall suitcases on rolling wheels.

"Did you forget anything?" Steve said, grumbling as he dropped one of the bags.

"Yeah, an empty suitcase for all the clothes I'm bringing back home."

"There's so many people, I can barely see the walls."

"Where are we going?"

"Toward carousel one, I hope — that's where the driver is supposed to meet us."

"Driver? Did you call for a cab when I was asleep?"

"No, Mr. Higashi is sending a car for us."

"You think Higashi will be there?"

"Nah, he's like royalty over here. He's not going to be bothered to visit an American wrestler at the airport."

Steve spotted a lanky man in a plain black suit and white shirt holding a sign with his last name on it. As he approached, the man dipped into a low bow.

"Greetings, Mr. Borgia," he said in excellent if slightly accented English. "I will take your bags."

"Uh, okay," Steve said as the man took the burdens from him. Autumn gasped indignantly at the man's failure to even acknowledge her.

"Not that one," Steve said, holding on to the carry on.

"As you wish, sir," the man said, struggling with what he was already carrying.

"What's so special about that bag?" Autumn said, huffing as she dragged the cases behind her.

"It has my ring gear in it." Steve took one of the cases from her grateful hand. "Pop says that you never, ever, *ever* let your ring gear leave your sight when you're traveling. One time the airline lost his luggage, and he had to do the whole Deathslayer from Hell thing in a black sweat suit."

"Oh my god, that must have been hilarious!"

"Yup, the lord of darkness, wearing 'give up on life' pants."

"'Give up on life' pants…that's what Crawley calls sweat pants." Autumn scowled. "Been spending a lot of time talking to her?"

"What's that supposed to mean?"

"Nothing, I'm just giving you a taste of your own jealous medicine." Her quick kiss on his cheek took much of the venom from her bluster.

They followed the man out of the airport. They passed by a string of waiting taxis, Steve looking expectantly at each one. Then he glanced up and saw Jiro Higashi, standing on the curb in front of a long black limousine. He was tall for a Japanese man, a legacy of his Western grandfather, and stood only a few inches shorter than Steve. His head was mostly bereft of hair, but he still had a ring of gray going around from ear to ear. Steve could respect that; he had not shaven his entire head, as many wrestlers did when they started getting sparse up top. A mustache peppered with gray hung over his thin but expressive lips, which he stroked lightly as they approached.

A woman of middle years who was still ravishingly beautiful stood nearby, her hair black as midnight. Two children of about high school age stood nearby, a boy and a girl. They, like their parents, were dressed very well in suits that probably cost more than Steve had made in a year teaching.

"Mr. Higashi," Steve said, striding up and offering his hand for a shake.

"Mr. Borgia," Jiro said, taking the hand in his own. Steve inwardly grimaced at the strength of the man's grip. Despite his age and semi-retirement, the man was obviously not lacking fitness. "Please allow me to introduce my family. My wife, Mariko, and my children, Ataru and Shinobu."

All three bowed to Steve, which he awkwardly returned.

"A-hem," Autumn said.

"Oh. Sorry. Allow me to introduce my fiancée, Autumn Winters."

"Pleased to meet you," Jiro said, barely nodding in her direction. Steve decided to ignore the way Autumn put her hands on her hips and cocked an eyebrow. "I am here to take you to my home."

"Can we stop by the hotel first? I'd hate to have our luggage cluttering up your house."

"Hotel?" Jiro blinked several times, and then light dawned in his folded eyes. "You are mistaken, Steve-san. You and your lovely fiancée will be my honored guests for the next four days."

"Honored guests?" Autumn said.

"Yes," Jiro said, actually flicking his gaze to her for a moment, "for the son of the legendary Deathslayer, we can do no less. We are honored that you have come to repay your family's debt."

"Debt?" Steve said. "Uh, I don't have much money—"

Jiro had already turned from him, and was speaking in rapid Japanese to the man who had taken their luggage. In short order their accouterments were stowed safely in the spacious trunk, and Steve was invited to precede Jiro into the back of the limo.

"We really appreciate your hospitality, Mr. Higashi, but we don't want to be a burden."

"There is no burden, Steve-san. My home is simple, but spacious enough to accommodate you as well as any hotel."

Steve nodded, feeling Autumn shift uncomfortably in the seat next to him. He was worried about the mention of a debt, but the man wasn't whipping out his bank book, nor had there been any mention of repayment in his twelve-page contract.

They rode to Jiro's home, mostly making small talk. The long flight had served a meal, but Steve was unable to stomach the *fois gras*. Autumn had graciously offered to eat his piece as well, which had a great deal to do with the way his stomach loudly rumbled. Ataru, the young boy, giggled at the sound, but a sharp glance from his mother silenced him.

"Your wife would make a great teacher," Steve said.

"I'm sorry?" Jiro said, eyes narrowing.

"Oh, it's just that…she seems to be good with children…"

"Ah." A brief smile crossed Jiro's face. "Mariko was once an elementary school teacher. Of course, she retired once we were married."

"Retired?" Autumn said, but Jiro did not pay any attention to her.

"Why did she retire?" Steve wondered. Mariko seemed awfully young to be retired.

"I don't understand," Jiro said. "I told you that we were married."

Shinobu spoke to her father in Japanese, which caused him to be taken aback somewhat. Her mother put a hand on her shoulder, probably a more serious gesture than it appeared.

"My daughter has reminded me that not all women, either from your country or ours, retire upon gaining a husband. It is…an old tradition."

"Forgive me, Mr. Higashi, but if I may say so, you seem to be a man who values tradition greatly."

Jiro gave a slight bow of his head.

"I would that all Japanese felt the same way. With so many Western influences, our past is slipping away like sand through the hourglass."

"I'm all about tradition—especially with regard to wrestling. My contract didn't say who exactly I would be facing. Could I speak with them before the match, work out some—"

"There will be time later to speak of *puroressu*, Steve-san. For now, let me and my family be at your service. Relax, my new friend, all will be handled in good order."

Steve leaned back in the seat, instinctively seeking Autumn's hand. She took it quickly, perhaps feeling just as out of place as he did. He was glad to have her with him.

For as long as she stayed. He squeezed her hand tightly, not wanting her to slip away.

When they first approached Jiro's home, neither of the Westerners were impressed with it. The walls around the homestead were low and quite plain. The only splash of color was along the top, where red slate had been arranged in an inverted V pattern. Nestled in the shadow of mountains, his abode was at least six miles away from the nearest neighbor.

When the limo turned onto a smooth, almost untouched blacktop road, Steve's mouth gaped at the domicile they were approaching. It was styled after traditional Japanese homes of the feudal period, with a series of shallow steps leading to a smoothly polished wooden deck. The deck looked as if it wrapped all the way around the structure…or structures, as when they approached more closely, several other buildings could be seen behind the main house.

The limo pulled into a circle drive and parked before the main building. Autumn whistled as she beheld Jiro's home, with its high ceilings and green tiled roof. Two fearsome looking statues of the

Shinto god Raiden stood flanking either side of the staircase. Several trees expertly manicured to conform to the shape of the house provided shade.

"Your home is beautiful," Autumn said to Mariko as she exited the vehicle.

"Thank you," the woman said, the first time she had spoken. Mariko's smile was warm enough, and she lacked the seemingly instinctive disdain that Jiro seemed to display toward Autumn.

Jiro led them up the steps, explaining the grounds as they went.

"The main house is the big one up front. That is where you will be sleeping the next few nights. Behind it are my dojo, gravel garden, and tea house."

"This place is impressive," Steve said. "Must have set you back a pretty penny."

"I am sorry?"

"I mean, it must have cost a lot of money."

"Ah, yes, it was quite expensive, but well worth it."

"I'm not disputing that," Steve said, casting his gaze all around. Every inch of the place, every timber of wood and every sculpted tile was clean to the point of gleaming. As they stood, a man Steve took to be a housekeeper ran by, shoving a white cloth on the floor before him.

They followed Jiro and his family as they strode toward a set of sliding doors. The family took off their shoes and left them on a metal rack next to the entrance. Steve followed suit, with Autumn a step behind.

Ataru's eyes went wide when he noticed the ink on Autumn's feet. Leaning toward his mother, he whispered something that made her laugh.

"I don't get the joke," Steve said, trying but failing to keep some irritation out of his voice.

"Forgive my son, he is young and foolish. He thought that since your fiancée has so many tattoos, she must be *yakuza*."

"*Yakuza?*"

"Japanese mafia," Autumn said. "They cover themselves with tattoos…of course, a true *yakuza* would never have ink that showed on his hands or feet."

Jiro's brows rose, and a tiny glimmer of what may have been respect shone in his eyes.

"Indeed," he said, turning away from Autumn before she could gloat.

Jiro took them down a hallway of the same polished wood as the deck. The walls inside appeared to be made of paper and flimsy wood. It occurred to Steve that it must be quite difficult to keep secrets in such a house. They turned a corner and Jiro stopped before a set of sliding doors.

"These will be your chambers. I hope they are satisfactory."

The doors slid open and the room that was revealed was simple but looked comfortable enough. Tatami mats covered the floor, providing some cushion. A very low table that no chair would fit under sat near one wall, a ceramic vase upon its surface. The vase contained a flower with a large red center and soft white leaves. A rolled up futon awaited their tired bodies.

"This will be fine, Mr. Higashi," Steve said.

"Good. I will leave you to refresh yourselves."

"Uh, Mr. Jiro," Autumn said, "where's the head?"

"I'm sorry?"

"The bathroom, uh, the toilet is probably what she's asking for…"

"Ah," Jiro said, a bit of embarrassment crossing his features, "but of course, it was a long drive."

After showing them the bathroom a short distance down the hall, Jiro left them, saying he would return shortly to call them to dinner. Upon her return Autumn kicked the futon and unrolled it, plopping down on its surface.

"Don't wreck the place," Steve said.

"There's no springs in these kind of beds. Besides, I'm not the one who weighs almost three hundred pounds!"

"It's mostly muscle!"

"Oh, I *know* it's muscle…"

She rose to her knees, hands vigorously stroking his leg. Steve took a step back and looked aghast.

"What are you doing? The walls are made of paper…*paper*, Autumn!"

"Pffft, the Japanese worship sex, Steve. Why do you think he took his family to the other side of the house? Why do you think he left us alone?"

"To refresh ourselves, like he said? C'mon, beautiful, don't get us deported!"

Autumn had not stopped her efforts at all, intensifying them instead. Her hands rose up to his belt buckle and unbuckled it.

"Stop," he said, half chuckling. "C'mon stop it—"

Autumn pulled down his shorts, leaned her head in close. Her eyes glanced up to him as she went to work, something that had always driven him crazy.

"Okay—don't stop!"

Steve reached down, put a gentle palm on the top of her head. He tilted his head back, gasped…

The sound of their room doors sliding open caused them to disengage. Mariko walked in, her eyes focused on the cloth bundle in her hands.

"I brought you some bath supplies…oh my!"

Steve and Autumn sheepishly stared back at her, he fumbling to buckle his belt. Mariko backed out of the room, bowing even as a smile spread across her fine features.

"I'm sorry," she said, as her feet trailed away.

"Great," Steve said, "now no one's gonna want to get us for dinner!"

Autumn clapped enthusiastically, even putting her fingers in her mouth and whistling, as Jiro finished a karaoke rendition of "Nights in White Satin." His accent was heavy, but he made up for it with poise and a clear, deep love of the song. They were sitting in what Steve would have called a living room but what Jiro referred to as a study. There was a flat screen HDTV on the wall, totally at odds with the more ancient surroundings. A soft mat cushioned their bottoms as they all sat on the floor. Mariko, Ataru and Shinobu had joined them, and the night was surprisingly festive.

"That was amazing," Steve said, adding his own applause.

"You humble me." Jiro was smiling from ear to ear. It was a different side of the seemingly serious, dour Japanese man, challenging Steve's assessment of his character.

"Our turn is up," Autumn said, rising to her feet. "You didn't pick that stupid song from *Grease,* did you?"

"Maybe," Steve said, grinning as he picked up one of the mikes and handed it to Autumn. She rolled her eyes and heaved a heavy sigh.

"Steve, I told you I hate that fucking mo—"

She stopped speaking when the first heavy riff from "No Sleep Till Brooklyn" wafted out of the speakers hanging flush on the wall. Her face broke into a wide grin.

"You get me, Steve. Somehow, you really get me."

"Don't make me mess up." He grabbed the other mike and sang the opening line. Autumn enthusiastically joined him on the other mike, throwing out phony gang signs.

Jiro and his wife seemed a bit taken aback by the hard rock-hip hop song, though their children were delighted. Steve and Autumn got a little bit loud on the chorus, and were joined by the Higashi siblings. As the song ended, Steve and Autumn high fived and took a bow.

"Very…interesting," Jiro said, loosening his collar a bit. He rose to his feet, Mariko copying him a second later. "If you will forgive me, it is getting late. My children do have to attend classes in the morning."

"We should retire as well," Steve said. "Thanks for the hospitality, Mr. Higashi."

Jiro bowed slightly, then he and his family took their leave. Jiro lingered in the study for a moment, his raised eyebrows enticing Steve to come closer.

"My children's rooms are not far from your own, so if you and your fiancée wish to…talk…it might be best if you did it in the outside garden. The sound of the running water tends to drown out noises, as my wife and I can attest."

He clapped Steve hard on the shoulder and left, a slight smile playing at the edges of his mouth. Steve turned around to face Autumn, his face reddening.

"What was that about?" Autumn said.

"I think we just got told to have sex in the garden, so we don't disturb his children's sleep."

"We could try duct taping our mouths shut…"

"I think only one of us is supposed to do that. Hanging out with Crawley at the tattoo parlor has made you even kinkier."

Autumn fluttered her eyes at him.

"*All* girls are into kink on some level."

"C'mon," Steve said as they walked back to their room, "that can't be true."

"Oh, no one wants to get raped for real…it's the *idea* of being powerless that's a turn on, not the actual powerlessness itself. I shouldn't have to tell you, you were hard as a rock before I finished tying you to the—"

"Shhh!" Steve clapped a hand over her mouth. "We're not outside yet!"

"I don't think their English is that good," Autumn said once her mouth was free. "But whatever."

They went to the end of the hall and opened the sliding doors at the rear of the residence. The scene that unfolded was almost breathtakingly beautiful. Bright pastel flowers ran in a hedgerow, forming an equator of sorts. The babbling stream that Jiro had mentioned came through a grate under the wall and meandered through the garden. It seemed as if Higashi had built his home around a natural creek. The dark stream ran over a waterfall and splashed into a large pool filled with colorful koi. An arched bridge stretched elegantly over the narrow waterway, paper lanterns shedding soft light on the scene.

Most wondrous of all were the fireflies. Dozens, maybe hundreds of the luminescent insects buzzed about the garden. The slower moving yellow flashes mingled with much quicker green ones. Their delicately glowing abdomens cast little spheres of light that reflected in Autumn's brown eyes.

"Wow," she said, her hand clasping with Steve's.

"Yeah." Steve felt that further vocalization was unnecessary. They walked around the garden for a time, silently enjoying both the natural beauty and each other's company. The smell of something akin to honeysuckle filled the air with an enticing aroma. Autumn's hand felt very small in his own, and not for the first time he worried for her health. It did not seem fair that their happiness might be taken away at any moment due to her disease. He let go of her hand and put his strong arm around her shoulder, squeezing her tight.

"What's wrong?" she said.

Steve kissed her gently on the forehead.

"I don't want to lose you, not ever."

"Then maybe you should stop giving me shit about leaving after my surgery."

Steve felt a vein throbbing in his forehead. Even here, surrounded by beauty, they couldn't be happy. They'd traveled to another country, but hadn't gone far enough to escape the specter haunting them.

"That's not what I was…Never mind. This place is beautiful."

"Yes, it is."

"But not as beautiful as you." Steve kissed her softly, enjoying the warmth of her breath in his mouth. She returned the kiss, wrapping her arms around his neck, and they stood for some time lost in each other's embrace.

After a while, Steve led her by the hand to a small nook in the hedgerow. A wooden bench painted with red lacquer sat nestled within. They sat upon its smooth surface and continued their amorous explorations.

Autumn hiked up her dress and pulled her underwear to the side, arranging herself on Steve's lap. She groaned as he slid inside her, his hands busy massaging her generous bosom though the thin fabric of her dress. They were in no rush, the sedate surroundings influencing their passion.

Autumn lurched forward, her hips moving like the sea at storm. Their eyes locked, and they smiled in unison. Their foreheads touched briefly, noses rubbing together, before Steve shifted his waist and she was racked with an intense wave of spasms. She leaned backward, his strong arms easily supporting her weight, dark hair brushing along the gravel walkway. Her cries mixed with his own, until she writhed in his arms. They were both exhausted and damp with sweat.

Steve slowly lifted her back into a sitting position. When her face was close enough he took her lips again, their mouths mingling together until they were as one. They stayed that way for over an hour, the fireflies and moonlight keeping them company.

Autumn eventually pulled back and stared him in the eyes. Her mouth was a tight line, unreadable as either angry or happy.

"What?" he asked.

"Nothing." She leaned her head on his shoulder.

"It's not nothing."

He felt her sigh against him.

"Steve, why are you with me?"

"Because I love you," he said quickly. His heart skipped a beat, and then thudded strong in his chest.

"Yeah, I know, but do you trust me?"

Steve opened his mouth. He intended to say that of course he trusted her. However, he couldn't lie to the woman he loved. The pregnant pause developed into an uncomfortable silence.

"That's what I thought." She kissed him on the cheek and rose to her feet. "Good night, sugar."

He sat in the garden until a faint red glow heralded the dawn. Then he lay down next to Autumn, rolled his back toward her, and pretended to sleep.

Chapter 23

After spending hours staring at the unfamiliar ceiling above him, Steve finally drifted off to sleep. Autumn, more used to shifts in her routine, had been swallowed by slumber almost immediately after getting back to their room. Steve, however, found himself struggling to relax, a victim of his own mind.

A cold, palpable terror had gripped his consciousness and would not let him go. Thinking back to the way he had been before she was in his life was like being blind to the beauty of the world all around him. He had felt some occasional glimmers of joy, living vicariously through the children he taught as they explored their world, but only after he and Autumn had found each other had he truly begun to live.

He had gazed over at her as she snored softly next to him. Her hair was unbound, spreading in a dark shadow beneath her head. She looked so vulnerable, so fragile, lying there on the floor of a stranger's house.

That was his last thought before sleep finally reclaimed him.

He awoke to the sound of Jiro's voice wafting through the paper walls of their room.

"Steve-san?" it said, polite but insistent. "Steve-san, are you awake yet?"

Steve groaned a bit, gently pulled Autumn's arm off of his chest and rose to his feet. He stumbled across the tatami mats to the sliding door. When he opened it he was greeted by the sight of Jiro, looking fresh as a daisy. The man was wearing a red track suit with broad white stripes down either sleeve. The corners of his mouth turned up with might have been amusement.

"Good morning."

"Morning," Steve said, yawning. "What time is it?"

"I'm afraid I'm getting a late start today, so it's just after six a.m. I was wondering if you would join me in the dojo."

"Uh, sure." Steve scratched the back of his head. "When?"

"Now."

"Okay," Steve said, biting back a retort about Japanese hospitality. "Give me a minute to pull myself together."

"I'll see you there." Jiro turned on his heel and walked softly down the polished hallway.

Steve sighed, grumbled, and dressed himself, wondering what he had gotten himself into. Autumn rolled over on her side and stared up at him as he was just about to slide the door open once more.

"Hey," she said sleepily, "where are you going?"

"To the dojo, apparently."

Autumn's face scrunched up.

"He's gonna, what, teach you kung fu?"

"I have no idea what he has planned. Go back to sleep, beautiful. I don't think…that is, I'm not certain that Jiro is, uh…"

"He doesn't like me much," Autumn said with a pout.

"That's not what I said."

"It's painfully obvious. Fine, go have your bro time."

"Autumn…"

"It's fine, Steve, we're strangers in a strange land. Do as they do."

"I love you."

Steve bent low to peck her on the forehead. He tried not to be upset that she didn't say it back.

Steve went to the outbuilding designated as the dojo. It was a one-story wooden structure, like everything else on the Higashi estate. The doors were open, and Steve gawked at the full size wrestling ring inside. Jiro was in the squared circle, doing deep knee squats like a champ. He turned to Steve as he entered.

"Excellent. Now let's…how do you Americans say…let's get this on, yes?"

"I'd have to know what 'this' is, first," Steve said, climbing on the apron and adroitly springing over the top rope.

"You are most agile for a giant. What this is, Steve-san, is something of a test. Many American wrestlers have an appalling lack of fundamentals, and I would ascertain that you are, as I hope you to be, a cut above that mold."

"Fundamentals…you mean, what, hitting the ropes? Learning how to bump?"

"No, fundamentals of wrestling, in the Greco-Roman style."

Steve grinned.

"Oh, well, I was an All-American in high school."

"Really?" Jiro said, dropping to all fours. "Show me."

"Uh, Mr. Higashi, with all due respect, I'm waaaaay out of your weight class, not to mention half your age."

"I'll go easy on you with respect to your youth and inexperience."

Steve's nostrils twitched. Youth and inexperience?

"All right, don't say I didn't warn you."

In short order, Steve learned that he was the one who should have been warned. Despite his own greater strength and speed, Jiro easily flipped him onto his shoulders with a move known as the plow. The Japanese man used his own head thrust under Steve's shoulder to send him sprawling. Jiro was on him quick like lightning, and the big man was hard pressed just to keep himself from getting pinned.

Steve felt humiliated, but Jiro seemed oddly impressed that the big man could, barely, hold his own. Still, Steve's shoulders were pinned to the mat a dozen times before a sweating, panting Jiro called a break.

"I do not find you wanting, Steve-san," Jiro said, offering a hand to help him to his feet.

"You're a wonder of the world, Mr. Higashi. Thanks for the lesson in humility."

"You are most welcome, Steve-san. Will you walk with me? There is something I would show you."

"Of course," Steve said, following him out of the ring. The big man was drenched in sweat, and he was surprised at how strenuous the brief encounter had been.

The two men walked out of the dojo and went back to the main residence. Jiro slid open a pair of doors to reveal a room with minimal décor. There was only a small black lacquered table bearing a vase with one of the red and white flowers that were growing outside. Above the table was a pair of swords, the curving type made famous in samurai movies. One was slightly shorter than the other, and both had opulently decorated sheaths.

"Do you know what these are, Steve-san?" Jiro said, walking over to the display and taking the longer of the two down.

"Swords?"

Jiro looked back at him and smiled.

"Astute, but not the whole story. This is a *katana*, and the shorter a *wakizashi*. Together, they are called daisho, the long and the short. They were crafted for my ancestor by the legendary smith Murasame. The legends say that every warrior who has wielded these blades with honor has left a piece of his soul within the steel."

Steve nodded, trying to be respectful.

"A *katana* is more than just a weapon," Jiro said, pulling on the hilt and baring a small span of shining steel. It reflected his intense gaze. "It is a symbol of the samurai's honor, of his willingness to lay down his life for his *giri*, his duty. Do you understand?"

"I think so. You're talking about manning up, right? Doing the right thing even when it's not the easy path."

"Indeed," Jiro said, snapping the blade back, "you impress me yet again, Steve-san. But there is more to it than that. *Giri* is not just fulfilling your obligations, it is fulfilling the obligations of your family, your company, and your country. Sometimes, these duties come into conflict, and it is then that you truly know if one has a samurai spirit. When your father reneged on his duty, and did not perform for us so many years ago, I was dishonored."

Steve swallowed. So this had been what Jiro meant by a family debt.

"That wasn't dad's fault, Mr. Higashi. The promoter he was working for—"

Jiro held up a hand to forestall the explanation.

"I am aware of that, and I am not saying your father is a terrible person, but he did neglect his *giri*. It is a debt which must be paid."

"I'm here. I'll do whatever it takes to settle things up."

Jiro put the sword back on the wall and turned around to face him. His expression was inscrutable.

"Will you? Steve-san, your opponent is to be me. We will have the match that your father and I were to have twenty years ago."

"A garbage…I mean, a Death Match?" Steve said, his mouth popping open. "I don't know if Autumn will let me…she doesn't even like it when I go off the middle rope!"

"Ah, so, you do understand *giri*. Much like the samurai of yore, your duties to your love and to your family are at odds. Tell me, Steve-san, why are you a wrestler?"

"Why? Well, mostly for Autumn, I guess, so we can be together and not have to live in a cardboard box. That, and, well, I guess I'm doing it for Pop…for my father, I mean. To carry on his legacy."

"That is a worthy motivation. Tell me, do they pay you well to dress up in that ridiculous costume and swagger around the ring?"

"Well enough. Hell, *I* didn't pick the damn gimmick."

Jiro smiled, clapped him on the shoulder, and led him out of the room.

"For our match, you will be the Deathslayer Jr."

"Deathslayer Jr.? That's kind of goofy."

"Jr. is a belittling honorific in the United States. Here, in Nippon, it is an honorable title."

"I don't care what you call me, I guess."

Jiro led him back outside into the cheery sunlight. It was already getting hot on the Kanto plains.

"Will you face me, Steve-san?"

"I…I should talk it over with Autumn first."

"Bah," Jiro said, making a strangled sound in his throat, "are you her man or not? American women all dress like whores and disobey their men."

"Don't call Autumn a whore," Steve said, his eyes narrowing to slits. He realized that he was a second away from throttling the little man.

Jiro's eyes lit up.

"Yes, Steve-san, yes…*that* is the passion, that is the samurai spirit! Oh, we are going to put on a spectacle for the ages!"

"What do you want from me, exactly? I don't get you at all. One second you're nice to me, the next you're insulting. Do you treat all your guests like this?"

"Only the ones who can handle it," Jiro said, clapping him on the shoulder once more. "Come, let us go to break our fast, as you Americans say."

"Breakfast, you mean." Steve followed the bewildering man.

Half a world away, the Crawley family sat around their gleaming, polished dining room table. It was family game night, and they were playing *Monopoly*, which Crawley had never much cared for but which her father seemed to enjoy. Tran had gathered most of the high end properties and was in the process of building hotels on them.

She herself wasn't doing badly, at least not as bad as her nearly bankrupt mother. Crawley picked up the dice and rolled, groaning when she ended up landing on one of her father's properties.

"Ha!" He made a come hither gesture with his hand. "Fork it over!"

"You should've bought Park Place when you had the chance, Ellie," her mother said teasingly.

"Yeah, well, no one can predict the future…"

Tran exchanged a meaningful glance with his wife, and cleared his throat.

"On that subject, Ellie," he said.

"What subject?" she said, counting out the faux money to hand to her father.

"The future…we were thinking about retiring."

"What?" Crawley said, the paper slipping from her numb fingers.

"Your father and I want to buy an RV and travel around the country while we're still physically able to do so."

"What about the lab? Dad, you're the one who talks to all the clients, who negotiates the contracts—"

"I've been trying to get you to do that yourself for years, but you're too busy hanging out with that rock and roll band to take it seriously," Tran said.

"It's time you grew up some, Ellie," her mother said, trying to smile to offset the harshness of her words. "Playing guitar and hanging out with…creative people is fine when you're a kid, but when you become an adult you have to manage responsibilities."

"But I love playing with the band! We're just starting to take it to the next level!"

"Growing up means losing things you enjoy," Tran said, sniffing. "That world is harsh, Ellie. Have you ever, even once, actually made a profit on any of your, your 'gigs'? Will a couple hundred dollars every other week pay the mortgage, the utilities?"

"Why are you doing this to me?" Crawley's bottom lip quivered. "What's wrong with the way things are now?"

"Ellie," her mother said, putting a hand on top of hers, "we know how much your music means to you, but you're so good at the lab work! Your father and I call you the Pied Piper of Spiders, you know."

"I enjoy working in the lab. I never said I didn't! I just don't do well with people, Mom."

"Oh, poo, you just need to give them a chance. I heard about how you ran out on poor Charlotte and her friends the other day. We raised you better than that."

"Poor Charlotte?" said Crawley, her nostrils flaring. "Poor Charlotte, mother? Really? Charlotte's a bitch."

"*Ellie!*" her mother said, aghast.

"Watch your mouth, young lady," Tran said, jabbing a finger at her accusingly.

"No, dad," said Crawley. "I am *not* going to watch my mouth! It's time you listened to me for a change!"

Both her parents closed their mouths and exchanged worried glances. Never had their daughter spoken to them in such a manner. Crawley turned her heated gaze on her mother.

"I told you a dozen times that Charlotte made my life hell in high school. Oh sure, she never laid a finger on me, but she didn't have to; she was perfectly capable of devastating me with just an insult, a snide laugh, or a nasty rumor. I don't want to hang out with that cunt."

Her mother's eyes went wide at the curse word, but she remained silent. Her father looked as if he were about to say something so Crawley headed him off at the pass.

"And as for you, dad," she said, venom rising in her throat, "I'm tired of you insulting my friends. They're good people, even if they don't all go to church, and I enjoy spending time with them."

With a loud screech, she shoved her chair away from the table and stood up.

"Go ahead and retire if you want, but I'm not giving up my music, or my friends, or my life."

"That's it," Tran said, standing up himself, "you're not going to talk to your parents like that. I'm your father, and you're going to do what I say."

"Oh, really?" Crawley said, striding over to stand inches away from him. "I suppose you want to dictate who I go out with too."

"Now that you mention it, you've never done very well in that regard yourself. How many boyfriends did you have in college? A dozen, at least. And once you opened your legs for them and they got what they wanted, they stopped calling. Even that Phil boy doesn't come around anymore because of your slutty ways."

Crawley stared at her father, dark eyes wide. She felt as if she'd been slapped across the face, punched in the gut, and then had her head stomped on.

"For the love of God, Tran," her mother said, equally aghast.

"So I'm a slut," Crawley replied, biting back tears. "Thanks, Dad, I feel so much better about things now."

"Ellie," Tran said, looking ashamed, "wait a minute, I—"

He was talking to her back. Crawley grabbed her car keys off of a peg near the door and patted her pockets to make sure she had her phone. She was sobbing now, unable to contain the streams of moisture running down her cheeks.

She got into her Eclipse and slammed the door, angrily starting the engine and pulling out into the street. It was inconvenient, living in the city when you wanted to drive somewhere to get a little solitude. Still, the traffic offered a kind of anonymity, and after twenty minutes of driving with no set destination she regained her composure somewhat.

Bitterly, she ran over her father's comments in her mind. He had been right, after a fashion. It was true that once she blossomed after high school, she didn't lack for male attention. Crawley never saw herself as a slut; rather, she saw herself making up for lost time. Oh, how she had envied girls like Charlotte, who could have their pick of any boy in high school! The only date she'd been on in high school was prom, and her date had been handpicked by her father. She couldn't even remember the mincing little prude's name. He had barely even pecked her on the cheek at the end of the night.

Wishing that Autumn and Steve were in town, she pulled over in the Greece Hut parking lot to figure out her next move. Again she wished she was one of them...

A rueful smile came to her lips. No, that would never work. What Autumn and Steve had was special, and didn't have room for her in it. What she really wanted was the same kind of love, her own love. Someone who, if they couldn't understand her, could at least accept her for what she was.

She thought about calling Phil, but she didn't want him to see her before, during, or after a crying fit. With a start she realized that she still loved him. Maybe he wasn't as hunky as Steve, but Phil was manly in his own way. A memory of him facing down three massive martial arts fighters at New Year's sprung to her mind. Phil was smart without being stuck up, kind without being obvious. And he was steadily improving in the bedroom...

She dug her phone from her pocket and flipped through her contacts. On a whim she deleted Charlotte completely, and felt somehow cleaner for it. Then she came upon Rex's number.

"What the hell," she said, hitting the call button. After a few rings she heard his voice, loud music in the background.

"Hey, what's up Crawley?"

"Hey, Rex. What are you up to? I hear music."

"Me and Sven are trying to put together a crib, actually," he said with a laugh.

"A crib?"

"Yeah, my old lady's pregnant. Looks like I'm gonna be a daddy."

"Wow, that's great, Rex!" Crawley's genuine smile broke through her tears.

"Yeah," he said, and she could sense his nervousness and joy in his voice. "I'm scared as hell, but then again, I've always wanted kids."

"Do you know what it's going to be, yet?"

"Nah, too early to tell, it's just a zygote or whatever. We're kind of jumping the gun on the crib thing, but my buddy Chet had an old one and Sven brought it over, as well as a six pack, and here we are."

"Uhm, I kind of, sort of had a fight with my parents. Can I come by and hang out for a while?"

"Uh, sure, that's fine. Maybe we could squeeze in a little practice."

"I don't have Molly on me."

"Oh, well, you can come over anyway. My old lady's making a mean three bean dip, and we even have some of that hard lemonade stuff you broads like."

"Sounds like fun. Thanks."

"No problem. I guess we'll see you in a bit?"

"I'm on my way. See you soon."

She hung up the phone and thrust it back into her pocket. Her heart felt lighter, and she realized how much she loved being with her friends. Pushing thoughts of her parents into the back corners of her mind, she pulled out of the lot, humming the new song she had written.

Never did she think that a musty basement could be a sanctuary from her problems. She found Sven and Rex easy company, and always had. Their interchange of insults and ideas kept her amused as she watched them piece together a wooden crib while bereft of the instructions.

Rex's wife Sally joined them, and Crawley had to admit the three bean dip was nothing short of amazing. She decimated nearly half the bowl, having skipped out on dinner with her folks.

The basement door banged open, and a blast of cool air accompanied Rich inside.

"What's up, you fucking fa—oh, hey Crawley. I'm glad you're here."

"Hey, Rich," Crawley said, standing up and wiping greasy dip from her hands with a paper napkin. "Listen, about the other night—"

"Nah, *you* listen," Rich said, his face more somber than she had ever seen it. "I happened to overhear some broads at work talking—"

"You were camped out in the ladies room again, weren't you?" Rex said over his shoulder.

"—*aaand,*" Rich kept talking, shooting Rex a smirk, "as it turns out, Phil was telling the truth. Gina really was trying to get him in bed, but Phil's motives were purely work related."

"I saw the police report," Crawley said, folding her arms over her chest. "Hard not to when you posted it online. I know what they were…up to."

"Yeah, she grabbed his boys," Rich said, "that's what made Phil wreck, dontcha know? He flung her hand out of his lap, then she slapped him, then *crash!*"

He clapped his hands together for emphasis.

"So, there you have it straight from the horse's mouth," he spread his hands out. "You gonna get back with my boy Phil or what?"

"That's my business," Crawley said, sneering at Rich. On the inside, though, she was bubbly and excited. Something about the story clicked, and made sense. She could definitely see Phil reacting that way to an unsolicited fondling.

"We are almost all here, *ja?*" They both turned to Sven. "Might as well call Phillip."

Rex glanced furtively at Crawley.

"I don't know about that bud —"

"It's all right," Crawley said, smiling. "In fact, I'll call him and see if he needs a ride."

She stepped outside to make the call, but not before she noticed Rich's jubilant fist pumping.

As the phone started ringing, her heart skipped a beat. Warm feelings she had not allowed herself to feel in over a month blossomed in her chest. Now that she had made her decision, it was as if she could breathe again. Even the fight with her parents seemed distant and inconsequential.

"Hello?" Phil's didn't even try to hide the excited nervousness in his tone.

"Hello, Phillip," she said, suddenly at a loss for words. "How are you?"

"Uh, bored, mostly." He cleared his throat. "Went on a Raid. People were asking about you."

"Well, unfortunately, if my parents get their way I won't be doing any WoW for a while."

"What happened?"

"I could eat up our data plans telling you now, *or* I could pick you up and give you a ride here."

She heard Phil's sharp intake of breath, and his phone jostled. It wasn't hard to imagine him pumping his own fist in the air, mimicking Rich.

"Phil? Are you there?"

"Yes! I mean, yeah, I'm still here," he chuckled. "Dropped my phone. What, we doing an impromptu band practice?"

"Maybe…if you're willing to go to my place and get Molly. Don't want to talk to my parents for at least twenty-four hours."

"Twenty-four hours?"

"That's how long it takes my dad to find something else to be mad about."

"Right. Well, I'm here."

"Can you meet me on the street outside?" She *was* going to get back with him, but really didn't want things to get awkward, and being alone with him in his apartment was going to be that.

"Yeah, no problem." He paused, and then blurted. "I love you."

"I love you too," Crawley said, and her heart danced at the proclamation. "I don't think I ever stopped. That's why this…this *thing* has hurt so damn much."

"I'm sorry." Phil loaded the simple statement with so much passion, it was almost comical.

"I know. For what it's worth, I think I always believed you when you said you were innocent."

"Then why—" Phil started harshly. He cleared his throat and continued more calmly. "Why did you leave me, then?"

"First off, my exact words were 'we're on a break,' and second—"

"Sorry to interrupt, but 'we're on a break' is commonly accepted to mean 'we're broken up but I don't want to tell you' in womanese."

"Maybe it is for some girls, but not for me. And second, you were a perfect ass right before you gave that little skank a ride home."

"Yeah, I guess I was. I just…I'm always afraid, Crawley. I'm always afraid that you'll wise up and realize you can have someone better than me."

It sounded so much like what Autumn had said, it brought a smile to her lips.

"That's debatable, but who says I *want* to do better? We click, Phil. I don't know why, but we just kind of click. In a lot of different ways…"

She let her voice gain a mischievous edge, and could imagine him turning as red as Steve.

"Yeah, we really do. You coming to get me now?"

"Yup. Don't get mugged while you're waiting."

"Got my Taser on me. Listen, Ellie…"

"What?"

"I'll make sure you never regret taking me back. I promise."

After that she turned off the phone and headed for her Eclipse. Maybe, just maybe, she wouldn't go back home tonight. Maybe she'd stay the night with Phil instead…

Chapter 24

Steve watched, highly amused, as Autumn fumbled with her chopsticks. She managed to glom onto a bit of crab meat that was swimming in the tiny porcelain bowl of rice she held cupped in one hand. Slowly, she brought it toward her deep purple lips, but then it slipped from between the thin sticks to plop onto the low table.

"Why don't you just ask for a fork?" Steve said, nimbly manipulating his own chopsticks.

"Because *shut up*." Autumn gave him a withering glare.

They were sitting at the long, low table the Higashi family used for meal times. Jiro was not present, having had to travel into Tokyo for business reasons. His two children had already boarded the train for school, so their only companion was Mariko.

Steve wasn't sure why, but he found himself really liking the often silent woman. She was soothing to be around, and seemed to bring out a similar quality in those around her.

Mariko smiled gently at Autumn's banter, but remained quiet. She reached across the table and helped Autumn get a better grip on the chopsticks. Steve watched their hands, Autumn's covered in finger bone tattoos, Mariko's unadorned digits smaller and more tapered. In two days, the women would watch while the men in their lives beat the living daylights out of each other in a "fake" fight.

Steve chewed the morsel in his mouth and swallowed it, trying to find the words to tell Autumn about the dangerous kind of match he would be involved in. As usual, he came up short. His father needed him to do the match, Jiro needed him to do the match. Even Autumn needed him to do the match, whether she agreed with it or not. Six figure paydays were rare in the wrestling industry, especially for a one night stand. Also, Jiro had mentioned a percentage of the gate, which, from what his father had told him, was where the real money was made.

"You look awfully serious, sugar," Autumn said, poking her chopsticks in his direction. "You're not thinking about backing out of our shopping excursion, are you? Because you *can't*."

"I wouldn't dream of it."

Mariko cleared her throat. When she had both of their gazes locked on her, she spoke softly.

"Will you be needing transportation?" she said in her measured, articulate English.

"No, we were just going to ride the rails."

"We can see more of the city that way," Autumn said, smiling.

"As you like," Mariko said, who did not press the issue. Something else Steve liked about her. Though he would never want Autumn to change, not in a million years, he did see the appeal of a different kind of woman. She did not strike him as submissive or mincing, but rather as supportive. No matter what her husband did, Mariko would back him on it to the hilt. If only he could feel that way about Autumn…

After finishing their breakfast, they returned to their room so Autumn could dress for the journey. She picked out a pair of tight, shiny leather pants. Steve watched, amused, as she literally had to jump into them. She ended up lying on the tatami mats, struggling to get them up to her waistline.

"All this Japanese food has me bloated," she said.

"Uh huh."

"What's that supposed to mean?"

"You knew those were a size too small when you bought them. But you were like 'my ass is gonna look fantastic,' so—"

"You're a man, so you don't know squat about sizing. Girl clothes are different."

"If you say so."

"Oh," she said, rising to her feet and crossing her arms over her chest, "I say so!"

She did a little pirouette, allowing him to bask in her shapely legs and bottom. He had to admit, she made the pants look really good.

She slipped on black sneakers after selecting a very faded Ramones T-shirt that she stubbornly refused to throw out. Steve smirked at the simple foot adornment, used to seeing her in boots and heels.

"What?" she said when she noticed his amused smile.

"I've never seen you in flat heels before."

She looked down at the black sneakers covering her feet.

"Going to be doing a lot of walking, and I'm serious about my shopping, god dammit!"

"Yeah, about that…" Steve dug in his wallet and took out a blue credit card. "Here."

"What's this?" she said, looking at the piece of plastic as he handed it to her.

"It's a credit card. You hand it to the clerk, they swipe it, and you pay the balance at the end of the month."

"Smart ass! No, why are you giving it to me?"

"Because it's yours. Well, my name's on it too, but the account is in your name. The limit's at about three grand, which in yen is… uh, I don't know."

"You're trusting me with this?" she said with a grin. It faded a moment later. "Hey, this probably won't work in Japan."

"No, it'll work fine, I checked for that specifically when I signed up for it."

"Can we afford this right now?"

"Let me worry about that, and you concentrate on shopping. Deal?"

"Deal. Now, let's go check out this *Bukkake* section of Tokyo."

"Uh, that's *Shinjuku*. *Bukkake* is…something else."

"Ugh," Autumn said, rolling her eyes, "of course it's something nasty. Where the hell did I get *Bukkake* from?"

"It's one of Rich's favorite words. Says it all the time."

After riding the smoothly running train into the heart of Tokyo, Steve and Autumn emerged from the subway station, mouths agape. Steve had seen the shopping district on television before, but the reality was far more impressive. Numerous lighted signs depicted familiar brands, like Coca-Cola, alongside strange logos and Japanese lettering. One of the largest took up almost ten stories of the skyscraper it was attached to.

All around them, the Japanese people went about their business. Most of them seemed to ignore the odd foreign couple, but a few stared intently at them without saying a word. A gaggle of schoolgirls tittered at Autumn, taking pictures of her with their cell phones. Autumn played it up, even rolling up her sleeve to display more of her ink.

"I could get used to it here. No one's giving me a hard time."

"There's people scarier looking than you," Steve said, staring at a young couple wearing bright red wigs and strange looking ninja masks.

"No one's scarier than me, not even Godzilla!"

She scrunched up her face and squinted her eyes, then ran back and forth on the sidewalk as if she were terrified.

"Run!" she said in an atrocious Japanese accent, "it's Godzirra! He rikes to eat rittle girrs!"

"You want to get us in trouble," Steve said, hating himself for his laughter, "don't you?"

"Trouble is just another word for fun!" She dragged him by the arm toward a boutique. "Come on, this looks like my kind of place."

Steve followed her into the clothing store. It was some sort of rock and roll apparel establishment, replete with exotic looking garments. Autumn took her time, carefully going through what seemed to him every rack in the store.

For a time he took pleasure in her exuberance, the way her eyes shone in the light as she oohed and aahed over one garment or another. Occasionally she would take one to the fitting room and try it on. Eventually Steve ended up sitting on a stool against one wall, watching with a bored expression as Autumn continued her shopping spree.

It was the same story as the morning wore on into afternoon. Autumn would stop in a store and they would be inside for at least an hour. The bags in his hands kept getting heavier, and still she wanted to check out "just one more" shop.

At length, his belly growled, reminding him that he was not used to getting by on fish and rice. He looked longingly at a steak house that had delectable aromas wafting out the open front doors.

"Want to get a bite?"

"What?" she said, staring longingly at a full length latex dress in a window. "Oh, sure, let's just hit one more place first—"

"I'm going to start eating Japanese people in a second."

"Oh, all right." Autumn glanced around. She spotted a kiosk on the sidewalk that appeared to sell snacks. "Get yourself a candy bar or something to hold you over. This won't take long."

"That's what you said two hours ago," Steve said, grumbling as he perused the selection. None of the brands were familiar to him, so he ended up taking a candy bar that had a picture of the product on the package. It looked normal enough, like a thick Hershey bar.

He unwrapped the silver package and followed after Autumn. The chocolate smelled enticing enough. Biting into it, he discovered that there was a filling of sorts. It did not taste like coconut, or nougat, or caramel. In fact, it tasted sort of like spicy gumbo. Very spicy.

"Ugh." He spit the gelatinous blob in his mouth into a nearby waste basket.

"What's wrong? Was it stale, or something?"

"No, it was hot!"

He examined the uneaten portion in his hand. There was a gritty paste within the confines of the chocolate, and when he sniffed it he realized what it was.

"It's freaking beans! Fuck, who puts spicy beans in a chocolate bar?"

"It can't be that bad," Autumn said, snatching it out of his hand. She took a big bite and chewed vigorously for a few seconds. Her expression changed to one of pure disgust and she spat a dark splotch onto the impeccably clean sidewalk. "Okay, yes it is."

"Autumn, this ain't New York. Try to spit in the trash cans, will you please?"

"No one even saw," Autumn said, putting her fists on her hips.

"He did." Steve pointed at an approaching police officer. At least, Steve assumed he was a cop of some sort; he had on a dark blue uniform bearing a shiny silver badge. The official left the car he was writing a ticket for and approached them.

The cop spoke rapidly in Japanese at Steve, gesturing toward but otherwise ignoring Autumn.

"I'm sorry...I mean, *Gomen*, uh, *Gomen Kamehameha*, er, dammit..."

The little man wrote furiously on a notepad while Autumn stuck out her tongue at him. With a jerk, he ripped off the top sheet and thrust it into Steve's chest. Then he was off, cursing in his native tongue.

"What's that?" Autumn asked.

"I think it's a ticket." He was unable to stifle a laugh. "I can't read it, though."

"Just wad it up and throw it away."

"I can't do that." Steve folded the paper in half and put it in his pocket.

"Why not? It's not like he asked for your license. He doesn't even know who you are!"

"Uh, I kind of stand out, beautiful," he said, gesturing around. Not only did Steve tower over the Japanese public, his bright hair and blue eyes marked him as well.

Autumn grabbed onto his arm and pulled insistently.

"Oh, whatever, let's go check out this place!"

"I'm never gonna get to eat," he said, staring back wistfully at the steak house.

Chapter 25

"Are you all right, Steve-san?" Jiro said, staring up at him with a wide smile.

"Never better," Steve said nervously, perched as he was on a twelve-foot tall ladder. The mat below him seemed very, very far away. Worse, the way the ladder constantly creaked and wobbled seemed to indicate it wasn't up to bearing his weight.

"Be sure not to spring off of the ladder, or you will knock it over and fall flat on your face."

"I've done ladder spots before." Steve did not add that it had been more than a decade ago. Men he and his father's size were just not meant to climb the flimsy structures. The aluminum ladder seemed solidly built, heavy in his hands when he was setting it up. However, once he had begun to climb it, he found that even the tiniest of motions would set it to rocking. He barely dared to breathe.

"Very good," Jiro said, flopping flat on his back on the mat. "Hit me."

Steve took a deep breath to steady his nerves, then stepped off of the ladder. He let out a grunt as his abdominal muscles twisted, turning his body to the side mid-air. His elbow came crashing down on Jiro's sternum, a little harder than he would have liked. Jiro did not seem to mind, coming to his feet almost instantly with an eager expression.

"Not bad." This was high praise from the middle-aged man.

Next they wedged the ladder horizontally in the corner, bracing it between the middle and top ropes. They took turns Irish whipping each other into the corner, experimenting with different ways to twist their bodies to make spectacular, but harmless, crashes. Steve was a tad overzealous with one of his attempts, slamming into the ladder back first at a high rate of speed. His bad shoulder was shooting torturous lightning through his arm, so bad he could barely breathe.

"Are you okay?" Jiro said, smiling at him as he groaned on the mat.

"Yeah, I hit it a little fast but I'll live."

"Let's take a break," Jiro said, tossing him a fluffy white towel.

"Sounds good," Steve said with sincerity. He and Jiro had been up since dawn working out the spots for their match. There was a kind of strange comraderie to be had, working on their particular brand of performance art. He had learned a great deal about Jiro in the past few days, though they had seldom spoken except about the match. The man had a strange sense of humor, and was also easily moved to emotion, even though he tried to keep it hidden like his culture required. Steve found himself not only respecting but liking Jiro as well.

"Steve-san, you are bleeding." Jiro didn't seem alarmed, but spoke as if he were stating a fact like *Steve-san, it is quarter till one.*

"Damn." Steve put a finger up to his forehead and felt sticky wetness. The wound had been torn open during his exertions.

"Nothing that will slow down one such as you, I am certain," Jiro added.

"It's just a scratch."

There was a faucet in the dojo, and Steve used it to run cold water over his head. Toweling off, he stepped back into his shoes and headed for the main house. He nearly ran into Autumn in his momentary blindness, stopping just short.

"Hey, sorry."

His smile faded when he saw the hard set of Autumn's jaw, the way her eyes were sharp as needles.

"What's wrong?"

"Want to tell me why there's a fucking *ladder* in the ring with you? Better yet, want to tell me what you're doing diving off of it like you were El Gato's size?"

"Uh, well, we're working a match where the ladder plays an integral part."

"You're doing a fucking hardcore match! You goddamn moron! I fucking knew it. Jiro wants to punish you for what your father did…" Autumn squinted and leaned forward, focused on his forehead. "Are you bleeding *again?*"

"He's not trying to punish me, Autumn." Steve pressed the towel against his cut and held it there. "Hell, most of the hardest spots are his. This is about repaying a debt. About duty."

"Duty?" said Autumn hotly, holding her finger an inch from Steve's nose. "Listen to yourself. He's brainwashed you into being one of them!"

"One of them, is it? I guess you'll accept their hospitality, but not their culture."

"Their culture sucks! It's misogynistic, antiquated and waaaaay too focused on how things look rather than how they actually are."

"Maybe, but it's their country, and they're paying me a small fortune for what amounts to one night's work."

Autumn drew herself up and crossed her arms over her chest. "Is that why you're doing this? For the money?"

Steve regarded her, the sun casting a red nimbus of light around her head. Even angry and admonishing, she was still beautiful. He felt himself starting to cave in, to change the match to a standard one. Then he remembered his discussion with Jiro, and he willed himself to stand his ground.

"No, not just for the money. Look, Autumn, Pop ain't in the greatest shape, financial or otherwise. He can't keep going forever, and barring a miracle contract with the WWE he'll never get rich in the States. But if he can come to Japan, he can pick up even bigger paychecks than mine."

"Your dad has enough money. He just bought a new car."

"That he's struggling to pay off. And that's not all. I want to do this Autumn. I want to do this for *me*. Everyone thinks I'm just in the business because I'm a legacy, that I had to come to it because I lost my teaching job."

"Well, if the shoe fits!" Autumn rolled her eyes to the sky.

"Gee, thanks. Look, I have to prove myself, Autumn. I have to prove I'm worthy of the main event, prove I can put asses in seats."

"You don't have to prove anything! I love you, Steve. One time, you said that was all you needed in the world."

Autumn flinched but didn't pull away when he cupped her chin in his thick fingers. "I still can't live without you, Autumn, but I need to do this. I have to."

"Fine." Autumn slapped his hand away harshly. "Just don't expect me to hang around while you kill yourself."

"Wait," he said, snatching her bicep in his massive grip, "don't just walk away from me. You said you believed in us…believed in *me*. Now you're just going to run away, again."

"Here we go!" She snatched her arm out of his grip and glared. "How dare you throw that in my face, day after day after fucking day!"

"How can I not? Every time the going gets tough, you get going—out the door!"

Autumn started to retort, then closed her mouth. Her fierce brown gaze scanned back and forth across his face, and Steve realized she was grudgingly starting to agree with him. Then her eyes welled up with tears, and she spun around on her bare heel and rapidly strode back into the main house.

"Are you going to be at the match?" he called after her. Autumn didn't speak, just disappeared inside Jiro's home.

Crawley glanced up from tuning Molly's strings to find Phil staring at her again. When he noticed her looking, he suddenly peered down at his keyboard, his mouth a thin line.

She wished he would stop looking at her, though. It was quite distracting, and not just because of the emotions involved. Phil was a handsome man, and her long drought had her feeling more antsy than usual.

"Sorry!" Rex said, his heavy footsteps heralding his arrival in the basement. "The old ball and chain had me looking at baby names."

"Oh?" Sven said, grinning ear to ear. "What you got?"

"Rex Jr., if it's a boy," Rex said sheepishly. "Michelle if it's a girl."

"If your son takes after you," Rich said, a wide smile on his face, "you should name him Needle Dick."

Everyone laughed, including Crawley, though she felt bad for doing so.

"Rich, that's terrible!"

"He could also name him Meatloaf," Rich said. "You know, because Rex looks just like that ugly mother fucker."

"Hey, I'll take his money and his fame, if that goes with the looks!"

Crawley smiled, energized by their banter. It was going to be a good practice after all…

Later, they packed up their instruments and congratulated each other on an outstanding practice. Rex was yawning as he attempted to fix a loose screw on his snare drum, and Rich was harassing him terribly.

"Have you ever held a screwdriver?" Rich said. "I mean, since they pulled you out of the trees and shaved you."

"Yeah, I'm real handy with tools. Just last night I used my love pump on your mom's ass."

"You guys are so mean," Crawley said, shaking her head.

"That's just the way we are," Rich said, seeming almost apologetic.

"Yeah," Rex said, "you women are all like 'oh, I love you, we're best friends forever!' Your friendships last an average of two years. Dudes are like 'pussy, cocksucker, asshole' and our friendships last forever."

"That's not even right," Crawley said, though she was laughing. "You know, I'm not tired. Do you guys want to go hit a diner, grab a bite to eat?"

"I'm bushed," Rex said.

"I could go for a bite," Phil said, smiling slightly at the corners of his mouth. Crawley found it quite endearing.

"*Ja*, I am hungry—oww!" Rich had punched Sven in the arm. "Hear my words and understand them later: do you want a can of ass whip?"

Phil and Crawley headed outside and stood in the driveway. After a few minutes of negotiation, they decided on a nearby all night diner. The drive was spent with them mostly talking about the band.

When they arrived, Phil got out and stretched his legs. Crawley turned on the car's alarm and cocked an eyebrow.

"What's with that look?"

Phil shrugged. His eyes ran up and down her form, and he licked his lips. "You look really pretty tonight."

Crawley beamed, blushing though it was hardly the first time Phil had said as much that evening. For some reason, his simple declaration made her happy. The sudden dampness of her palms let her know that yes, there was still something between them, an electric chemistry that had her feeling a tad giddy.

"You can be so sweet." She slipped her hand into his. The gesture seemed to surprise him, but he folded his hand over hers anyway.

"Don't tell Rich. He'll make fun of me," Phil said with a laugh.

"My lips are sealed," she said, startling him again by pecking him on his smoothly shaven cheek.

That was all she intended. A quick kiss there in the cold parking lot. Once her lips brushed his skin, however, she didn't want to stop. Phil turned his head and their lips mingled. After exploring each other's mouths with their tongues, they pulled back for a moment and met with half-lidded gazes.

"We should go in," he said.

"Yeah, we should."

"Getting really hungry…"

"Me too."

"Or…"

"Yes?" She smoothed her palms over his chest, feeling the lean muscle there.

"I do have a—" he laughed, "a can of SpaghettiOs at my—"

"Done deal!" She practically ran around to the driver's side and flung open the door.

The ride to his apartment was the most agonizing thirty minutes of her life. Phil kept dropping his hand into her lap and rubbing her between the legs. If there had been anywhere that she felt safe enough, she'd have pulled over and jumped him right then and there.

As it was they got started early, in the mirror-walled elevator. Infinite Crawleys and Phils snuggled close and devoured each other. Phil pressed a hand against her lower back and crushed her to him. She gasped, belly heating up, and fervently tugged at his clothes.

They had to pause, laughing like school children, when another couple got on the elevator. Once they reached Phil's floor, she took him by the hand and led him down the hallway. She put her hands behind her back as she walked, a submissive gesture that was their non-verbal code that she wanted to get kinky tonight.

Phil had a hard time getting his keys into the lock. Of course, that was probably because Crawley had her hand down his pants. The familiar feel of his member in her hands made her giddy and excited and warm all at once.

When he at last managed to get the door unlocked, they sprawled on the sofa. Crawley ended up on top, straddling his lap and smothering him with kisses. Phil's hands clutched at her breasts, kneading them forcefully. With a smile she reached behind her head and seized the hemline of her shirt. She peeled it off slowly, enjoying his sudden gasp at the sight of her small but firm breasts.

"I'll never get tired of this view," he said, smoothing his hands along her bare skin.

"They're so small," she said with a titter, "not big like Autumn's."

"They're the *perfect* size," he said, popping his mouth over her nipple. "Phee?"

She giggled, then moaned as he increased suction. Maybe Phil had learned a thing or two about suction from her own efforts below the belt; he mixed up the pressure, and added little nibbles with his teeth that had her fingers pulling painfully on his hair.

Phil took her entire breast in his mouth, then dragged his lips off slowly. With a grunt he grabbed her around the waist and rolled to his side, pinning her beneath him. Crawley put her hands up over her head and sighed as Phil peeled her tight jeans off. Her hand played with his soft hair as he kissed her gently on the belly.

"You're so beautiful," he said, "and so fucking hot…"

Crawley arched her back, mouth flying open as Phil's tongue found her clit. Gently probing fingers spread her wide, sliding around inside her. She reached behind her and grabbed the cushion under her head. Phil used his fingers like a cock, while his lips and tongue worked over her clit and hood. It was good—very good—but it wasn't enough.

"Phil…" she breathed in a whisper. He looked up, face glazed with her moisture. "I want you inside me."

Phil stood up quickly and peeled off his pants. She stared at his slim hips, framing his shaved genitals. A drop of moisture hung from the head of his shaft, and his hands shook a bit as they reached beneath her hips and lifted her pelvis.

The feeling of his entry was intense. His bulbous head slid in slowly until his testes bumped against her labia. Crawley clutched at his back, digging in deep enough to leave red welts. Then he dragged himself about halfway out, and shoved back in much more quickly.

Phil's apartment must have had better soundproofing than Steve's, as there was no way to silence her grunts and cries of pleasure and there wasn't a single thump of complaint heard from upstairs. He pulled her into his lap, both their pelvises swiveling rhythmically. Though it had been over a month since they'd done this dance, it was as if they'd never stopped.

Crawley grabbed the back of the sofa and rode him for all she was worth. Phil gripped her ass tightly, helping to support her weight as she ground into him. A loud scream that had nothing to do with pain or fear reverberated off the ceiling when she finally came. A deluge of fluid squirted past his member, drenching both of them from the waist down.

"Dude," she said, giggling and sweaty, "your poor sofa…"

"I can just flip this cushion over, too," he mumbled into her chest. The little kisses he left told her he wasn't finished yet. For that matter, she wasn't finished either…

Pulling herself off of him with a wet pop, she slid down to her knees, smiling the whole way. Placing her tongue on the bottom of his sack, she ran it all along the shaft until she reached the tip. Her mouth opened wide and she took the head inside, eyes fixed on his. Pleased sounding grunts and coos came from her muffled mouth. Demeaning? Not hardly. There was no doubt in her mind about who was in charge.

Crawley pushed herself down on him deeper, until he was almost tickling the back of her throat. Then she bobbed her head, slowly at first, and then picking up speed. Her undulating, wet gurgles mingled with his hot panting. When he came, it filled her mouth and nearly caused her to sputter.

Nearly. Pointedly looking him right in the eyes, she swallowed and wiped her mouth. The look of wonder and awe in his eyes was something she'd missed terribly.

"You're so bad," he said, pulling her back into his lap.

"I know," she said, kissing him. Some men didn't like to kiss her after she'd given head, but Phil didn't seem to mind. "I'm so very, very, very bad…what ever will you do about it?"

"I suppose I could tie you to the bed and spank you," he said, rising to his feet with her in his arms. Crawley pretended to consider it and shrugged.

"It's a start," she said, throwing her arms around his neck.

Chapter 26

Steve sat in the locker room, wiping the sweat that was pouring from his palms on a white towel. It was a place where the Tokyo pro baseball team normally dressed, and their logo was on almost every surface. Since he was in the main event, he rated a private dressing room, and he did not know if it was an honor or a slight to be placed in the same locker room as the baseball stars.

He felt an uprising of bile in his belly and strove to swallow it back down. True, he was worried about getting hurt; Death Matches involved the participants hitting each other with steel chairs, ladders, garbage cans, and even metal baking sheets. While the match, like all professional wrestling, was a performance and not a real fight, the objects hurt just the same. He and Jiro had worked out the specifics in advance, and he had to admit that it would probably be an exciting match.

He sighed, wishing Autumn were there. Seeing that he still had almost thirty minutes before the match, he picked up his phone and called his father.

There was an answer almost immediately, and Deathslayer's familiar gruff baritone was soothing in his ear.

"Steve! Did you have your match yet?"

"Not yet, Pop. Sitting in the locker room right now."

"What's wrong, son?" Deathslayer had picked it up from his tone. "You're not working hurt, are you?"

"Yeah, but that's not why I called. Autumn," Steve said, sighing miserably. "She's gone, Pop. Cleared out her stuff before I woke up this morning."

"She snuck out?"

"Yeah, we were…she asked our hosts for separate sleeping arrangements after we had a fight."

"I see." Deathslayer didn't pry, remaining silent so Steve could continue.

"We've been doing that a lot. Fighting, I mean. Ever since we got back together."

"What about?"

"About this crap!" Steve felt the fire rising in his belly. "Once again, things get a little bit hard and she takes off. I've spent the past year and a half chasing after her, it seems."

"Well, if she's the right one, you should keep chasing."

Steve scoffed.

"And that's not all. She keeps giving me the business about working 'snug' and taking chair shots to the head."

"Son, *I'm* about to give you the business for that. You're too good to tear up your body in those crap matches."

"You're taking *her* side?"

"I'm not taking anyone's 'side.'" Deathslayer chuckled. "Look, Steve, I know it fucked you up when Autumn left. Why don't you look at it from her point of view? Would you want her to have to watch you get hurt, or even die?"

"Of course not!"

"Well, she don't want to, either."

"Well, she could have said something about it instead of just ripping out my heart and stomping on it in the same damn hospital room she was dying in a week before."

"I see," Deathslayer said, and Steve thought he detected a note of disapproval.

"You see what?"

"Autumn hurt you really bad, and you want her to suffer for it."

"That is so — I do fucking not!"

"Well, suffer might not be the right word. Maybe 'atone' might be better. Look, Steve, you and she can't change what happened. All you can do is move forward and try to be more supportive of each other."

"Didn't you listen? There's no moving forward. She's gone. She's… gone…"

Steve choked on the last work, feeling tears well up in his eyes. It wouldn't do to smudge his makeup—he was wearing eyeliner just like his legendary father—so he stifled his woe as best he could.

"Steve…" his father sounded miserable and helpless. "You want me to call Autumn? Maybe—"

"No, Pop." Steve sighed. "If Autumn's made up her mind about something, well, she won't change it because someone else tells her to."

"Okay, son. Good luck in your match."

"Thanks, Pop." Steve forced himself to smile. "Are you going to watch?"

"Wouldn't miss it! My PC is having trouble with that link you sent so I'm using your mother's tablet."

"Yeah, I think Rex and the gang are watching it too," Steve said. "Hope I don't embarrass myself."

"You'll do fine, son. Be safe out there! I love you."

"Love you too, Pop. I better get off here. It's getting to be that time."

"Man, getting ready to walk down the tunnel in the Egg Dome. I'm jealous as hell!"

"Yeah, it's something else." If only Autumn were here, so he could feel happy about it! So he could feel happy at all…

After he got off the phone, he did a few knee bends to limber up. A pounding on the locker room door drew his mind back to the present. Nervously, he wiped his hands once more and went to open it. A short, balding official informed him that it was time.

Steve thought he was used to crowds, but the sight of the Tokyo Egg Dome filled to capacity made his breath catch in his throat. Grateful that the lights had been dimmed low in imitation of Deathslayer's legendary entrance, he began the long walk to the ring. The Japanese crowds were strange, he had been told, applauding when either the babyface or the heel executed a move well. Their eyes stared at him coldly, giving him nothing to work with. That was just as well, because he was in the Deathslayer Jr. persona now. Deathslayer did not care for adulation or derision; he was a walking murder machine.

I am a walking murder machine he repeated to himself mentally on the way down the ramp. The sight of the galvanized folding ladder, nearly fourteen feet tall as it stood outside the ring, made his belly do flip flops. There would be pain tonight, probably the most pain he had ever felt — physically, at least.

He entered the ring, wishing for a moment he was tall enough to step over the top rope. His father had done that during his entrance, an easy feat for a man over two meters tall. Steve stretched out his legs, awaiting the arrival of Jiro.

Jiro's entrance music hit the speakers, and everyone in the crowd stood in unison. Flash bulbs went off all over the arena, and it occurred to him just how big a deal it all was. Here he was, about to face arguably the biggest star in Japan, and all he could think about was Autumn. He glanced over at the corner where she would normally stand, then turned back to Jiro.

The man walking to the ring bore little resemblance to his host of the past several days, though they had the same face. This was not Jiro Higashi, doting father and peaceable businessman. This was Jiro "Hero" Higashi, striding purposefully toward the ring with his jaw set and shoulders back. Their eyes locked as he entered the ring, and Steve felt a bit of fear in spite of himself. Maybe there was something to what Autumn had said after all, and the Japanese man *did* want to punish him…

The bell rang, and they circled each other. At first they applied amateur style grappling holds upon each other, building up anticipation for the more spectacular maneuvers later. Jiro moved well for a man of his age, and he was more than able to keep up with Steve's youthful quickness.

As they had planned, Steve was the first one to go for a weapon. After planting Jiro solidly with a gorilla press slam, a crowd pleasing move that involved holding the Japanese man over his head for nearly a minute, Steve slid out of the ring. He selected a folding steel chair and banged it loudly on the steps a few times, which seemed to play over well with the crowd. Sliding back into the ring, the crowd sang out in alarm as he bore down on the still-felled Higashi.

Jiro suddenly popped to his feet and leaped into the air. His boots made contact with the chair, slamming it into Steve's face. It *hurt*. More than he had been expecting. As he fell to his back, hands covering his face, he made a promise to himself to respect the man's power more.

The match went on, going back and forth between them. Jiro was soon bleeding from his forehead, supposedly due to Steve running the ladder into his face but actually the wound was self-inflicted—Jiro had used a small razor blade to gash himself when he was lying face down on the mat.

You can smell your blood different from the other guy's blood he remembered his father telling him years before. Soon, Jiro had turned the tables, and Steve was the one who took a ladder to the face. Steve reached into the wrist band on his right arm and withdrew a tiny sliver of metal.

Stick it in all the way to the bone and give it a quick jerk, his father had once said.

That was the secret of "blading," you didn't want to make a shallow cut because those could scar more easily. A deep, clean cut would bleed for a good while but would close up more quickly than a longer, shallow one.

Steve almost broke character and smiled as drops of red stained the tape on his fingers. The wound on his forehead had opened up once again, eliminating the need for the razor fragment in his fingers. He stuffed it back into his wristband and sold the bump.

The blood mixed with his sweat, making him look truly ghastly. He lay on the mat, feigning unconsciousness so Jiro had time to prepare for the next spot. Steve was particularly dreading what was coming…

Jiro rolled out of the ring and lifted up the apron, drawing a murmur from the crowd. He rummaged around underneath the ring for a moment and stood up, holding up a small black bag. The fans seemed to know what that entailed, their voices raising in volume. Jiro rolled back into the ring and opened the bag. He spilled its contents out onto the mat, a glittering stream of silver tacks. Steve heard the sound, rolled over onto his face as Jiro approached. Taking a handful of Steve's long hair, Jiro dragged him to his feet. The Japanese man picked up Steve and twisted him in the air, slamming him back first onto the tacks.

As the crowd groaned in sympathy, Steve felt the hundred tiny fires burning in his back. He was not quite in as much pain as he had expected, but when Jiro lay across his torso to pin him, they ground into him further. Steve kicked out of the pin at two, just as planned, the agony of his stippled back adding vehemence to the action.

Steve rose to his feet and staggered, only partly faking. His forehead was a bleeding wreck, as his earlier cut had opened back up. Knifing pain in his shoulder only added to his misery. They were building to the crescendo, the final high spot of the match, and it was going to be spectacular. Jiro hit his finishing move, a brutal looking hold called a brainbuster that actually dropped Steve onto his muscular shoulders rather than his head. He lay there, pretending to be knocked out while his half lidded eyes watched Jiro climb to the top of the tall ladder.

He's going to kill me, thought Steve. *Why am I even here? I've lost everything I care about...*

Jiro stood on the precipice for a moment, basking in the cheers of the capacity crowd. Then he leaped off the ladder and landed squarely on Steve's abdomen with both feet.

Steve had prepared to receive the bump, curled his stomach up and tightened his muscles as much as he could, but the impact was still terrible. Jiro flipped off of him right away to eat up some of the kinetic energy, but Steve still felt something give inside of him. Jiro dragged himself over Steve's form and covered him for the pinfall.

Steve kicked out at two-and-a-half, just as had been scripted, but agony shot through his torso. Suddenly, his shoulder was just a distant twinge compared to this new torment. He gasped for breath while Jiro rose slowly, giving him time to recover.

I can't do this, thought Steve, forcing himself onto his hands and knees but unable to rise further. *Something's wrong...just can't...*

That was when he heard the pounding on the mat. Turning his head, his eyes went wide when he saw Autumn standing in his corner. She wasn't dressed as Candy Pain, but in her street clothes — which were admittedly exotic — and her face seemed upbeat, even jubilant.

"C'mon, Deathslayer!" she shouted, pounding her hands on the mat. "Get up! Don't let that little bastard beat you!"

She's here. She came back to me.

It was a performance, not a real fight. Still, when Steve saw her, he felt inspired to move past the jolting pain. First one foot, then the other, was placed on the mat and he levered himself erect. It was hard to breathe, and even harder to move, but he assumed a fighting stance and faced off with Jiro.

Steve lashed out with a vicious looking kick to Jiro's midsection, which the man sold well. While he was bent over, Steve lifted him to his shoulders and delivered a Death Valley Driver onto the tacks. The crowd gasped in shock as their national hero writhed in pain beneath him. Autumn hollered and pounded the mat, her voice so loud it was breaking up.

Of course, Jiro the Hero wasn't going to go down like that. As Steve dragged the man to his feet, laughing as if he enjoyed Jiro's pain, the smaller man used the momentum to deliver an *enziguri*, a spectacular move that involved a flying kick to the head. Steve dropped like he'd been shot, then allowed Jiro to roll him over for the "one-two-three."

Jiro stayed in the ring to soak in the crowd's adulation, while Steve rolled out to the floor to begin the "walk of shame." He almost collapsed when fire shot through his ribs, but Autumn was there to help support him.

The walk back to his locker room was arduous. The pain was bad, worse than he had ever felt before, but he managed to keep on his feet thanks to Autumn. It overwhelmed the jabbing, sharp pain in his back from all the thumbtacks, though now his shoulder was raging again. If Autumn were not there beside him, he'd have collapsed for sure.

Autumn. He turned his head to look at her, face screwed up with the effort of holding even a portion of his weight. It was hard to dispel the notion that what he was seeing wasn't real, that she'd just been conjured up by his imagination.

The other wrestlers were waiting for him, shaking his hand, slapping his shoulders, and telling him in Japanese and English what a terrific match it was. He did his best to be polite, but the pain made it difficult.

"For fuck's sake, back off!" Autumn snapped. Some of the boys snickered, some looked offended, but all of them made way before the furious woman. Her lips quivered as she spoke again. "He's hurt, you douchebags! He's hurt…"

Once they were ensconced in his locker room, Steve felt his legs giving out. With a hasty shuffling, Autumn managed to get him seated on the bench.

"You came." It was all he could manage.

"Yeah." She looked at the shining tacks impaled in his back. "Jesus Christ, Steve!"

"It looks worse than it is."

"I don't see how." She carefully plucked one tack out, then another, Steve hissing each time. They rang musically off of the concrete floor as she added more to the pile.

"I thought about the other day, when you told me that I didn't believe in you. You're wrong. I believe in you, Steve. I believe in us."

"I'm sorry, I never should have said that."

"No," Autumn said, shaking her head slightly as she worked another tack free, "I needed to hear it. I needed that kick in the ass."

"For the record, I agree with you that no one should go through this kind of beating. My hardcore days are over."

"Hindsight is always twenty-twenty. Oh, don't think that I'm still not mad at you, because I totally am. But you don't always like my decisions, and you stick by me anyway. It's only fair if I do the same for you."

Steve flinched as she plucked yet another tack and added it to the shining metal pile on the smooth concrete floor. He glanced up, eyes widening in alarm, when the door opened and three dour looking Japanese men came rushing in. Relaxing when he realized they were the EMTs, he allowed them to clean the cuts on his forehead and apply a smear of antibiotic salve before affixing a gauze bandage. The EMTs poured peroxide solution over the multitude of holes in his back, which foamed up like the vinegar and baking soda volcanoes he had made in his back yard in childhood. Autumn stood back, arms crossed over her chest, and clucked her tongue as Steve hissed.

"Be a man, tough guy," she said as they applied a wide swath of bandages over his back.

"I don't wanna be a man," Steve said as one of the EMTs poked him in the ribs. "It really hurts!"

After squeezing Steve across the torso, the trainers suspected that his ribs were cracked but not badly broken. In halting English, they managed to convey to Steve that he would be cleared to wrestle in two weeks.

"Uh, wait," Steve said, "you know how long two weeks is, right? Are you sure you don't really mean two days?"

"No," said the heavyset man, who Steve took to be the senior member of their team. "You wait two weeks. Two weeks, ribs heal okay. Go back in ring now, very risky."

"This isn't good," Steve said, grunting in misery as they wrapped his ribcage in ace bandages. "I have to work for WWL in three days!"

"You'll have to cancel," Autumn said, striding over to his side and fixing him a glance that said she would brook no argument. "You're not risking your health for that scumbag Reilly."

"Reilly gave me a break, when the Macs and the Carters wouldn't even touch me. I owe him, Autumn."

"You owe him two things: Jack and shit."

"But—"

"No buts." Autumn grabbed his face roughly and forced him to look in her eyes. "You are not going to get hurt worse than you already are. Understand? I can't live without you either, you know. I've known that since the first time you lumbered into my life."

"I lumber?"

"In a very nice way," she said, kissing him on the cheek.

"Showing up like you did," Steve said, trying not to gasp, "it means a lot. Everything."

"It had better. I mean, for God's sake, Steve, I just stood by and watched you get mauled in front of a bunch of bloodthirsty maniacs who probably think the wrong side won World War II!"

Steve laughed, slapping a hand across his midsection when the motion caused him pain.

"Don't make me laugh!"

"Sorry."

Steve shook his head, a sad smile playing at his face.

"Hey, as hard as it was to watch, it was worse to live through. I did it all for us, though."

"Bullshit," Autumn said, taking a step back. "You may think that in your twisted little brain, but you did that for yourself, and maybe for your dad too, but mostly you just wanted to prove to your hero Jiro Higashi what a man you are."

Steve opened his mouth for a hot rebuttal, then closed it. She was right; he had done the match as much for himself as anything. The money would certainly help, as would the notoriety and exposure, but most of all he really had been trying to impress Jiro. Maybe he wanted to have a father figure who he could please. It often seemed that his father, the legendary Deathslayer from Hell, gave out his approval too easily, while keeping his real feelings secret.

You want to be a teacher? Steve remembered him saying many years ago. *That's great, son.*

If his father had truly thought it was great, why had his smile seemed so tense, his happy tone forced?

He was drawn out of his reverie by Autumn, who waved a hand in front of his face.

"Earth to Steve! Those painkillers must be kicking in, huh?"

"No, you were right on the money. I did the match for myself, okay? I wanted to impress Jiro Higashi, and I'm a selfish jerk…yadda yadda yadda."

"Okay," Autumn said, looking a bit sheepish, "don't beat yourself up about it too much, sugar. That's my job!"

She hugged him around the waist, which he would have found sweet and comforting if not for the agonizing pain.

Chapter 27

Steve looked over his shoulder, though twisting his torso still caused him agony. He was taking one last look at the Higashi compound before he got into the rear of the Jiro's limo.

"Penny for your thoughts, sugar," Autumn said, hovering nearby so she could assist him with his painful entry into the vehicle.

"Just thinking that Jiro's really made it, you know: house, career, wife and kids, the whole thing."

"Give it time, we'll make it, too."

Steve smiled at her, putting his hand on her cheek. Their lips met in what he intended to be a quick kiss, but his mouth lingered upon her own. Worries about missing his scheduled dates drifted away as her tongue explored his mouth.

"Steve-san," Jiro said, startling them. They turned sheepishly to face him.

"Sorry," Steve said.

"Don't apologize for loving your woman, as she's a good woman."

"Well, thanks," Autumn said. "I kind of thought you didn't like me, Mr. Higashi."

"I was wrong about you, Miss Winters. I thought you were overly proud and willful, but you ended up playing a properly submissive role in the end."

"Properly submissive?" Autumn said, anger flashing in her eyes.

"Thanks for everything, Mr. Higashi," Steve said, shaking the man's hand and interjecting himself between the two of them.

"Thank you, Steve-san," Jiro said with a smile. His hand gripped Steve's tightly but not painfully. "You and your father are welcome to work in Japan. Perhaps we might see you for the Nippon Super Tournament?"

"Yes," Steve said, shaking his hand more enthusiastically, "yes, that would be awesome!"

"Properly submissive?" Autumn said, but both men ignored her.

"Oh," Jiro said, leaning forward a bit, "don't worry about Reilly. I am the main investor in his operation. It is for that conflict of interests that the WWL cannot work in Japan in an official capacity."

"What?" Steve said, scratching his chin. "You're one of the investors in WWL?"

"Indeed. I plan to send my children to work there—after they graduate from college, of course."

"Why send them to the United States at all?"

"The properly submissive woman is getting in the car," Autumn said. "Get your feeble, crippled ass in by yourself."

"Because," Hiro said, "no one in Japan will treat them the way they need to be treated—harshly. So many will fear drawing my ire that they will not learn their craft properly."

"Ha! So you want them to pay their dues! I can respect that, Mr. Higashi."

"Please, if you would, call me Jiro-chan."

"Okay," Steve said, laughing, "Jiro-chan."

"I bid you farewell, Steve Borgia, Deathslayer Jr., and will see you in the spring when the tournament begins!"

"Take it easy, Jiro-chan," Steve said, turning toward the limo. "Autumn? Weren't you going to help me get in?"

"Are you commanding me, oh lord and master?" Autumn said, sneering from within the limo.

"This is going to be a long ride to the airport, isn't it?"

"Oh, I wouldn't know, I'm just a properly submissive woman."

She glared up at him as he painfully eased his way into the car.

"You're so cut off."

"Autumn, I'm pretty busted up right now, so you cutting me off is meaningless."

"Oh, okay, then I'll just wait until you're all healed, and then I'll cut you off."

"You're evil," Steve said as she grinned wickedly.

Epilogue

"You have to admit," Rex said as he shoved his snare cymbal on top of the growing heap in Crawley's family van, "it's a sweet gig!"

The plain featured man was dressed in a blue tuxedo that had been out of style for some time, possibly before he had even been born. Nearby, Sven carried a heavy amplifier up to the cargo doors, lips pursed in annoyance as he realized there was no more room for such a bulky contrivance.

"Playing at another dive bar?" Sven said.

"No, you foreign bastard," Rex said, rolling his eyes. "I'm talking about Steve getting us that job writing theme music for WWL."

"Yeah," Phil said, coming around the side of the van with a sack full of business cards, "but now we have to write like thirty new songs."

"It won't be that hard," Rex said with a grin. "Writing a wrestler's theme music is easy. They're all just different ways of saying 'worship me!'"

"Where's Crawley?" Sven said.

"Right here, Sven," Crawley said, coming around the side of the trailer bearing Molly. "I had to send a text off to my dad."

"How's that going?" Rex said. "Did you guys ever work things out?"

"Yeah," Crawley said. "I'm going to take over the family business, but I'm not giving up the band. I'll try to find time for both...and for certain special people."

She turned her head and pecked Phil on the cheek as she passed him. Grinning ear to ear, his cheeks burned red, no doubt remembering the steamy night they'd spent together.

Growing up was terrible, wonderful, and inevitable. But you didn't have to do it alone.

"Your dad looks nervous," Steve said.

"Uh huh. Handsome, but nervous."

He had to agree with her that Jonathon Winters cut a dapper figure. Jon had shorn his bristly gray hair until it was sleek against his scalp, and the tuxedo's satin cummerbund hid a bit of his paunch. Steve had on a similar tux, though he had went with a red bow tie. Autumn was dressed in a nice indigo sleeveless dress, the skirt coming just below her knees. Her hair had been put up in a formal style, baring her slender neck and its myriad tattoos.

They approached him, walking across the hotel lobby. The ceremony would be simple and brief, but the reception promised to be a memorable affair complete with an open bar. Autumn had cursed, however, that it was probably going to be draft beer only.

When Jonathon saw his daughter, he smiled and stopped his pacing.

"It's almost time," she said. "Are you nervous?"

"A little," Jonathon said. "You look beautiful, my dove."

"Dad!" Autumn said, scrunching up her face. "*So* not a dove!"

"Well," Steve said, "being nervous is normal on your wedding day."

"Speaking of weddings," Jonathon said, "when am I going to be giving you away? Steve hasn't even given you a ring."

"Daaaaaad," Autumn said, rolling her eyes. "I don't need a piece of carbon dug out of a godforsaken hole in the ground by an eight-year-old Nigerian boy to know my man loves me."

Steve joined his future father-in-law in a deep sigh.

"She does like to see the negative side of things, doesn't she?"

"I have no comment," Steve said. "My ribs still aren't healed all the way and she might hurt me."

"You can both suck it!" Autumn stuck her tongue out at them. Then she poked Steve in the ribs with her sharp nail.

Jon followed them into the chilly winter sunlight. The hotel pool was closed for the season, but the elegantly carved gazebo was available for use. As they made their way toward the structure, he plied them with questions.

"So what is the deal with you two?" Jonathon said. "Are you officially engaged? Or are you going to cohabitate for a while longer?"

Steve and Autumn stared at each other and then quickly looked away. Jonathon noted their awkward silence with a pained grimace but did not press the point.

The chilly wind made Autumn lean against Steve as they watched her father say his vows to Brad. There weren't many others there to witness the ceremony. John had wanted to keep it intimate so as to avoid any protests, either for or against their union. Brad's brother was there, a big heavyset man with an easy smile, as well as Jonathon's boss from Jenoine Contracting. And of course, Autumn and Steve.

"Are you crying?" Steve gently lifted her chin to see moisture glistening on her cheeks.

"Is my mascara running?" Autumn sniffled, her voice sounding thick with emotion.

"No, not really," Steve said.

"Good, I didn't get ripped off when I bought the name brand shit." Steve offered her a handkerchief, which she sullied with a heavy load of snot. She tried to hand it back to him, and he tossed it into a nearby trash can.

"Oh, you can touch my pussy but not my snot?"

"Autumn!" Steve glanced up at the gazebo. The party was a good twenty feet away at the bottom of the stairs, but it seemed that no one heard her.

"I'm just saying, what if—what if I get pregnant? Then you'll have to change diapers. Do you want to change diapers, Steve? I certainly don't."

"What…" Steve looked at her askance. There was a relaxed, easy smile on her face. "What are you getting at?"

"Kids, dumbass," she said, snuggling close. "Now *shhh*, the good part is coming up."

After John put a ring on Brad's finger, the two of them kissed and the small gathering applauded. The two of them got in a horse-drawn carriage and trotted around the block. Steve and Autumn followed in a similar carriage, taking turns making jibes about the cold and humiliation.

"Seriously, this is the most touristy thing I've ever done," Autumn said.

"Yeah, might as well go to the Statue of Liberty."

"I've lived here my whole life, and I've never been there."

"Really? I think I went on a field trip once, but it was all under construction or some such. Couldn't go up in it."

"And of course the weather, which has been mild all winter, has to turn freezing on this of all days."

"Naturally! We're just playthings in the hands of uncaring gods."

They both laughed, and she stroked a gloved hand through his hair. "You think my dad and Brad are going to make it?"

Steve noted the tension in her voice, the slight tremor of her lip. She was asking about her father's marriage, but he could tell she had a lot of emotional investment in his answer.

"Yeah, I think so. I mean, they complement each other well. Bring out the best in each other while compensating for each other's… weaknesses."

"Weaknesses, huh?" Autumn grinned ruefully. "Like running out when the going gets tough?"

"Or being a jealous asshole who can't forgive and forget?" Steve laughed.

"So…do *we* do that?" Autumn chewed her lower lip. "Complement each other? Make each other stronger?"

"Yeah, it's like we're the Wonder Twins. Form of an Ice Eagle or some such."

"The Wonder Twins were brother and sister, Steve. Do I need to worry about you and Susan?"

"God no!" Steve laughed, though he was somewhat revolted as well. "You know, you're pretty dang evil sometimes."

"I'm not evil, I'm just unpredictable. And you love it." She leaned over and kissed him as the carriages made their final approach to the reception. "There's one thing about me that you *can* predict, though."

"And what's that?"

"That whatever happens, I'm going to be right here with you. Forever."

"Forever?" Steve smiled putting his hand over her shoulder and pulling her close despite the jabbing pain of his ribs.

"Forever, dumbass. You know, eternity, in perpetuity, the endless—"

Steve shut her up with a passionate, fierce kiss, but Autumn didn't seem to mind.

Acknowledgments

The author would like to acknowledge Jennifer, Colleen, Sean, and the rest of the hardworking staff at Omnific for all their time and energy dedicated to the release of a novel that features leg humping little people in cat costumes.

About the Author

Christopher Scott Wagoner: Strange visitor from another world! Jettisoned from his planet at an early age, he was adopted by a kindly midwestern couple and taught to fight for truth, justice, and the Native American way!

When he's not busy saving the Galaxy, Chris finds time to pen fiction novels. *Forever Winter* (the sequel to *Forever Autumn*) makes it two books without dragons in them. He is rumored to enjoy professional wrestling, cartoons, and jokes that fall on the "offensive" side. Unsubstantiated accusations that he used to teach preschool have never been confirmed by him, but he has a lot of pee stories.

New Adult Romance

Three Daves by Nicki Elson
Streamline by Jennifer Lane
The Shades series: *Shades of Atlantis* & *Shades of Avalon* by Carol Oates
The Heart series: *Beside Your Heart, Disclosure of the Heart* & *Forever Your Heart*
by Mary Whitney
Romancing the Bookworm by Kate Evangelista
Flirting with Chaos by Kenya Wright
The Vice, Virtue & Video series: *Revealed, Captured, Desired* & *Devoted*
by Bianca Giovanni
Granton University series: *Loving Lies* by Linda Kage
Missing Pieces by Meredith Tate

Paranormal & Fantasy Romance

The Light series: *Seers of Light, Whisper of Light* & *Circle of Light* by Jennifer DeLucy
The Hanaford Park series: *Eve of Samhain* & *Pleasures Untold* by Lisa Sanchez
Immortal Awakening by KC Randall
The Seraphim series: *Crushed Seraphim* & *Bittersweet Seraphim* by Debra Anastasia
The Guardian's Wild Child by Feather Stone
Grave Refrain by Sarah M. Glover
The Divinity series: *Divinity* & *Entity* by Patricia Leever
The Blood Vine series: *Blood Vine, Blood Entangled* & *Blood Reunited* by Amber Belldene
Divine Temptation by Nicki Elson
The Dead Rapture series: *Love in the Time of the Dead, Love at the End of Days* &
Love Starts with Z by Tera Shanley
The Hidden Races series: *Incandescent* & *Illumination* by M.V. Freeman
Something Wicked by Carol Oates
Chronicles of Midvalen: *Command the Tides* (book 1) by Wren Handman

Romantic Suspense

Whirlwind by Robin DeJarnett
The CONduct series: *With Good Behavior, Bad Behavior* & *On Best Behavior*
by Jennifer Lane
Indivisible by Jessica McQuinn
Between the Lies by Alison Oburia
Blind Man's Bargain by Tracy Winegar

Historical Romance

Cat O' Nine Tails by Patricia Leever
Burning Embers by Hannah Fielding
Seven for a Secret by Rumer Haven
The Counterfeit by Tracy Winegar

←··→ Erotic Romance ←··→

The Keyhole series: *Becoming sage* (book 1) by Kasi Alexander
The Keyhole series: *Saving sunni* (book 2) by Kasi & Reggie Alexander
The Winemaker's Dinner: *Appetizers & Entrée* by Dr. Ivan Rusilko & Everly Drummond
The Winemaker's Dinner: *Dessert* by Dr. Ivan Rusilko
Client N° 5 by Joy Fulcher
The Enclave series: *Closer and Closer* (book 1) by Jenna Barton
The Adventures of Clarissa Hardy by Chloe Gillis

←··→ Anthologies ←··→

A Valentine Anthology including short stories by
Alice Clayton ("With a Double Oven"),
Jennifer DeLucy ("Magnus of Pfelt, Conquering Viking Lord"),
Nicki Elson ("I Don't Do Valentine's Day"),
Jessica McQuinn ("Better Than One Dead Rose and a Monkey Card"),
Victoria Michaels ("Home to Jackson"), and
Alison Oburia ("The Bridge")

Taking Liberties including an introduction by Tiffany Reisz and short stories by
Mina Vaughn ("John Hancock-Blocked"),
Linda Cunningham ("A Boston Marriage"),
Joy Fulcher ("Tea for Two"),
KC Holly ("The British Are Coming!"),
Kimberly Jensen & Scott Stark ("E. Pluribus Threesome"), and
Vivian Rider ("M'Lady's Secret Service")

←··→ Sets ←··→

The Heart Series Box Set (*Beside Your Heart, Disclosure of the Heart &
Forever Your Heart*) by Mary Whitney
The CONduct Series Box Set (*With Good Behavior, Bad Behavior &
On Best Behavior*) by Jennifer Lane
The Light Series Box Set (*Seers of Light, Whisper of Light, Circle of Light &
Glimpse of Light*) by Jennifer DeLucy
The Blood Vine Series Box Set (*Blood Vine, Blood Entangled, Blood Reunited &
Blood Eternal*) by Amber Belldene

←··→ Singles, Novellas & Special Editions ←··→

It's Only Kinky the First Time (A Keyhole series single) by Kasi Alexander
Learning the Ropes (A Keyhole series single) by Kasi & Reggie Alexander
The Winemaker's Dinner: RSVP by Dr. Ivan Rusilko
The Winemaker's Dinner: No Reservations by Everly Drummond

Big Guns by Jessica McQuinn
Concessions by Robin DeJarnett
Starstruck by Lisa Sanchez
New Flame by BJ Thornton
Shackled by Debra Anastasia
Swim Recruit by Jennifer Lane
Sway by Nicki Elson
Full Speed Ahead by Susan Kaye Quinn
The Second Sunrise by Hannah Downing
The Summer Prince by Carol Oates
Whatever it Takes by Sarah M. Glover
Clarity (A *Divinity* prequel single) by Patricia Leever
A Christmas Wish (A *Cocktails & Dreams* single) by Autumn Markus
Late Night with Andres by Debra Anastasia
Poughkeepsie (enhanced iPad app collector's edition) by Debra Anastasia
Poughkeepsie (audio book edition) by Debra Anastasia
Blood Eternal (A Blood Vine series single, epilogue to series) by Amber Belldene
Carnaval de Amor (*The Winemaker's Dinner*, Spanish edition)
by Dr. Ivan Rusilko & Everly Drummond

coming soon from
OMNIFIC PUBLISHING

Twice Upon a Kiss by Jane Susann McCarter
The Ground Rules by Roya Carmen
The Keyhole series: *Keyhole Kinklets* (short story anthology)
by Kasi & Reggie Alexander

www.ingramcontent.com/pod-product-compliance
Lightning Source LLC
Chambersburg PA
CBHW020403120726
47904CB00002B/680